At The

Father John Martin, age 47, black hair with silver specks, graying at the temples, lay on the floor his open dark eyes fixed on the ceiling. His blue-striped pajamas were ripped and bloody, his rather muscular arms were crossed over his chest rigid in defeat. *He must have stayed with some kind of exercise program,* thought Russell, *though he had told me two Christmases ago he was giving up golf.*

On his arms rested a Bible opened to Matthew, Chapter 26. The faint hint of the smile frozen on his face was so utterly out of place that Russell found himself momentarily paralyzed. He willed his eyes away from the body for a few seconds, only to hear the booming laugh that had often come out of this man. Swallowing his gulp of grief, he leaned over closer to the body and counted the stab wounds; there were twelve. He added that information to his notes. His eyes went back to the face and lingered on the smile. *Who did you see, Father? The angels, a friend, your parents?*

Coleman was also looking at the dead priest. He found himself full of questions for God, which did not make much sense because he had decided a long time ago that God was uninvolved in life here on earth. The remnant of his childhood faith prevented a total dismissal of the idea of God, but life had taught him that God had no power. The only way to survive was to be strong and self-sufficient; if you were careful and did the right things, if you were fair, you would be safe. His insides squirmed; he knew that was not true; he had seen too many good people killed. Which, of course, merely proved his conclusion about God. God could not protect you; no matter how much you prayed, how good you were, or whatever else you did to please Him.

So, he asked himself, *what happened, here, Father John? Were you a good priest and your God did nothing for you? Or were you something else? Why was someone so angry with you? Was your life a lie and God just gave you up? A God of justice; that might explain a few things for me, but a God who does not care explains a lot more.*

What They Are Saying About

At The Last Supper

"At the Last Supper is a gripping story by a master story-teller who knows the inside (church) story well. A great read!"

—Dr. Thomas H. Groome
Director Boston College Institute of Religious
Education and Pastoral Ministry
Professor of Theology and Religious Education
at Boston College
Author: What Makes Us Catholic

Wings

At The Last Supper

by

Sr. Christine Kresho

A Wings ePress, Inc.

Cozy Mystery Novel

Wings ePress, Inc.

Edited by: Lorraine Stephens
Copy Edited by: Shena Skinner
Senior Editor: Lorraine Stephens
Executive Editor: Lorraine Stephens
Cover Artist: Richard Stroud

Wings ePress Books
http://www.wings-press.com

Copyright © 2005 by Sr. Christine Kresho
ISBN 1-59088-615-1

Published In the United States Of America

August 2005

Wings ePress Inc.
403 Wallace Court
Richmond, KY 40475

Dedication

To my mother, Mary,

and

my niece, Lori,

who live in Eternal Mystery

One

The candles on the altar in St. Joseph's Church had been burning for fifteen minutes; the footsteps of the latecomers had ceased. Restless fidgeting stirred apologetically among some of the morning faithful; others were transparently annoyed.

"Why is it," Diane groaned under her breath, "that whenever I have a doctor's appointment that priest is late?" The jab of her sharp elbow into her dozing husband's side woke him; he gave her a so-what shrug as she pointed to her watch. 8:10 and no Father John in sight.

Maggie Wendell, who was recognized by all as the resident owner of the front pew, twisted her weary and lumpy body towards the back of the church; she squinted until she located Joe and Charlie sitting at either end of the last pew. With a poke of her wrinkled, quivering finger to the clock above the exit, she then jabbed the air towards the rectory; they nodded to each other and simultaneously rose straight into the air, ready to follow her orders.

Joe's chuckle when they got outside made Charlie grin to himself. "Father John's going to be embarrassed that we had to wake him up again; second time this month."

Charlie nodded his agreement, as they walked the short azalea-lined sidewalk to the rectory; he tried to brush away a twinge of gloom tugging at his heart. A faint breeze whimpered through the huge oak that stood guard in the front yard. "I guess these two years without Father Bill is wearing him out; remember when we had three priests here?"

"Sure do; things were a lot different back then."

Joe pressed the doorbell and they waited; no answer, no sound from inside. After the third time, both men shaded their eyes as they leaned into the long window on the right side of the door. Their eyes focused first on the grand oval rug that defined the entrance and then moved to the imposing crucifix on the far wall. Suddenly, Charlie shivered from an unexpected chill and he rubbed his clammy hands together. He stared at Joe and just as he opened his mouth, he heard a car approaching.

Charlie winced as he twisted his ankle and turned to see Joe's granddaughter arriving for work; she was the computer coordinator at the parish school. He smiled when he saw that red Mustang; he remembered the day Joe had told him about it.

When Jen noticed her grandfather, she braked with a screech and rolled down her window. "What's wrong, Grandpa? Waking up Father John again?" Her teasing grin faded away as soon as she saw their anxious steps and heard the worry in her grandfather's words.

"Jen, we rang the bell three times."

Jen swung back her long cinnamon hair and grabbed for her cell phone. Joe looked with such pride at his lovely young granddaughter; for three years she had been making a lot more money working in the county school system; that's when she bought that car. But last summer, when Father John told her that her former grade school was hurting for a computer teacher, she gave up the great money, "but not my car," she had said with a serene smile.

She would forever be grateful to Father John; two years ago, the day before her wedding, the priest, her favorite priest at that time, Father Bill, had left the parish without a word. How could he? Why did he? Didn't he know how brides want every detail planned and perfect? Father John had stepped in; he did everything she had wanted and even more than she expected; everyone at the wedding had been impressed with his charm; her words of praise for him knew no limits.

The answering machine came on. The three frowned at each other, their breaths in short puffs, their hearts pounding. Jen bit her lip and punched in 911. *Oh, God, please, please, please, don't let anything be wrong with Father John,* she begged silently.

Within minutes Detective Chris Coleman and his partner, Rick Russell, careened into the driveway of St. Joseph's parish. Following them Alice Manning stumbled out of her car, banged her knee on the edge of the car door and muttered to herself for being so clumsy. She usually made it in time for Mass, but everything had gone wrong this morning. She would just have to live through a bad hair day and promised herself an appointment at the beauty salon before the weekend. "Oh, please, not Maggie," she whispered as she watched a dark-suited broad-shouldered stranger coming straight towards her.

She heard Joe yelling in the background. "Alice, open the door; we can't seem to waken Father John."

A deep voice above her asked, "Who are you?" and she looked up into the darkest deep-set brown eyes she had ever seen; the badge he pulled out of his jacket, and the heavy hand that felt so light on her shoulder, made her realize her hands had turned to ice.

"I'm Alice Manning, the secretary, what's wrong?"

"Would you open the door?"

"Of course." She fumbled for her keys; with her left hand steadying her trembling right hand she felt the lock click its release and she shoved to open the heavy door.

Her stomach twisted itself into knots so tight she heaved for breath as she stepped aside for the detectives. *Just like walls,* she thought, as she stretched her neck to see first around the one, then his partner.

"Father John Martin! Father John Martin!"

He'll be so embarrassed, Alice told herself, to see these officers standing at the foot of his steps. She strained to hear his footsteps, but nothing except a forbidding silence filled the room. The fright in her stomach was churning out dread.

Coleman turned to Joe, Charlie and Alice; again those deep-set eyes spoke control and security as he asked them to wait outside. Walking out in a straight line, they saw Jen still in her car, her head on her hands clasped to the steering wheel.

When the screech of the police car had punctured the stillness inside the church, the twenty or so people gasped as one. They stumbled out of their pews in their rush towards the door, bumping elbows, tripping over themselves and one another. Some stopped long enough to mumble a quick *sorry* while a few shoved their way through every empty space; a young child began to cry.

As they pushed through the church doors, Joe and Chuck waved to them to stay where they were. Huddled at the entrance they watched the two detectives emerge from the rectory and walk towards Alice.

Even though 500 yards separated them, they heard Alice's broken-hearted sobs and watched her shoulders rising and falling as she tried to breathe. Father John Martin was dead; before they could cry out from the pain that stabbed at them, they overheard one word in Jen's phone call to her husband. "Murdered."

Their grief burst into panic. Shivering from head to toe, on a warm May morning, they clutched at one another. The child had stopped crying while his wide, wet blue eyes moved around the circle of faces surrounding him; he stared at faces wrenched with anger; he reached out to several heads bowed in disbelief; he was too young to be surprised that even some of the men were wiping away the dampness from their cheeks.

Soon a steady stream of cars flooded the driveway as parents arrived with children who attended St. Joseph's School. Disbelief and stunned anguish traveled from one car to the next. They looked around for Sister Ann, the school principal. "There she is," came a shout from one of the eighth grade boys. Everyone rushed towards her, stopping only inches away from this small woman commanding their attention while hastily wiping her eyes.

Mothers and fathers panted for air and pulled their children close to them as they cried out with one voice, "Not Father John! Tell us what happened."

A single voice from the side shouted, "Why are we being punished? Why has evil come here?"

Sr. Ann raised her hand and said simply, "Please, take the children home. We know nothing yet. Please. Go home and pray with your children."

Dazed parents turned and walked to their cars. The bus pulled into the driveway with all the student faces pressed against the windows. Sr. Ann raised her hand again; even the bus driver knew he must stop right where he was. Seeing Sr. Ann headed for the bus, the students dropped into their seats, their eyes darting from one friend to another.

As the door opened, they watched Sr. Ann as she forced her legs to carry her up the three steps; she looked into their bewildered faces. She failed to smother the tremble in her voice as she spoke her terrible message.

Tears began to flow immediately as the youngest children hugged each other; some older students bit their lips in defiance while stinging trickles ran down their cheeks. A few eighth grade boys pounded the seats shouting "Why? Why?" An eighth grade girl sitting in the front seat screamed, "No, No, No. Not Father John."

Sister Ann squeezed her hand. "I wish I could send all of you back home right now, but I know most of your parents are already at work; the secretary is contacting them and it is on the news." She took a deep breath, motioned for them to follow her to the cafeteria and promised to stay with them until their parents could come to pick them up.

In the parking lot, the tragic scene had already been invaded by TV vans and pushy reporters loaded with cameras and microphones. Shoving their way into small clusters of parishioners, some weeping, some looking around in silence and a few women clutching their stomachs, they began asking the mindless "How are you feeling" questions.

One reporter shouted to the crowd, "Was there evidence that Father John was not alone when this happened?"

Glaring looks stopped his next question. Some shook their heads and walked away; others began shouting their disgust.

When two more detectives from homicide arrived, they were grateful that the crowd had thinned. Coleman called them upstairs to the priests' bedroom. He began to speak, but paused and coughed to clear his throat. His partner, Russell, stared in disbelief at this unfamiliar behavior in his always-in-control partner.

"Be extremely careful here," Coleman began. Again, he cleared his throat. "We can't miss a single clue, do not overlook anything, no matter how small," he continued with an urgency that implied a personal obligation.

The chaos he sensed in Coleman puzzled Russell. St. Joseph's was Russell's parish; Father John had visited his home and the two men had shared many good laughs. Russell had admired his pastor and knew how devastating this murder would be to the congregation. He understood why his encounter with this crime was personal, but what was Coleman's struggle?

His eyes roamed around the room of the dead priest. In the chilled room, the lamp lay on the floor, the light bulb shattered where it fell. The yellow blanket and top sheet had been wrenched from the bed and the phone cord yanked from the wall. From the crack in the screen it was obvious the laptop had slammed to the floor along with everything on the table—notes, books, pens, paperclips—were scattered in all directions.

The large mahogany dresser had been shoved across the room, leaving a cruel check-mark scratch on the shiny hardwood floor and now it sat at a desolate angle near a wide rectangular window. In the mournful stillness the smashed mirror reflected a fractured image of the room.

Father John Martin, age 47, black hair with silver specks, graying at the temples, lay on the floor his open dark eyes fixed on the ceiling. His blue-striped pajamas were ripped and bloody, his rather muscular arms were crossed over his chest rigid in defeat. *He must have stayed with some kind of exercise program,* thought Russell, *though he had told me two Christmases ago he was giving up golf.*

On his arms rested a Bible opened to Matthew, Chapter 26. The faint hint of the smile frozen on his face was so utterly out of place that Russell found himself momentarily paralyzed. He willed his eyes away from the body for a few seconds, only to hear the booming laugh that had often come out of this man. Swallowing his gulp of grief, he leaned over closer to the body and counted the stab wounds; there were twelve. He added that information to his notes. His eyes went back to the face and lingered on the smile. *Who did you see, Father? The angels, a friend, your parents?*

Coleman was also looking at the dead priest. He found himself full of questions for God, which did not make much sense because he had decided a long time ago that God was uninvolved in life here on earth. The remnant of his childhood faith prevented a total dismissal of the idea of God, but life had taught him that God had no power. The only way to survive was to be strong and self-sufficient; if you were careful and did the right things, if you were fair, you would be safe. His insides squirmed; he knew that was not true; he had seen too many good people killed. Which, of course, merely proved his conclusion about God. God could not protect you; no matter how much you prayed, how good you were, or whatever else you did to please Him.

So, he asked himself, *what happened, here, Father John? Were you a good priest and your God did nothing for you? Or were you something else? Why was someone so angry with you? Was your life a lie and God just gave you up? A God of justice; that might explain a few things for me, but a God who does not care explains a lot more.*

"Any thoughts so far?" Russell's question cut through the muddle in Coleman's head.

"Not much. You?"

"Looks personal to me."

"What makes you say that?"

"The Bible; I think it was opened for a reason to Matthew, Chapter 26. Plus the twelve stabs; one or two would have been enough to kill him; someone is giving us a message."

Satisfied that they were collecting the evidence and doing everything right, Coleman realized it would be late in the afternoon before the coroner's office could remove the body from the rectory. "I guess we'll know more after the autopsy. Come out back with me."

8

The back door leading into the kitchen was open; the lock had fresh scratches; maybe the crime lab would find something useful there. No dead bolt. Coleman pointed to the security system, in working order but it had not been armed.

Some marigolds under the kitchen windows had been tramped on. Russell called for the photographer to take a picture of a large footprint. Two deep impressions from something else were another few feet away.

The lid for one of two trashcans hung slanted on a bulging trash bag. *If he threw the knife away I doubt he took time to tie up the bag,* thought Coleman. He lifted the other lid; only an empty Cheerios box.

They continued to search under all the shrubs and hedges. "Get someone on the roof to look at those gutters," yelled Coleman.

"I don't see anything else, Rick. Do you? I guess we might as well head back to the station."

Chris Coleman and Rick Russell had been partners for three years. Coleman was 42, two years older than his partner. Coleman was exactly six feet tall; Russell was a mere half-inch shorter. Both gave themselves high marks for being in good physical shape. Coleman tended to ignore a minor detail, as he called it; only fifteen pounds overweight, a fact his wife reminded him, every now and then, he could change before it got worse, but only if he chose to do so; she never bugged him, though, and that he appreciated. *She's a patient woman,* thought Coleman, *especially with me. I wish I could tell her what I feel, but I don't want to lose her; she's such a believer, how does she put up with me?*

He and Russell worked well together sharing an unwavering dedication to the ideal of justice for all. They despised any sign of weakness within themselves but both became very protective of anyone who was clearly vulnerable. Each man always brushed off any compliments to his tender side.

Coleman especially would never admit, least of all to himself, that tears, especially a woman's tears, stripped him of objectivity. To be honest, eyes pulled him into their inescapable mysteries. What he did not realize was how his eyes gave strength to others.

The partners talked about their wives and kids, sports and politics. They thought they knew each other well, but were typically masculine when it came to sharing their personal beliefs. So it was a reticent Coleman who said, "What do you think that priest did to make someone so angry?"

"What he did? What do you mean? You think this is about some kind of revenge? Are you suggesting that he abused someone?"

"Isn't that the first thing you thought? You said yourself it was personal."

"True, but I didn't mean something like that. I know... I knew, Father John; he was my pastor."

Wow, thought Coleman; *you sure kept that part of your life a secret.* "You're a Catholic! I didn't know. What did you think of him?" *What would Russell think if he knew I was Catholic, too? Well, in name anyway,* Coleman laughed to himself.

"He was a great man and a remarkable priest. We trusted him completely; no reservations."

"So, then you must question how God let this happen."

"No, I don't." Russell avoided Chris' stare. He never felt comfortable questioning God about anything; somehow, he always tried to believe what he had been taught as a child—it was always God's will and God knew better than we did.

"Well, what good is a God who does not or cannot protect you?"

That's the question Russell had never faced and he had no answer now. "That's not why I believe in God; I don't spend a lot of time thinking about it, but I do acknowledge that there is a higher power in my life." *That sure was weak,* Russell admitted only to himself.

"Well, this might be hard for you to accept, but maybe Father John wasn't the priest you thought he was. Many priests have fooled a lot of people."

Anger and resentment swelled within Russell; he and Coleman had never had this type of conversation and he did not like where this was headed. "Not so with Father John; I just know it could not be."

Coleman would not let go. Knowing that Russell was Catholic made him even more insistent. "You saw the results of rage back there, Rick. I'm just saying we have to be open to any possibility."

"O.k., I know what you're saying and usually I'd agree with you. But, I can tell you with certainty; this crime has nothing to do with any secret life of Father John. This is something else; I'm positive. I'd stake my life on it."

"Take it easy, Rick; we'll find the truth. And I hope you're right; I really do." A yawning surge of loneliness erupted in Coleman's stomach. He shoved it deep into an internal cavern with all his other questions.

An anxiety spasm shattered Russell's insides but he pushed it away as Coleman pulled into his parking spot and they hurried into the station. Chief Joe Flannery and Captain Randolph motioned them to a conference room. Once inside, the Chief, in his no-nonsense fashion, gave them the expected announcement. "I know you realize that solving this murder is our top priority. So the first item on the agenda is setting up a task force."

Before Flannery could ask for volunteers Coleman spoke up. "I want to head this task force, Chief."

"Any particular reason?"

"No, not really; Russell and I were the first on the scene. I do guarantee this my total undivided attention."

Russell squirmed and got lost in his doubts. *We're starting off with two different views; I'm afraid we're almost at opposite ends on this. I wonder if this will be the end of our partnership. Chris is a great guy, but I just don't understand why he's on this God-has-no-power thing.* He all but regretted the Chief's answer.

"O.k., it's yours. I'm depending on you for a swift resolution. Anything to add, Captain?"

"Just that you'll have full cooperation, including state level support. Coleman, let me know by the end of the day how many men you will need."

"Thanks, Captain; you, too, Chief."

"One more thing," said Chief Flannery. "The bishop is issuing a statement at 6:00. You should be there."

Throughout the day as reports of Father John's violent death spread, people began gathering at St. Joseph's to seek solace from other friends and parishioners. When workers left their jobs, they also headed for the church. A mysterious pull was drawing them to the place where they had celebrated Mass with their beloved priest just two days earlier.

The darkened church comforted yet confused them. How would they continue believing in a loving God? Was it possible for the pain to go away; could their anger be quelled? Why did the Almighty allow this to happen? How could anyone expect forgiveness for such an evil?

Everyone was anxious to hear the evening news. What would the bishop say and what would he do with their church? Six years ago St. Joseph's had three priests residing there. The oldest one, Monsignor Robert Wetzel, had officially retired, but continued to say Mass on a daily basis until he died three years ago; there was no one to take his place. Then Father Bill had gone away a year later; no one seemed to know why. Now they had no priest.

By 5:40 Coleman and Russell were in the bishop's office, jammed against the back wall behind the swarm of reporters. Coleman studied the gaunt figure of Bishop Steele as he sat at his desk staring down at his notepad; not one strand of his thinning white hair was out of place. Even at this distance Coleman could see a persuasive kindness softening his solemn face. As the program manager signaled the countdown of seconds, the bishop put on his rimless glasses and cleared his throat.

Bishop Steele clutched his notes in front of him. The unsteadiness in his well-manicured hands was barely perceptible. Coleman moved his head back and forth to see around the microphones and cameras and he could see determination in the whiteness of the bishop's knuckles. He wondered if the bishop's uneasiness meant more than the obvious. His voice was tense but unwavering; his aging body claimed an unexpected strength.

"Good evening. As you have no doubt heard; Father John Martin of St. Joseph's Church was found brutally murdered this morning."

He paused, swallowed the lump in his throat, and sipped from the glass of water nearby.

"We ask your prayers for Father John's family, and for the congregation of St. Joseph's. The mystery of evil is always a challenge to our belief in a loving God."

Coleman stole a quick glance at Russell; his eyes were fixed on the bishop; his jaw was rigid; his shoulders were pulled back, locked in attention.

"But I urge you to put yourselves with your questions, your pain, and your anger into God's embrace."

Coleman's whole body tensed. *What! What was that word he used? Embrace? He had said to put yourself in God's embrace. If you could do that,* Coleman argued with himself, *then how could you suffer evil? If there were such a thing as God's embrace, why didn't he protect those who were faithful?* Faithfulness was what he saw in his mother and his wife. *I guess those words work for some people,* he thought; but he was glad that at least his wife didn't bug him about this, either. His mother, though, had been a different story. And being her only child, made it worse; she had tried so hard to convince him, but once he had learned of God's impotence, he would not let anyone be his savior.

"Funeral arrangements will be made after the autopsy is completed."

The bishop hesitated. He lifted his head and looked into the camera; his blue eyes, wet and raw, aroused again the loneliness and once more Coleman sent it back to its cave.

"All I ask of you now is to pray. Pray for this city, pray for yourselves, and pray for the police. Pray for me. And I join my prayers with yours. May God give us peace."

He bowed his head, his sad sigh missed as the camera faded away to a reporter.

Coleman found himself both fascinated and perturbed by Bishop Steele. *How well did you really know Father John,* he thought. *And how do you know about God's embrace,* he heard himself screaming inside. *I am sure, Bishop Steele, we will meet face to face very soon.*

Two

Twenty-four hours after the discovery of the body, the church was packed with parishioners although they knew there was no one to say Mass. In the last pew knelt Detective Chris Coleman. *Just part of the job,* he told himself; *the killer could be here to relish the effect of his work.*

But, why the hell, am I kneeling, he mumbled silently.

Memories of himself as a child flashed before him. His First Communion day; he felt so holy that day; Jesus was his friend. Now he's an altar boy; his parents look so proud when they see him all dressed up in his white robe. God was so strong then; he felt safe and special.

Until the day his father was killed. His mother said that God knew best and that his dad was with God now; but he wanted his dad at home. *How come God didn't know that? Why did God take my dad away?* The priest at the funeral had said that God had taken his father to heaven. *How mean of God,* Coleman remembered thinking. He was so mad at God. But he never spoke any of his terrible thoughts out loud. How he wished for an older brother or sister; maybe they would understand; at least, he imagined, they would have listened to him, without crying like his mother would; *if she only knew what I was thinking, would she still love me?*

She said they had to keep going to church; he would feel better, she said. He did feel better, for a while, so he decided she must be right about the other stuff, too. God had his reasons; humans would have to wait until they got to heaven to know why.

All the words worked for a while. *I did try to believe in you,* he thought. A hushed applause caused him to raise his bowed head; a tall, robust man with excellent posture was standing at the podium.

"Good morning."

"Good morning, Deacon Cummings."

"Although I have served here at St. Joseph's for three years, some of you may not know me. I have been a deacon for fifteen years; my wife Sarah is very active here in the parish; we have three grown children, two boys and a girl. They are all married and live outside of the state. With your kind permission, I would like to lead us in prayer and have a communion service."

The thunderous applause brought a tear to his eye as he made a profound bow to the congregation.

"I would also like to offer this suggestion: a continuous prayer vigil from now until the murderer is found."

Again thunderous approval.

During the ensuing service, they prayed for themselves, for Father John, for his family, for the police; and they prayed that the killer would come forward. Coleman could not get a clear view of the deacon's eyes from where he was seated, but the captivating calm of his voice united these morning worshipers. As the people lined up for communion, Coleman noticed that two others, besides himself, remained in their pews.

After the final prayer and a loud Amen from the group, the deacon announced that he would put a sign-up sheet on the table at the back of the church and asked people to write their names in the half-hour slots; they would keep vigil and pray for as long as it took to solve this crime.

One by one people began leaving; as each passed the table, another name was added to the list. Coleman scribbled his name for the 5:00 am period, more than a little amused at his own impulsiveness. *I wonder what Russell would say if he knew what I just did.* He jerked his head to see whose warm hand was on his shoulder, but there was no one there.

Coleman pulled into his spot as Russell got out of his car. Coleman looked for the Dad-mug his partner carried every morning; his kids had given him that for Father's Day two years ago. He treasured that cup; one day when he saw him staring at it, Coleman asked him what he was thinking. He still remembered the melancholy in Russell's eyes when he said he hoped he would live long enough to take it with him to the nursing home someday. Coleman came so close that day to telling Russell about his dad, but instead made some joke about going to the same nursing home.

Coleman understood the absence of Russell's every-day smile but his usual confident stride was also missing.

"Let's talk," he said when they met inside. "Is this case too personal for you, Rick? I want you to be my right hand on this task force, but not if you think you can't give it your all, like usual."

"You're right about it being personal, but that won't be a problem. You should know me by now. I won't let anything distract me from my duty."

"O.k., just so you're sure."

"I'm sure." Then came the usual grin, "Just because you look younger than me, don't think I can't keep up with you."

Russell did not waste time dwelling on Coleman's heavy-duty mop of hair, but they did tease each other once in a while. Russell would always needle his partner by reminding him what Deb, Coleman's wife, had told him after he shaved his head. Michael Jordan's twin; those were her exact words he would say, amused at Coleman's feigned scorn.

"Hey, the captain's motioning for us to come to his office. Maybe there's a break in the case already."

However, all the captain wanted was to pass on the names of those who would be on the special task force. The first meeting was scheduled for tomorrow afternoon. The coroner's office had called; forensics expected to send over the autopsy report in the morning.

Coleman and Russell spent the day planning for the task force meeting. The air between them fluctuated between strain and straightforwardness. Coleman knew their partnership was being tested and he felt guilty for pushing so hard the day before. By 5:00 they called it quits. Russell forced a smile and was taken aback by an unfamiliar confusion in Coleman's eyes.

Coleman grabbed for his jacket. He groaned as he remembered his early morning commitment.

"Are you in pain?" asked Russell.

"Nah, just thinking about tomorrow."

They walked to their cars, each wondering what the other was thinking.

A strange calm tugged at Coleman as he opened his car door and he remembered the warm hand on his shoulder that morning; he stood still for a moment, but shrugged it away without another thought. Russell stared at him, but decided against another question.

Three

Thursday morning Coleman quickly smacked the alarm button when it jarred him awake at 4:15; Deb remained asleep until she heard him in the shower. She rolled over to check the clock, groaned out loud and wondered how much this case would cost him.

She wished he were not so driven by his desire to protect everyone; she remembered how often she told him, *you can't save them all; and you can't always make it better. Bad things do happen.* She had never allowed her tongue to go further and remind him that he could not always be in control.

She feared this case would extinguish the last spark of hope that she was positive lurked in his soul; she knew what he would not admit, that he was searching for a power in his life that he could depend on. She did not know how to help him find it. *O God, she prayed, I know how much you love him. I believe you will never give up on him.*

Twenty minutes later just as she was dozing off, he tiptoed over to her side of the bed, planted a tender kiss in her tousled ash brown hair and was out the door. She hugged her pillow and felt a tear seep out of each eye. "I love you, too," she whispered as she buried her face in the pink silk pillowcase.

At 5:00 he slipped into the last pew. On his knees in a position he had not forgotten, he admitted it felt strange after all these years. Only one other person was there, in the front pew; in the early morning darkness it was hard to make out who it was, but it looked like another man. Coleman was glad there was so much distance between them.

His angry confusion about good and evil, justice and mercy, feeling safe and feeling vulnerable wrung cries of why from the depths of his soul. *Why are you so far away, God? Can you even hear me? Are you even there? Why am I even trying to speak to you?*

The half hour passed slowly, yet at 5:30 Coleman wondered why he was reluctant to leave.

This is crazy, he told himself. *Why am I disappointed? I knew that nothing would happen. I heard no answers, felt no embrace.* He looked at his watch again and noticed two women coming in the side door. Time to go.

Traffic was heavy but he arrived at the office before Russell. *Good,* he thought. *This will give me time to review my notes, and think about motives.*

. Fifteen minutes later Russell stuck his head into Coleman's office and lifted his Dad-mug in greeting. *He's looking more like himself today,* Coleman said to himself.

"Morning, Rick."

"Morning. How did you get here so early?"

"Just lucky, I guess." *You'd be shocked if I told you the truth,* Coleman grinned to himself. "Want to review your notes with me? I'm hoping the autopsy report gets here soon."

"Sure, I have them with me." He grabbed a chair and pulled out his pad.

An hour later the autopsy report arrived. Coleman scanned page one. The time of death was set between 11:00 pm and 2:00 am. Death came with the most severe wound, a gash in the throat. This was the stab that killed him but it was impossible to say which stab was first. The pattern was so haphazard giving no clues to the sequence. He passed the page to Russell.

On the next page he read that resistance bruises on his arms and legs proved that Father John had fought a vigorous battle for his life. His left ankle was broken.

Unfortunately, he had not scratched his attacker; there was no skin under his nails.

But there was another blood sample on his pajamas. *In his fury,* pondered Coleman, *did the killer realize he had cut himself?* That might help if they found a suspect soon.

Coleman erupted. "Tell me all you know about this priest. Why would anyone hate him so much?"

"I have no clue, Chris, I already told you; I know he was a good man."

"This wasn't random violence; this was deliberate and personal."

"Look, Chris, I know you like your cases neat and tidy; cause and effect; you like it when it looks like evil is a payback for something bad. But there are no guarantees in life; I told you the other day, yes, I do believe in God, but I don't think that entitles me to any promise that nothing bad will ever happen to me."

"So, no promises, not even if you dedicate your life to God as a servant?"

"Right. I know it would be easier for you to accept that Father John was guilty of something."

"Wait a minute, now; that doesn't mean I think his murder is justified."

"I know that. But I'm telling you, he was innocent."

"But someone hated him for something."

Coleman was silent for the briefest of moments. On the one hand he wanted to confirm his partner's trust in Father John, but he admitted in a deep space within himself that it would be a simpler case to solve if Father John was not all that he seemed to be.

My viewpoint could be prejudiced, he confessed to himself. Moreover, shoving it down Russell's throat was certainly not the way he wanted to go. "Well, we'd better get back to work. I have a lot to do before the task force meeting at 2:00. We can't afford any mistakes and I want the first impression to leave no doubts in anyone's mind."

"You're right about that." As he stood up to leave, Russell hesitated before turning to walk away.

When he got to the door, he turned back. "I can't give you a sensible answer, Chris, about evil, but I know this case isn't about revenge; and I have a suspicion that we'll both be changed by the time we solve it."

Chris nodded and waved him out the door, not wanting to explore that thought and not knowing what else to say.

The evening news on all channels carried Bishop Steele's announcement of the finalized funeral arrangements. Coleman sat in his favorite lounge chair and glanced at his wife; their two children huddled on either side of her. He watched his son lean forward as the reporter spoke of the throngs of mourners anticipated; his daughter's eyes were red from crying again. He hoped that neither his wife nor his children would be disappointed in him if he discovered a truth they did not want to hear. The reporter continued in solemn tones about how Father John's influence extended far beyond his parish; throughout the city, government and business leaders and people of all faiths had called this man friend. Coleman twisted in his chair as he listened to how Father John's inclusive projects for justice and peace, his welcoming attention to all he met, and his engaging sense of humor, revealed an available and loving God. *So they all proclaim,* he thought, immediately sensing an unwelcome guilt as he looked again at his wife and children.

He heard, as if from a distance, how fitting that Father John's funeral would be held where many had gathered before; Holy Spirit Cathedral, in the center of the city, had often been the chosen place for rallies, demonstrations and prayer vigils. On Saturday at 11:00 it would be the sad host of a profound farewell.

Following the funeral announcement was a news clip from Detective Coleman's brief afternoon press conference. "Look Daddy, you're on TV," his daughter squealed, her moist brown eyes, so full of pride.

He gave her a wink and turned his eyes to the TV. Stating that at this stage the police had little evidence, and were seeking help from the community, he ended with, "The savage violence of this crime indicates someone with a deep personal grudge; we are also convinced that the killer sustained bruises during the fierce struggle. Anyone with any information along these lines is urged to call the anonymous hot line any time of the day or night. Please!"

Alice Manning shivered as she turned off her TV; *I'm sure the police will be coming back to ask me questions. Father John,* she prayed, *how much do I tell them?* Alone in her own house, she threw herself on her couch and wailed, pounding her fists into the brown plaid cushions.

Four

Friday morning found Coleman again on his knees. He swore he was not coming back, but after all, he did sign his name to that sheet. *It means nothing more, nothing less than being true to myself,* he said. *I am always faithful to my word.* His partner's promise about this case changing both of them nagged him with its threat of certainty.

He got a little better look at the man in the front pew. The questions came flooding back again with the same result. Again at the end of the half hour, he knew some force, some spirit, wanted to hold him there. But its grasp was fragile, and he hurried out the door.

Back in his office he reviewed the notes from yesterday's task force meeting. He felt so lonely when he looked at the name they chose, *Operation Soul Search. Why,* he thought, *does it sound like my personal obligation? Was it Rick who came up with that?* He looked over to Rick's office and saw that he was on the phone. *Was he there when I came in? I don't remember seeing his car in the lot.* He tapped on Rick's door just as he was hanging up the phone. "Can we talk some more about the stuff we shared with the task force yesterday?"

"Let's do it in the car. I called St. Joseph's; Alice, the secretary, and the deacon can't believe that a member of the parish would murder Father John, but they said we can talk with them this morning."

"Good. Let's go right now."

"Did you notice how chilly it was this morning?" Rick grabbed his jacket and followed Coleman to his car. "I hope the weather is better on Tuesday for the funeral."

"So, now, tell me again your ideas about that Bible passage."

"As I said yesterday, Matthew 26 tells the story of the Last Supper; the traditional belief is that Christ ordained the apostles as priests that night. That was also the night that Judas betrayed him.

"So, what do you think made Father John a Judas?"

Russell kept silent long enough to force his partner's swift glance off the road. "I'm only saying this once; Father John was not a Judas. Someone may have judged him a betrayer, but he was not. He did not betray God, he did not betray the church; he did not betray anyone."

"Rick, come on. We have to explore every possibility, no matter how disgusting."

The strain in their conversation continued to grow. For every betrayal possibility that Coleman imagined, Russell maintained its impossibility. He was relieved to see St. Joseph's coming into view. *This conversation will take a different turn after this meeting,* he assured himself. Coleman and Russell pulled into the parish driveway. Alice was hanging up the phone as Deacon Cummings opened the door and welcomed the detectives inside.

"How are you?" asked Coleman.

Deacon Cummings sighed. "As well as can be expected, I guess." Coleman looked into his dark eyes; he saw a depth of determination that stabbed at his own loneliness and wondered how deep a man's belief could go.

Alice nodded her head hurrying to wipe away a tear from her cheek. "I still feel as if I'll wake up from this nightmare, yet I know I am awake. I wish I weren't."

When Coleman saw her eyes, he glimpsed a terror that shadowed a secret. *She must have cried half the night,* he thought. "I understand. We're grateful that you're both willing to give us this time and your insights into any possibilities. Don't think anything is too insignificant to mention." His gaze locked onto her eyes for just a moment.

"Well" the deacon began. "I've been racking my brain trying to make some sense out of this. I guess I should mention a group of young boys that Father John started to help when they were 12 or 13. By now I think some of them are out of high school. In fact, both priests that we had back then did a lot for those kids. They are not labeled by anyone that I know of, as a gang, but they do hang out together; they've been in trouble a few times for doing drugs and were suspects in several robberies. I can't remember if anyone was ever convicted of anything."

He looked to Alice who shrugged her shoulders. "I don't know about that, either."

"They're always seen going into an abandoned house on the outskirts of town and they call themselves The Plumbers. The leader is called the CEO; I don't know his real name."

"Was Father John involved with them in some way?"

"I know he went to court a few times to testify."

"Was he testifying for or against?"

"Oh, I'm sure it was for; he always could see the potential for redemption when the rest of us were ready to call it quits. I just hope one of them didn't misinterpret his virtue for naiveté."

Alice wiped away another tear. "Father did visit them, sometimes two or three times in a week. Several of them came here one day. I could hear angry words and it sounded as if someone was pounding on the wall, but when they left, they seemed quite peaceful. They even smiled and wished me a good day."

"When Alice and I were talking about this, you know it's hard for us to point fingers at anyone; this is just so unbelievable. But, you said to mention anything; I wasn't aware of this but Alice said we should tell you about Dan Salvage."

Coleman raised an eyebrow. "The guy released a few months ago from death row? Something about new evidence, or lawyer incompetence. He was the one convicted of planning the murder of his wife and little girl. How do you know him?"

Alice gulped. "Father hired him, maybe six weeks or so ago, part-time. He's been doing some maintenance work around here. I heard on the TV that you said the killer might have bruises." She inhaled a deep breath. "I noticed yesterday that Dan's arm was black and blue; he even had a band-aid on his right thumb." She looked up at the deacon.

"I've never seen him; he just came up in our conversation this morning."

"Was he here yesterday? I never saw anyone else come in while we were here."

"Oh, Detective, he didn't come in until late afternoon; after the coroner." She bit her lip to stifle the sob that trembled in her mouth. "He had heard the news and stopped by. He usually came only when Father called him about something needing to be done."

"We'll need an address on him."

Alice nodded. She opened a side drawer. "I have his file in here." Alice had been the parish secretary for more than twenty years; now a widow, she had raised four children and enjoyed being a grandmother. Russell admired the pictures on her desk.

"Beautiful children," he said.

"Thank you; they're such a joy. I keep telling my daughter to enjoy every minute with them because they grow up so fast; too fast." She wiped away another tear.

"You must have seen a lot of growing up with all the families in this parish over the years," said Coleman.

"True." A shadow passed over her face as her eyes went first to Coleman and then to Russell. "I feel awkward about this; even disloyal. Father John always told me how much he trusted me. He knew that I kept many secrets."

"What is it? We need all the help we can get; anything at all might give us a lead."

"Sometimes I overhear things." She rubbed the palms of her hands together. "I make it a point to not be a snoop, but sometimes people get very loud."

"Was someone angry with Father John?" asked Coleman. "It's o.k.. We'll check it out and decide if there's reason to investigate. Your name will never come up; I promise you."

Those eyes, she thought. *He can see; he will know.* "This is so hard for me to do. I've never talked about anyone who came here for help. Both of these problems happened several years ago."

Coleman and Russell waited and watched the struggle with her conscience; her eyes darted back and forth as she balanced what she considered betrayal to those families with the enormity of her pain of losing Father John.

Coleman searched for the right words. "Sometimes, when people have a lot of anger and feel that God has abandoned them, they transfer their anger to someone they see as God's representative. They can strike at that person; they can hurt that person; they can't do anything to God because God is too far away."

Russell was grateful that Coleman was being prudent enough not to suggest his other ideas.

"No, it didn't sound like they were angry with God; they were really angry with Father John."

Her voice became calm and steady; her conscience had given her the green light.

"Michelle Mahoney had an abortion; her parents were so terribly upset. I never saw Michelle come with them, but I often heard her mother, Susan, crying; her father, Michael, was usually loud and intimidating. He has a temper. I could just imagine what went on in that home when they found out what she had done."

Alice bit her tongue. *That sounded so judgmental,* she reprimanded herself. *I better stick to facts, not my opinions.*

"I gave them so much credit, though, for continuing to see Father. It took a while, months really, before their meetings quieted down. And, except for that, which you can understand why it was so upsetting, they were a perfect family. Mike and Susan are so religious, always at Mass and involved in church functions. I just can't believe that Mr. Mahoney would let his temper turn to that kind of violence."

She caught herself wringing her hands.

"Oh, maybe I shouldn't have said anything. I'm sure he, Mr. Mahoney, couldn't have done such a terrible thing."

"Don't worry; you're doing the right thing. We'll find the truth. What's the other story?"

What is it about Coleman that put her at ease even though she felt guilty? His eyes cut into her soul, yet they relaxed her. *This isn't gossip,* she convinced herself. *Father John would tell me to trust him. Isn't that so, Father John? I have to help him find your killer.*

"The Anderson's. Their daughter, Cindy, had a baby while she was living with her boyfriend, the Collins boy. Mr. Anderson wanted Father John to tell them they had to get married, but Father refused."

"Was Mr. Anderson angry?"

"Oh, was he. Mike and his wife, Carol, had quite a few sessions here; I've known Carol for years. She was torn between keeping peace with her husband and holding on to her daughter. One time I heard Mike yell, 'It's your job, Father, to keep them from living in sin!' After a few months, they broke up."

"Do you think Mike Anderson blamed Father John for his marriage failing?"

"Oh, Mike and Carol didn't break up; Cindy and her boyfriend broke up; Cindy and Wayne; that's it. His first name is Wayne."

"Thank you, Alice. This gives us a place to start." As she walked over to her files, the deacon described the location of the abandoned house where *The Plumbers* hung out.

Having thanked them again for their help, Coleman and Russell headed for the door. Deacon Cummings said, "We're praying for you. God bless you."

"You seem to be doing a good job holding the congregation together." Out of the corner of his eye, Coleman saw the bewilderment on Russell's face as they walked towards their car.

Out of earshot of the Deacon he said, "What the heck was that all about?"

"Nothing, really. The day after the murder I went to the church to check things out; I thought that maybe the killer would show up to see how upset people were. The deacon led a service; the people seem to like him."

"I never thought about that. I take it you didn't see anyone suspicious."

"No, but a couple people didn't go to Communion."

"Oh, I don't think you can read much into that."

Coleman started getting nervous. *If we keep talking about this, I might end up telling him I'm going there every morning.* "Where should we go first?"

"Let's go with The Plumbers. I've heard some of the guys talk about them; there's been lots of rumors, but always a suspicious lack of witnesses. Maybe Father John was too trusting. Maybe one of them demanded even more than he could give and things just got out of control."

"But how would you explain the absolute hatred that we saw. I mean, why, if things simply got out of control, why was there so much violence? Why did he keep stabbing him, most likely even after he was dead?"

"I still don't think it was personal in the sense that you do. Put drugs into the picture; then there's no logic to anything."

"You're right about that." He glanced at Russell and decided this might be a good time to get something off his chest. "I've been wondering about something else. Do you mind if I ask you; it might be a little personal?"

"As long as it isn't any more of your disgusting theories. Did you hear how good he was with people; even with people who were upset with him? And you're going to hear more stories like that, too."

"This is on another level. What do you think Father John did in those last moments, when he knew he was going to die? Do you think there was a moment when he cursed his killer?"

Russell was more than pleased to give his viewpoints on this. These were the types of conversation he could only hope would increase.

"No; not at all. I think that at the worst moments of your life your best side comes through. Remember 9/11; what did all those people say on their cell phones—*I love you*—they didn't speak words of hate. I believe you die the way you live, so I am certain he prayed. When he first realized he was being attacked,

I'm sure he prayed to be saved, but I think when he knew he was going to die, he just prayed. Now, I can't give you any proof, but I also believe that he wasn't alone at that moment; I think that he saw God and he just let go."

"Damn! You really believe that God is that involved? I don't buy it."

"I do. Ever think that you just might be afraid to allow a stronger power into your life. You've made self-sufficiency your life's work; you always have to be in control."

"It's the only way I can feel safe; if I'm in control, I can protect others; it's all that I know how to do. But I have to admit that a small part of me, just a tiny part, mind you, envies you, Rick. Sounds like a terrific way to live if you believe that you're not alone in this world. But believing doesn't make it true. That is what I know. Wait a minute; this is the address the deacon gave us. This is supposed to be The Plumbers' residence right over there."

Both detectives stared in awe at this so-called abandoned house; a one-story wooden house boasting a recent coat of light green paint, a precision-trimmed hedge, framing a freshly mowed lawn that Coleman admitted looked better than his. *The empty porch could use some white resin chairs,* he thought as he rapped on the door.

A very tall and lanky teenaged boy, with a slouch that made Coleman think of an al dente noodle, gave them and their badges a once-over glance. Bowing low with a dramatic flourish, he welcomed them inside.

Off to the right the detectives observed a spacious sunny kitchen where a large empty box of pizza had been thrown on the table and empty soda cans filled the trashcan labeled RECYCLE NOW! The sink was empty; the lemon smell added an unexpected accent. In the living room area, six boys huddled around a computer. The CEO stood up; all the others stopped what they are doing and gave him their full attention.

"Why are you here?"

"We're clean," said the one in the middle facing the computer. Indeed, as the detectives scanned the room they saw one worn couch, three mismatched cushioned chairs, a small TV, no carpet, and no signs of drug use.

"We're here to talk about Father John's death."

A unified shout rattled the detectives with its intensity. "We don't know nuthin' about that."

A lone voice added, "Nuthin' at all."

The CEO pointed to the couch and invited the police to sit down. He was tall, a head taller than Coleman, with spiked blond hair tinged with dark brown and piercing green eyes. *A too perfect fit for the so-good-looking, popular, and dangerous cliché,* thought Coleman.

The detectives seated, the CEO dragged a folding chair to a spot in front of the couch, sat down facing the back and wound his legs around the front legs. He leaned over the back, his lips spread into a confident smile, and with a keen, cool look in his eyes, began, his voice unwavering.

"Listen, Officers, we loved Father John; he was our friend and our mentor. You should have seen this place before he helped us. It was a mess. We were a mess. This was our place to hang out, to do some drugs, to plan our next project, if you get my drift. But Father John, he listened to us; he met with the teachers at our high school; he talked to our parents. He convinced all of them to give us a chance to change. That was three years ago."

Every boy nodded his head. The CEO pointed his right hand towards the computer.

"He loaned us the money to get that computer; he even came after we set it up so he could see what we were doing.

And to tell us, in no uncertain terms, what he never expected to see us doing on there. Plus, he helped us work with a drug counselor at the school and another one at the hospital; we didn't really get it at first; we still got in trouble more than once, but he never gave up on us. So you gotta believe me, nobody here would hurt Father John; he was our friend."

"What about the money for the computer; how were you going to pay him back?"

"Well, even though we knew we had changed, and Father John knew we had changed, other people still didn't trust us. Besides, we didn't know how to do much of anything. So he thought that a computer would help us; we had computers in school but there was never enough time to use them. Father John, he said he didn't care how long it took to pay him back; it was just the idea that he wanted us to work for something. I'm telling you, he was our good friend. No way anybody here would hurt him."

"By the way what's your first name and why do you call yourselves 'The Plumbers'?"

"Matt's my name; Matthew Ryder. We named ourselves The Plumbers because we were going to unclog the money in this town; get it? Unclog the money; drain it away from the rich."

His choked snicker evaporated into the air, as his whole face became one solemn protest.

"But, Father John, he taught me another meaning; he told me plumb could mean to go into the depths to get to something. He actually said he wanted me to plumb the meaning of my life; no one ever said nuthin' like that before—that my life had meaning."

His eyes glistened; he had never taken his eyes off Coleman or Russell.

"Then he told me about the Matt in the Bible; he was a tax collector, so he was like doing what I was doing—you know, he was draining money from the people, but Jesus came along and called him away from that kind of life."

He stopped for a wistful second, leaned closer and whispered, "That Father John sure had a way with words; he made us all feel like we was somebody. Father John; he was like a real father to us."

Matthew became even more subdued. He lowered his eyes to the floor and shook his head, "No way!" He murmured three times. "Just no way could anybody here do something so awful to Father John!"

Silence. The computer said, "You have mail."

"How good are you with that thing?" asked Coleman.

"We're very good. We have our own Web site; we've posted our pictures and our job qualifications; the pictures are mainly for the girls, of course. We write reviews of local high school sports and just some other fun stuff."

"I have an idea," said Coleman, "if you're that good. We might be getting back in touch with you." Both detectives stood. They thanked Matt and the other boys for their help.

After Russell attached his seat belt, Coleman asked, "What do you think?"

"It sounds too good to be true, but I don't think he could have made up that story about plumbing. Who knows about any of the others that we didn't see there today. You like to believe the best when you see what we saw in there, but someone could have held an old grudge about a priest; or someone could have thought that if Father John had money for a computer, he had a lot more."

"Anything is possible, of course. If all Matt said is true, I can see that you might be right about Father John. But he made someone angry about something; I just hope it wasn't one of them. Well, let's move on; maybe we'll learn something from Dan Salvage."

Dan Salvage clicked off the remote when he heard the doorbell. Opening the door his stoic face drew Coleman's attention to his vacant eyes; the graying hair and the ashen complexion made him look much older than he was. "I figured you'd come. I guess from now on my role will be that of the convenient suspect."

"We just need some information, that's all. Can we come in?"

Salvage stepped backward into the hall entrance.

"Since you've been doing some work around the rectory we thought you could tell us when you last saw Father John."

"I was there that night, Monday, but we just talked. Don't get me wrong now, I'm glad to be out of prison; shouldn't have been there anyway, as you know. But now, what kind of life do I have?"

Coleman and Russell followed him into the living room, an undefined room that seemed to answer his own question. A newspaper lay scattered on the floor; an empty beer bottle sat like a vase on the end table. If a robbery had occurred during the murder, Dan Salvage would be a prime suspect.

"I'm alone, don't have a job, and because the real murderer is still out there, I know I'm still guilty as far as a lot of folks are concerned. Others are just plain scared to be around me."

His hands twitched as he went through his pockets for a cigarette. When he didn't find one, he grumbled under his breath and chewed the inside of his cheek.

"Father John was helping me get into school so that I could learn some new skills. Because I don't like to accept charity, he gave me some part time maintenance work to do around the parish; that's why I was there Monday evening. I had just finished some roof repairs and I really needed to talk with Father before I went home."

Must have been his footprint, thought Coleman. *Looks like the right size. And those other impressions must be from a ladder.*

Salvage turned his face away for a brief moment. "I miss my wife and little girl so much. I hate coming home to this empty place. Father John understood that and he often invited me to stay for supper, just like he did on Monday. But like I said, I really wanted to talk, too, so I stayed even longer than usual. After we ate, we watched some TV. Then I came home. He was fine when I left."

"What time was that?"

"Well, we watched some of the news; I left after the sports part, so it was a few minutes before 11:30."

"By the way, how did you get that bruise?"

Salvage stared at his arm for a moment. "I don't remember; must have been when the ladder started to fall; I grabbed it and got my finger caught; even bled a little." He held up his thumb.

"While working around the parish, had you observed anyone recently that was angry with Father John; any strange characters showing up?"

"Not really; there were always people coming and going. I really didn't pay much attention. And I never heard anything."

"If you remember something, anything that might suggest someone had a grudge against the Church or God, whatever, let us know.

"Sure thing, officers; if I think of anything. I'd like to do something to change people's attitude about me."

Salvage stood at his door and watched them leave; as they pulled out of his driveway he slammed shut the door.

"Where next?" asked Russell.

"The Mahoney's. What did you think of Salvage?"

"He didn't try to hide the bruise so he was either unaware or he did get hurt with the ladder. I saw you looking at his feet when he said he did roof repairs; guess that means we don't have anything."

"Doesn't prove he didn't do it. It's lunch time. The secretary said that Mrs. Mahoney is usually home in the afternoon. Let's grab a quick bite to eat first." They pulled in front of the McDonald's drive-up window.

"Hey, what's with the grilled chicken sandwich?"

"Deb's finally convinced me that I have to be the one who makes the choice about getting this weight off before I start hanging over my pants. Look, no fries."

"She's right, you know. Are you going to exercise, too?"

"One thing at a time. But, yeah, I know she's right about that, too."

Just as he was putting the empty containers into the car's garbage bag, Rick said, "Turn right, here. The Mahoney's are the first house."

When Mrs. Mahoney opened the door, both detectives were captivated by her charm. Having calculated that she must be in her 40's, they did not expect someone who looked 30, petite, shoulder length light brown hair with golden highlights and striking sapphire blue eyes.

Coleman heard once that your eyes enlarge when you are looking at something pleasing. *I can actually feel them getting bigger. I hope she doesn't notice.* He fumbled for his badge.

"Ahh, Mrs. Mahoney, I'm Detective Chris Coleman, this is my partner, Rick Russell. May we speak with you?"

"Please, call me Susan. Of course, Officers, come in. What's this about?"

They followed her into the living room. *No ambivalence here* thought Coleman as he surveyed a white couch and love seat with black pillows placed with precise care. Coleman tripped over the white carpet.

With all this bright sunlight, what is his problem, Russell hooted to himself. *He even dropped his badge.*

Coleman recovered in record time. "Mrs. Mahoney, we are talking to people in the parish, trying to gather information from anyone who may have had a particular relationship with Father John."

"And you think I did?" Coleman noticed a momentary frost in those sapphire eyes.

"Well, we know that you and your husband went to Father John for counseling after ah, after…"

"After our daughter's abortion; yes. You've evidently talked with Alice Manning."

Coleman rushed to defend the secretary, saying that he and his partner had access to all the parish records.

Susan lowered her eyes. "Of course, you do. I should not have said that. Alice is a wonderful person; I've never known her to betray a confidence. I guess that the abortion still embarrasses me. Every day I think about it and every day I regret what our Michelle did."

Her entire body stiffened. She forced herself to smile. "But, we don't brood about our failure as much anymore. But somehow, we did fail; our daughter made a decision that contradicted everything we believed in and everything we thought we had inspired in her. But how can there be a connection?"

"We're not saying there is."

Coleman proceeded with caution. "What were trying to do is develop a picture of how Father John dealt with predicaments and difficulties in his parishioners' lives; somewhere in that picture might be a clue as to why someone would find him unsuitable for ministry."

"And that judgment would give them permission to kill him?" For a second time Coleman caught the iciness in those eyes.

"We've learned to never be surprised by people's justifications."

"I suppose you're correct."

Her eyes lowered again, she continued in a voice that cracked with disappointment and heartache.

"We had been very upset about the abortion. And I'm sure I was even more upset because Michelle had not confided in me. My husband was furious with Father John, because he thought Father had been too easy on Michelle, telling her about support groups that she could join and that she could be forgiven for this sin without revealing the name of the father—that hit Mike the hardest."

The fingers of her one hand twisted and turned her wedding ring. She took a moment to decide how to justify her husband's pain.

"Mike's a senior partner at the law firm downtown and he has this impassioned sense of right versus wrong; he didn't think it was fair for the boy to 'go free,' so to speak. But that was four years ago."

"Did your husband ever change his mind?"

Her eyes were still focused on the rug. "I'm sure he still grapples with it; we never discovered who the father was. But Father met with us numerous times, he prayed with us, grieved with us and was helping us to learn how to forgive. Our relationship with Michelle is still strained and Father had just lately helped us move closer to a real reconciliation with our daughter."

"Does your daughter live with you?"

"No, Michelle has her own apartment near the downtown area, just ten miles away. She works at Optimize, Inc., a computer software design company."

She lifted her head, her eyes fluid with sadness. "She's in another relationship at the moment, but we haven't met him." A delicate smile warmed her face for just a moment.

As if being driven to clear up any doubts, Susan went on. "My husband was more in tune with Deacon Cummings because the deacon emphasized the sin and Michelle's need for repentance; he didn't seem to make the forgiveness aspect so easy."

She clenched a fist and sighed. "But again, that was at the beginning when Mike was consumed by his anger and just couldn't let go of the fact that he could not prosecute Michelle's boyfriend. He felt betrayed not only by his daughter's apparent rejection of all she had been taught, but also by Father John's firm insistence that he release his anger at the unknown boyfriend. However, I believe that in his heart my husband recognized that forgiveness is the true message of Jesus, and though it was not easy for him, he was gradually coming around to Father John's way of dealing with the matter. I'm sure of it; I really am."

Her voice changed from energized to persuasive. "It's going to take more time, of course, but I have no doubt that our family will become closer, that this ordeal will make us more honest with each other."

The blush that tinted her cheeks betrayed the insight she had just admitted to herself, perhaps for the first time—it had always been more important to the Mahoney's to be admired as the model happy family than facing their communication issues with Michelle.

"But," she clenched both fists, "We needed more time with Father John; he had been so patient with us; helping us understand how we had to first forgive ourselves. Now I'm not sure if we have the strength to continue without his help."

Coleman and Russell expressed their sincere gratitude to Mrs. Mahoney for her honest conversation and asked her to call if she remembered anything that might be helpful to their investigation. The embarrassment in her eyes told them she was worried that she had already shared too much.

Neither Coleman nor Russell believed Susan was hiding anything, but something made them nervous. Maybe Susan was seeing in her husband the transformation she wanted to see. Maybe he had not released as much hostility as she hoped, or had convinced herself to believe. No doubt, Michelle's side of the story would be a compelling part of this family picture, if they ever needed to fill in the missing pieces. Coleman wondered if she had inherited the sapphire eyes.

They had been with Susan Mahoney much longer than planned. Tomorrow was Saturday but this day had been long enough; they decided the Anderson visit could wait for the morning.

Five

On his way to the office the next morning, Russell found himself going back again to the scene and looking at that incompatible smile on the dead priest's face; that was enough proof for him that Father John was the good man he believed him to be. "But it doesn't make it any easier to accept," he said aloud. In silence he prayed, *O God, you know that I do not doubt you, but I'm having a hard time with this one. I'm afraid of what the truth might be and I don't know what to say to Chris.*

Coleman was also reviewing the violent evidence he saw; he remembered what he told Russell after their visit with The Plumbers. He wanted to believe it when he said it, especially for Russell's sake. Yet, it was harder to believe that if Father John Martin was that good, that he died the way he did. It just wasn't right and it made no sense. *What would happen to Russell's faith if the truth turns out to be closer to my suspicions,* he asked himself.

At 9:00 Coleman and Russell entered the Anderson's circular driveway; they did a quick study of the brick and stone two-story mansion centered on a wooded corner lot. *My kind of style,* thought Coleman as he checked out another downhill driveway leading to a three-car garage. When the secretary had mentioned the Anderson name, Coleman never made the connection until now. Mike Anderson was a well-respected cardiovascular surgeon and his wife had been written up in several magazines for her work in cancer research.

Two rings of the doorbell. When Mike opened the door he didn't even try to hide his surprise at these unexpected visitors. The detectives produced their badges and asked if they could come in; he nodded with a subdued greeting and invited them inside. The spacious foyer dominated by a huge vase of fresh flowers, led to a circular staircase.

Coleman and Russell followed him into an enormous living room. *Nothing but the best,* thought Coleman as he admired the luxurious maroon leather furniture. The Anderson's daughter, Cindy, with her blond hair falling into a wave touching her shoulders, had an engaging smile, and was standing in the hallway leading to the family room with curly-haired, four-year old, Bryce.

Mike called to his wife and signaled Cindy to come along. Mike and Carol sat close to each other on the couch and Mike pointed to two, very comfortable-looking chairs for the detectives. Cindy put Bryce at a little table in the far corner of the room; she left for a moment and returned with some books and model cars and joined her parents on the couch placing herself near her mother. Coleman noticed that her dark brown eyes hinted at the tension of being a young and single mother living with her accomplished parents.

"How can we help you?" Mike ran a nervous hand through his thick brown hair.

I'll bet he had transplants, thinks Russell; *he must be around 50.*

"I'm assuming you're investigating Father John's murder. Are you visiting all the parishioners?"

"Only the ones who had some recent encounters with Father John."

Anticipating his next question Coleman continued, "We have no suspects at this point; we are merely trying to gather information about how Father John dealt with families in crisis, to help us understand if his approach to problems and religion could inspire anger or hostility in someone."

Mike's eyes darted from Carol to Cindy. He strained to control the tension in his voice as he acknowledged that he did indeed have a problem with Father John when he would not marry Cindy and Wayne Collins.

Mike confessed that he had even had a secret conversation with the deacon regarding the possibility of having him perform a private ceremony in their home. When Deacon Cummings showed him the folly of that decision, Mike gave in. "Besides, Father John said forcing them to marry would invalidate the marriage and when Cindy and Wayne insisted that they were not ready to marry I resigned myself to the situation."

He looked over at Cindy but their eyes never made contact.

"But I wasn't willing yet to forgive Wayne. However, I was beginning to understand the truth of something Father John had told me—again and again—the work of forgiveness would be the toughest job I ever had to do. If I hadn't had Carol beside me, I don't know what I would have done."

He instinctively grabbed for her hand, as he asked, "Do either of you have a daughter?"

As both detectives nodded in the affirmative, Mike said, "Then I think you understand what I'm saying as a father."

Coleman nodded his agreement. "But what I want to know is did his preaching about forgiveness rub people the wrong way? Did people think he was too tolerant of sin?"

"No way. Everyone loved Father John. But he was very open and accepting of everyone." Mike's inner conflict slipped out. "I guess there were others, like myself, who thought he was too lenient, especially with the teenagers and children. I confess I wished he had talked more morality with the kids. He had a lot of group activities and dances and so forth, but I didn't hear much about right and wrong."

"Oh, Daddy," Cindy broke in. "He did talk with us a lot about that; but he tried to help us see God as a loving God, not a check list judge."

"Maybe there was too much love talk; maybe you and Wayne should have heard more about sinning rather than about..."

Cindy lowered her eyes and Coleman tasted her embarrassment; Carol curled her fingers around her husband's and squeezed his hand; Mike bit his lip.

He reproached himself with every word that came out of his mouth. "Cindy, honey, I'm so sorry; I shouldn't have said that. I'm sorry. Forgive me. Cindy, please. I didn't mean that."

Cindy raised her head and acquiesced with a weak smile. "I know Dad. It's o.k.."

"What about Wayne's parents? Did they feel the same way? Did they want your daughter and him to get married?"

"No. They agreed with Father John from the beginning."

As her husband hesitated to go on, Carol jumped in. "Wayne is adopted. He had been a particularly difficult foster child and had been in the system from the time he was abandoned at age 2. They were upset just like we were, right, Mike?" She patted his hand.

"Yes, they've even insisted on helping Cindy with expenses and they made Wayne get a job and he gives her money every week. Even though we would have no difficulty providing for our grandchild, we felt he should take some responsibility. I don't believe in making it too easy to forget your mistakes."

46

He looked at both detectives; his next words revealed his submission to a situation he could not change.

"So I can honestly tell you that we're working together. This was a hard lesson for everyone, including myself. But I love my daughter; and I love my grandson. We're taking it day by day, but we're finding our way."

An hour of candid conversation wound to a close; Coleman and Russell thanked the Andersons for their cooperation, waved good-bye to Bryce and left.

"A lot of personal struggle, but Mike's efforts at forgiveness seemed genuine, don't you think?" asked Russell as both detectives hurried to their car. Coleman nodded. Time would disclose the truth, but it was enough for a Saturday.

Coleman's son had a soccer game at 1:00 and he promised him he would be there. Russell's son was on the same team and he had made the same promise. They agreed to take five minutes for a quick check-in at the office.

Both detectives roamed around their own thoughts all the way back to the station; Russell remembered a good priest who had shown him that holiness was an everyday opportunity. Coleman still had the same questions swirling around inside, yet was surprised that he regretted not knowing Father John and wondered what kind of God he would have found with him.

Will Operation Soul Search bring me any kind of satisfaction or will it be merely another detour? Will I find out all over again that I must only rely on myself, that hope and trust and faith might work for others, but not for me? Those words sound like surrender and that, I will never do, he promised himself.

Earlier that morning at St. Joseph's Deacon Cummings informed the congregation that, Father Clarke, a chaplain from the local high school who had served the parish on weekends, would continue to come for the Saturday evening Mass and two

Sunday Masses, but there were no other priests available during the week. When he announced that there would be a special service tomorrow, Sunday at 4:00pm because Father John's body would be returned to them, a collective heartache hung in the air. After pausing with his head bowed, the deacon intoned the opening prayer.

Dan Salvage sat in the last pew. He put his head in is hands and wept silently. Yesterday, he had introduced himself to Deacon Cummings.

Six

By 3:30 on Sunday the parking lot overflowed with cars and vans; parishioners, walked in twos and threes, some held small children by the hand, others carried quiet babies, a few people in wheelchairs and others struggled with walkers and canes; all made their sad and somber journey toward the open church door.

Coleman and Russell were sure the killer would be attending the service but they had no reason to hide their presence as they stood near the open doors. Task force members were scattered throughout the church.

No one gave in to impatience today when the parking spaces all around the church were filled; people headed for the school playground and also began lining their cars along both sides of the street.

Inside the church people squashed and squeezed into every pew; most sat and stared ahead, some knelt, some held their heads in their hands, others were bowed in deep concentration.

Five minutes before the service was scheduled to begin Coleman and Russell slid in beside so many others cramped against the walls along the back and sides of the church. The late afternoon sun shimmered through the stained glass windows and Coleman followed its path to a pew on the far side. Dan Salvage sat, alone, his head bowed into his chest. Beside him were Matt and the Plumbers, their faces riveted to the picture of Father John on top of his casket.

Russell observed Mr. and Mrs. Anderson close to Cindy who was holding Bryce; she stole a covert glance at Wayne who was seated across the aisle with his parents. His stare was fixed on the altar.

Carol Anderson leaned her head close to her husband and pointed to where Father John's family sat and prayed. Russell recalled the fun times when the parishioners had welcomed Ed, Father John's only brother, his wife, Jenny and their three children; because they lived in a nearby city they were frequent visitors for various parish events.

Russell searched for Sister Rosemary. How proud Father John was the day he gave his youngest sister his special blessing before she left to serve in Brazil.

He noticed his other sister, Donna and her husband, Paul; each parent had an arm around a child. Two pews behind them were the Mahoneys.

Deacon Cummings walked to the podium; an aura of influence surrounded him and fascinated Coleman. He noticed that he gave a hint of a smile to a younger woman in the front pew. *Is that his wife,* wondered Coleman. *Maybe she is the one who keeps him so calm, like Deb does for me. Except, they're both on the same side.* His soul's loneliness stirred like a soft and sad whimper of a boy child; Coleman turned his attention back to the deacon who spoke gracious words of welcome to the bishop, parishioners and visitors.

As Bishop Steele began with "In the name of the Father," Russell winced as he looked at his family, seated across from the Mahoneys. He regretted that his wife often had to fill the roles of both father and mother. Noelle sat between their daughter, who was the older one and their son; their family had enjoyed so many good times with Father John. He studied their sad faces and worried about the possibilities his partner had forced him to consider. *Oh, God, please, don't let any of it be true.*

Coleman was having a difficult time concentrating; his eyes sought out his wife and children sitting near the windows. They seemed to belong here in this church. *Of course, they do*, he reminded himself. *I'm the one who doesn't belong.*

The service concluded at 5:30; immediately a line formed to pass by the casket.

Fingers trembled as they touched the coffin; some found it difficult to move on; they wanted to cling.

As they walked by, each member of Father John's family squeezed a hand or was embraced by a compassionate hug.

As the crowd of parishioners spoke of their devotion and love for Father John and his impact on their lives, his family heard many loving descriptions repeated over and over—dynamic, gentle-hearted, charismatic, compassionate, loving.

But the image that most consoled their hearts and soothed the ache in their souls was the banner that hung near the altar: "We encountered God face to face when we met Father John." Coleman was struck by it, too. *What if I missed my chance,* he asked himself. The thought was so frail he forgot it as he turned his attention to Dan Salvage, who stood for an extra long time at the casket. *Is it guilt or pain of loss,* thought Coleman? *I wish I could get a handle on a motive.*

On Monday another wake service was held at Holy Name Church, Father John's first parish. Father Bill Williams welcomed the bishop and the congregation.

Russell talked with him after the service telling him what so many other St. Joseph parishioners said that evening—how much he was missed. Sentiments he treasured, he told Russell, but how he wished the circumstances for hearing them could be wiped away.

Coleman made sure that Russell saw that Dan Salvage was there. Russell tended to believe Salvage's story and told Coleman that Salvage may only be trying to stay away from an empty house, or may even be hoping that he was making himself more acceptable to the people. Coleman was not ready to let go of his suspicions.

St. Joseph's remained open all night; determined, resolute men and women continued to come every half-hour. Only a week ago, and yet it seemed so long a time since Father John had left them. They would bury him tomorrow, with still no clue about the evildoer.

Tuesday morning a final prayer service was scheduled before the funeral. The regular morning group that always attended that 8:00 Mass was lost in the huge crowd that arrived that day; no responsibilities of work, school, or home, could keep anyone away that morning.

The dark blue haze was interrupted by streaks of light fighting to control the struggling sun. When Coleman and Russell got out of their car, they were confused at the crowd outside the church looking into the sky. Their eyes followed the pointing fingers and they gasped. The biggest rainbow they had ever seen formed an arch over the entrance to the church. Russell smiled as he whispered, "Thank you, God."

Coleman was irritated at the joy he saw in Russell and also felt within himself. He recalled words from some forgotten source about a sign of a covenant with God. *This means nothing; it's only a coincidence,* he assured himself. He pulled on Russell's arm. "We'd better get inside."

Coleman could hardly wait for the service to end. The church was so packed he had a hard time checking for his favorite suspect. As soon as they got outside Coleman checked the sky. The rainbow was gone. "Thank goodness," he mumbled under his breath.

As if the heavens wanted to send another message, a downpour began without warning. Husbands let go of their wives' hands as the women tried to shield their hairdos; teenagers stopped their group hugs and little children hung on to their mothers' skirts; everyone dashed to their cars.

Police escorts waited in front and at the rear of the line, which extended a full mile down the road. All along the way people watched, umbrellas and newspapers covering their heads. Tears slid down the faces of many as the procession wound its way downtown to Holy Spirit Cathedral.

By 10:30 the hearse pulled into the wide tree-lined driveway leading to the entrance of the cathedral. Parking lots all around the cathedral were soon packed.

Since the cathedral was only two blocks from the shopping mall, many opted to park there and walk the short distance to the cathedral.

At 11:05, the organ erupted with the notes of *I Am the Resurrection* as Bishop Steele, with bent shoulders, followed dozens of priests down the aisle. The Mass began.

As the bishop prayed, Coleman studied his face; it was that terrible night last week when he made the shocking announcement on TV that Coleman first became aware of the bishop's strength; it was odd to say that someone had a kind mouth, but Coleman didn't know how else to describe what he saw there. *Interesting man,* he concluded.

Father John's sister walked to the podium. As Sr. Rosemary read from Ecclesiastes, Chapter 3, *"There is an appointed time for everything,"* her voice trembled like a leaf letting go of its attachment to the tree. When she pronounced the words, *"A time to kill, and a time to heal,"* she paused for a second to silence the protest in her soul. She continued in a tone of forced resignation, *"a time to be far from embraces."*

Why did that word punch Coleman in the stomach? Why did *far from embraces* sound so personal? He hated the longing that was quivering within him.

When the children's choir sang the Psalm response echoed by the Congregation, *"I will bless the Lord at all times,"* the atmosphere was vibrant with affirmation and consolation. Russell hoped that others were feeling the same comfort he was—that Father John was in their midst singing and smiling with his people.

Next, Father John's brother, Ed, walked to the lectern. With a heavy-duty voice that called forth hope and expectation he began the second reading from Thessalonians, Chapter 4: *"We would have you be clear about those who sleep in death, brothers and sisters; otherwise you might yield to grief like those who have no hope."*

By the time the choir sang *Alleluia* Coleman realized his anger had peaked; the rainbow was nonsense, now this ritual that summoned joy in the midst of torment. *What kind of God could look on as people sing and brush away tears at the same time?*

Had God watched him when he said good-bye to his father? Did God see his tears? His father's killer had never been found; even after all these years his mother was still faithful, going to Mass every day now. They never talked anymore about his father's death, or his own loss of faith; for days he could not forget her pained face when their visits ended in anger and he hated himself for causing her more pain.

So one day he made a pact, one that existed in his mind only. No more confrontations with mom about church; her faith was good for her; and so were the grandkids. Their games, their good grades; that's what he would concentrate on; he could always be counted on to ignore the elephant in the room.

Even so, he knew his mom still loved him, but he would never tell her what he really thought about God. He was grateful that he had a wife who had the same unconditional love, but he could not go to church just to make either of them happy. The day he had realized that his attendance at Mass was based on fear, he dismissed it as he did with so many other fears in his life. *What difference does it make in my life? Nothing, as far as I can see.*

Familiar words brought him back to the Mass when he heard Deacon Cummings read from the Gospel of Matthew Chapter 26: *"When it grew dark, he reclined at table with the Twelve. In the course of the meal he said, 'I assure you. One of you is about to betray me.'"*

It had to be about betrayal no matter what Russell said. But everything he had seen and heard since the murder gave no hint about betrayal. He heard a priest introducing himself as Father Peter Hodges, Father John's best friend. *I'm sure a best friend isn't going to give me a clue,* thought Coleman. Nevertheless, he found himself wondering again what he had missed by not knowing this priest.

"John was the name of the beloved disciple and it is fitting that today we talk about my friend, Father John Martin, as the beloved of Christ. He did the work of Jesus not only in his parish, but also throughout this city. He was immersed in many outreach, government, and youth programs; in addition, he was personally absorbed with individuals and families whenever and wherever they were in crisis."

More of the saint stuff, groaned Coleman to himself. *Well, God, if you're hearing this, I think you made a big mistake not stepping in for this stellar guy.*

"But he not only was present in times of sorrow and need, but also like the Jesus that he resembled, he enjoyed time spent with people in celebration. He may not have been able to change water into the best wine at weddings, but at every glad occasion he would generate so much delight and fascinate us with his charm that we can not imagine how we will celebrate without him."

Father Hodges heard his own voice crack at that sentiment. The audience held its collective breath as he paused to regain his composure.

"His ability to have fun was a quality we will never forget. I remember when we were in the seminary together; he convinced our group of twenty to borrow the huge cookie sheets from the kitchen and use them as sleds on the hill behind the chapel. Unfortunately for us, sliding down that hill added permanent dents to every one of those cookie sheets and we, being men who don't pay attention to such things, returned the sheets to the kitchen, never dreaming that the cook would notice anything. We had even washed them."

Lighthearted laughs rippled around the church.

"After all, we did have some sense that using cookie sheets as sleds was somewhat creative."

More laughs. *Isn't it strange,* thought Coleman, *that memories of the dead make us laugh rather than cry?*

"The next day, the rector summoned us all into his office. He had one cookie sheet on his desk; we took one look and knew we were in trouble. But even though the twenty of us had to give up cookies and cake for a month, that story has given us volumes of good memories and laughter over many years. Of course, it was John, Father John, who pointed out to us that during that month more cookies and cakes appeared on the dessert menu than ever before."

The congregation laughed wholeheartedly now, nodded their heads in agreement and remembered how often he had made them laugh.

It felt good to savor how much fun Father John had been. They recalled how many children invited him to their birthday parties and First Communion celebrations.

On Halloween a visit to the rectory was mandatory; Father John designed his own costume every year; sometimes it was scary and other times just plain hilarious, but he always had a huge basket with the best treats in the neighborhood.

The reality of the present returned as Father Peter's tone became sober.

"We know that his spirit is here with us, that his life is changed, but so is ours. We are all more complete, more effective human beings, for having known him. We also understand that our grief holds within itself anger because he was taken from us in such a brutal way. Some of us may question how a good God could let this happen."

You're right about that, thought Coleman. *I am eager to hear this explanation.*

"Let us allow that question to pierce our hearts so that we may be opened to a more convincing insight. I want you to think about this, to reflect on this, to pray about this. God's will did not cause this violence. I am going to say that again; God's will did not cause this violence. Rather, God honors the gift of free will so much that we might indeed say that God limits God's own power so that we can be free; but with that freedom, we come face-to-face with consequences. Some will use their free will to destroy, to kill, and to hate. But with your free will, you and I can pursue—I use the word pursue because it will take work to change our old ideas about God's will—pursue the image of God strengthening you, loving you, walking with you, grieving with you during this time of loss and most of all embracing you."

Not again, moaned Coleman. God embracing you. *Did anyone ever, ever experience that?* He itched to get out of there now, but the preaching continued.

"You do have the freedom to choose how you will see God. With that picture in your mind, think how God, the one we often name as Father, but whom we can also call Mother— think of God's agony when Jesus died his violent death. God did not demand Jesus' death; God had never closed heaven to us; but we did not know how to live or love. That is why Jesus came to our world; to show us how to live. Jesus loved so well. Let us then thank God today for the gift to us that was Father John; he loved us all so well."

Coleman sensed a peaceful presence engulfing the whole assembly, all except him. He felt strangled by desires and doubts.

The embrace word was bad enough, he thought, *what was this stuff about free will? What did he mean? How can I allow myself to trust a God who gives human beings the power to mock their Creator? How can I relate to a God who is so inept and impotent? Why would I want a God to share my struggles when I prefer a God who would make things right?*

The words of the final blessing broke through. He battled an irrational consolation that came over him.

Father John's family walked down the aisle following the draped casket.

He stared at their pain-wracked faces. Desperation screamed inside of him. He wanted to grab them by their shoulders, shake them and shout, *tell me how you can endure this? How can you still believe that God cares about you?*

He observed the individual faces of the crowd as they filed out of the church, mindful that he was supposed to be alert to the possibility of looking into the face of the killer; if he were here, what would he have to say about an embracing God? *Is he laughing at you, God, at the thought that You are powerless to stop him?*

A small group of parishioners, drained from the funeral, returned to St. Joseph's to resume the prayer vigil. The emptiness they tasted defied description. They appreciated the consolation that came during their prayer, but the moments were fleeting. Worry and fear were the emotions in charge. Someone pointed to the deacon coming to join them; they were surprised that he had not gone to the reception back at the cathedral.

"I would rather be here with you," he told them. "You know that the work of healing is not a work that can be rushed; like grief it must be given time."

A few parishioners nodded their heads in agreement. They had learned that truth in their own lives; they were the ones who knew that when this crime was solved, healing might demand a radical faith. Others had learned that sometimes the horrors in life were so evil that they could strangle the need to forgive. They asked the deacon if he thought they would be capable of being reconciled to the truth when it was unearthed.

He replied that he was sure their faith would save them. "Let's pray together," he suggested and they walked arm in arm into the cool quiet of the church.

Operation Soul Search was scheduled to meet at 2:00. Russell's daughter had left her umbrella at St. Joseph's, so they stopped to check if someone had put it in the lost-and-found cupboard in the church vestibule.

Inside the church they saw the group kneeling in silence with the deacon. Coleman noticed one figure in the front pew; all of a sudden he realized this was the same person that was there every morning, but now, in the afternoon sun he saw who it was.

As Russell held up the umbrella, Coleman rushed him outside. "Did you recognize who's in the front pew?"

"I didn't really look."

"That's Dan Salvage; he's here every morning."

"How do you know?"

"I've been stopping in every morning before heading in to work. And he's been here, in that same pew, every day."

"So, how does that make him any different from anyone else that comes every day and why are you here every day?"

"Just a hunch. I think he was hiding something the other day. And since he believes that people still think he is guilty, he does this real religious thing to throw them off."

"I don't see it that way, Chris. Maybe, he just can't sleep. *Why are you doing this real religious thing?*"

"Just checking out all angles, that's all. I keep thinking that if the killer is feeling guilty he might show up here seeking forgiveness. Don't read something else into it; I'm not getting religion."

"O.k.; if you say so. We better get moving. The Operation Soul Search meeting begins in forty-five minutes." Russell allowed his thoughts to turn into hope as they headed back to the station. He imagined how great it would be if his partner joined his church.

During the meeting the team examined the scant evidence gathered so far. The interviews with The Plumbers, the Anderson's and Mahoney's, and Dan Salvage had offered negligible hints for further investigation and Father John's reputation was still intact.

Coleman suggested they share their ideas for motives stemming from the bible selection. "You've all been studying that passage; anyone come up with some clue that would give us an insight into the killer's thoughts?"

"I have," remarked Officer Kelly, the youngest member of the task force. "We've been concentrating on the aspect of betrayal. What about greed? Judas betrayed Jesus for money."

"We didn't see any evidence of that; Father John sure didn't have a luxury car and what he had wasn't new. But that doesn't mean he didn't have some secret wealth." Coleman glanced at his partner.

"You won't find any," said Russell.

"Maybe not personal riches, maybe the wealth of the church."

Russell said, "I think that's the wrong interpretation. You know, there was another apostle who did something wrong. Peter lied. What if Mahoney not only found out who was the father of Michelle's baby, but that Father John knew?"

"That would also fit in with the betrayal aspect. My money is still on Dan Salvage, except that I have no clue for a motive."

The meeting ended with Coleman's thanks; they had done a good week's work, he reminded them; three motives and two suspects.

After the meeting he and Russell returned to the rectory. They had no idea what to look for; both had an obsession for meticulousness and it drove them into every nook and cranny of Father John's home.

Frustrated they retraced their steps outside the residence. Coleman wheezed as he wiped away the sweat from his forehead. "I can't get Dan Salvage off my mind; I know it makes sense that his fingerprints were found inside, but he would know that, too."

"True, but I have an important question right now; have you started exercising yet?"

"No, but I promised Deb, next week. Let's not miss something obvious here; just because Salvage had no reason to lie about being in the rectory, does not mean he's innocent."

"What about motive? He needs money, but there was no robbery."

"I wasn't the one who worked his case, but didn't he become the main suspect because he was not at home the night his wife and daughter were killed."

"Right. He was here that night, at the parish, presenting a fundraiser project to the school parents to raise money for a computer lab. But the prosecution claimed he had set that up as his alibi; his daughter went to St. Joseph's School, but yet his wife did not attend that meeting; he said his daughter was sick. They even got Father John to admit that the meeting had been called on a special night."

"I'll bet that night was his suggestion. No imagination needed for him to see Father John as a betrayer; think of all the anger he would have built up all those years."

"Something's not right, other than it sounds too easy. Besides, we have nothing solid to back it up."

"It works for me. You get to keep your good priest and I have proved again that God, if there is a God, has no power over evil."

Russell was irritated; it had been a great conversation up to now. His mouth said, "Let's not jump to any conclusions." His heart prompted him to hold his other thoughts; the journey to truth had just begun.

Seven

Father Jim Clarke, the chaplain at the local Catholic high school, arrived again on Saturday for the evening Mass. He always looked forward to his weekends at St. Joseph's. He greeted the faithful gathered before him, the finality of emptiness sinking into the pit of his stomach. *Time,* he thought, *especially the passage of time, is a cruel master; how could this already be the second weekend without Father John? Help us, O God, to believe that he is with you and you are with us.*

After his homily, he remained at the microphone, silent, knowing the impact of what he was about to say. People started looking at each other; they looked at him; they waited.

"I have some news from the bishop; this Saturday evening Mass will remain on the schedule but the Sunday Masses will be reduced from four to two."

"Oh no, no," rumbled throughout the congregation. Two white-haired women in the front pew leaned their heads together and began whispering to one another.

"I'm the only priest available at this time. I have served you at this parish every Sunday for the past two years as a weekend helper. You know of my great affection for you. I will continue to be available to you as we all walk this journey of grief;

ultimately, I promise you, we will find healing together. Now, let us continue our Mass."

Father Jim possessed a rare combination of sensitivity and acumen that enabled him to minister to a parish family grieving for their priest. He celebrated the liturgy with such devotion that he was able to center their attention on the Mass; muffled gulps coming from several sections of the church told him that images of Father John appeared again and again before their eyes.

Painful days turned into weeks with no clear progress in the case. The first month anniversary coincided with the last day of school. The parish and school planned a special memorial service with Father Clarke.

By 9:45 the church was packed with adults. Dan Salvage sat in the last pew; his daughter would have been in the fifth grade. Russell found his wife and slid in beside her. She reached for his hand and pulled it onto her lap.

The first twenty pews were empty waiting for the students to come. Heads turned as the first child began walking up the aisle.

The children entered in a silent single file with their teachers leading them; their heads were bowed as they walked into their pews. No shoving, or giggles today; not one student glanced around or waved to their parents.

The children's prayers during Mass attested to the incredible fervor of children in circumstances that battered the seasoned faith of the adults.

Father Clarke stood for the closing prayer; without a sound students and adults rose with him; the air was filled with a conspicuous anticipation.

In previous years, right before he gave the final blessing Father John led a glorious round of applause in gratitude to the teaching and administrative staff. And then he urged (his actual word was commanded) everyone to have a grand summer while reminding them, with that gracious smile of his, that he would be looking for them in church on Sundays.

This year Father Jim Clarke intended to carry on the custom; however, before he said a word, a gasp echoed throughout the assembly; hands covered open mouths; everyone saw him. Father John was standing beside Father Jim; he smiled as he started clapping.

The applause from the assembly began. It grew; it thundered. Like mighty water breaking from its dam, it filled the entire church.

The final hymn, chosen because it was Father John's favorite, burst forth like fireworks.

Russell thought about his partner; how he wished he were present. *He will not believe me, I know, but I am going to tell him anyway.*

He caught a glimpse of Dan Salvage, wiping away his tears. *Coleman will only be interested in him, but my gut tells me that Dan Salvage is just lonely.*

Russell was right about Coleman's reaction and he remained convinced that solving this case would reveal more than the identity of the killer. Would Operation Soul Search bring his partner the answers he needed? *Will it bring me the answers I want,* agonized Russell?

That night a raging storm enveloped the city for two hours. Joe and Charlie, with their wives, made it to the church; they were a part of the 11:00pm group since the first day. They took their usual seats near the middle of the church; another man sat alone in the front pew.

The lightning was more brilliant and startling than anyone could remember. Thousands throughout the city and neighboring areas had already lost electrical power.

The group cringed as a furious roar accompanied a glowing bolt of lightning followed in less than a second by the boom of thunder.

They rushed from the church gasping with dread; arms locked together in a voiceless panic they peered into the dark night.

The next blazing flash of lightning wrung a piercing scream from the group. The huge tree in front of the rectory had crashed through the roof into what had been Father John's bedroom.

Although it was a humid hot night, they shivered and clung to each other, unaware that they were drenched. Without a word they clutched each other's hands; as if they had melded into one unyielding person, they turned to walk back into the church.

All five huddled in the same pew as they attempted to resume their prayer; their words for hope and healing choked on their mounting fear of what was coming.

They kept turning towards the back door, watching for anyone from the 11:30 group to arrive. Only two showed up; Henry and Helen Collins, both in their 60's, were always the first to arrive. They struggled with the umbrella that insisted on pulling them away.

The group rushed to greet them; they pointed towards the rectory. Another flash of lightning brought a scream from the newcomers. Now the seven hugged each other and sobbed. They stood motionless, frozen together; after another five minutes passed, they presumed that the storm was preventing the other two, both men, from coming.

The five original witnesses, numbed in body and spirit, paced back and forth not wanting to leave. Mr. and Mrs. Collins were shaken. Mrs. Collins finally said, "I think this is an omen; I don't know what it means, but we have to be strong, right, dear."

She looked up at her husband; he nodded and put his arm around her. They straightened their rounded shoulders and stood valiant as they convinced the others to go home.

Mr. Collin's powerful arm drew his gutsy wife closer to him; they turned and walked back into the darkened church.

The next morning, the cloudless blue sky and the radiant sun accented the devastation throughout the city. Although repair crews had begun working even before the storm died down, immense branches obstructed many driveways and most traffic lights remained out of order.

Word of the collapsed tree at the rectory brought out a larger than usual crowd of worshippers for the 8:00 am prayer service. As they stared at the grim picture, its cruelty stared back at them; they were unnerved by their uncanny suspicions of impending disgrace.

Promptly at 8:00 Deacon Cummings approached the altar and shouted, "Repent!" Then he lowered his voice as he requested that the people kneel; he led them in prayer with Psalm 51, beginning with, "A clean heart create for me, O God, and a steadfast spirit renew within me. Cast me not out from your presence."

After concluding the psalm, he remained kneeling in silence for a long time; he prostrated himself on the floor before he stood and faced the congregation and then motioned for them to be seated.

Making no attempt to hide the tremble in his voice he began, "I share with you this morning that I was shaken to the depths of my faith last night. However, as I prayed in my confusion during that storm, I was given a revelation. I understand now that God is speaking to us, the people of St. Joseph's."

He nodded his approval as he saw many people hurriedly blessing themselves.

"God has a message and that message is 'Repent.' We, here at St. Joseph's, are obliged to scrutinize our collective and individual consciences to determine how we have offended the Almighty King. I call on all of us to examine our beliefs and our conduct, so as to learn what has called forth God's fiery wrath. We have seen the effects of sin, some terrible sin!"

The mood of the worshippers at once changed from fright to turmoil. Such words of wrath and transgression were alien to their ears.

Many of them had been at the children's Mass on the last day of school. They remembered the joy.

They remembered now how often Father John had emphasized the immeasurable love of God for them; he always said that humans waste too much time worrying about the past and condemning themselves for sins and failings.

They remembered that he told them to look at Jesus and listen to the stories he told to prove God's extravagant love for them.

Nevertheless, the deacon's severe message made sense, and they, as one, fell to their knees.

How could they ignore the grave message of the storm? They prayed with attention focused on each word, "Our Father, Who art in heaven…"

When the deacon opened the tabernacle for communion, people began glancing at one another with questioning eyebrows as they repeated the words said so often before, "Lord, I am not worthy." Today they believed that with their whole heart and they thought twice about approaching the altar.

When the deacon saw their doubt, he said, "No, no, you must come; we are never worthy; it is the Lord who invites us;

he knows our sins. And now he also knows that we are going to repent. Come, do not be afraid."

Heads bowed, in silence, they moved forward to receive. Dan Salvage was the last in line. The deacon pressed softly on his palm as he put the host in his hand. After the service concluded, many remained in church on their knees, their heads buried in their hands.

The following day a tree service chopped up the tree and disposed of it. Roofers assembled a temporary cover over the gaping hole.

Diocesan officials had already made a decision to demolish the rectory. Even though the storm damage simply advanced the date for tearing it down, many saw the storm as a sign from God.

In their conversations now, people described the rain as a symbol of their abundant tears; the fury of the lightning and thunder as their fierce and desperate cry of pain. Many agreed that a new rectory might help to blur their memories, but few believed they would ever be able to forget.

The numbers gathering for the morning communion service began to increase. The call for repentance seemed to be taking hold in the hearts and souls of more believers every day.

Subtle but meaningful changes were taking place; the greeting of peace was replaced with a prayer of contrition for sins of commission and omission.

Each day before they approached the altar to receive Holy Communion, the assembled again begged for forgiveness of their sins.

During the time of thanksgiving after receiving the sacrament, they petitioned God for guidance and divine inspiration so that they would be submissive to His will.

It took but a very short time for guilt to begin accomplishing its purpose. Many became convinced that their numerous sins and their wanton neglect of penance had encouraged evil to settle within their midst.

They now believed that they had taken God's love for granted and had aroused His anger. This severe chastisement was God's way of demanding their conversion.

By the end of the second week, a small group requested a meeting with the deacon. They declared their support for his moral strength and implored him to advise them as to how they might proceed to develop a new direction for St. Joseph's.

Deacon Cummings barely smiled as he told them how grateful he was for their recognition and acceptance of his leadership. He was delighted to see Dan Salvage in the group; *maybe this is God's way to fill Dan's life with meaning,* he thought to himself.

"I have been praying every day for just this kind of response. I am humbled by your trust and I am confident that a parish meeting will bring more like-minded parishioners together and then we can devise a plan for a spiritual reawakening."

The group agreed and the following Sunday a flyer was included in the church bulletin announcing that all those interested in moral restoration were invited to a meeting on Tuesday evening at 8:00.

Discussion, it stated, would focus on what remedies might be fundamental in obtaining God's favor on St. Joseph's parish. All were invited to pray for the grace to understand how they could make reparation and thus bring a moral rebirth to the parish.

Not everyone was enthusiastic about this proposal. This uncomfortable and unfamiliar approach to God was alien to some and others experienced an appalling dread settling into their souls.

When Chris Coleman's family returned from church on Sunday, the first thing he heard was the front door slamming.

His ten-year-old son, John, who never had anything to say about Mass, stared at his father, seated on the couch with the Sunday paper in his hand and shouted at him.

"Why don't you come to church with us; you're going to hell."

He burst into tears and raced out to the back yard. Another slammed door.

His daughter, Lori, stood straight in front of him for what felt like a full minute, chewing her lip; then she turned and raced up the stairs to her room.

"What the hell is going on?" Chris flung the paper to the floor and looked at his wife. "What happened, Deb?"

"Oh, Chris." Her lower lip quivered.

He took her in his arms. "Tell me what happened."

They fell into the couch together.

"I didn't realize the kids were so upset. Today's bulletin had this flyer attached and some of us were talking about it after Mass. It seems that the storm the other night and the fallen tree have scared some people into believing that God is punishing us. I didn't know the kids heard what Dan Salvage was telling Mike Mahoney."

"Which was?"

"I could only hear bits and pieces because I was talking with Susan Mahoney. I heard something about missing Mass, and sin, and…"

"Who made Dan Salvage judge and jury? I'll have a word or two with him."

"No, don't do that. We need to talk about things here, in our family. You know that I do pray that someday you'll go to church with us."

Chris squirmed and began to stand up. He and Deb had never argued about religion; he was already making comparisons to how it used to be with his mother. As Deb grabbed him and pulled him close to her, Chris couldn't deny the swell of loneliness that filled his soul. He was going to lose her, too.

"Please, listen to the rest of my sentence, which is, I hope you know that I also love you. And I believe that it has to be your free decision; I would never force you, you know that."

Chris nodded, relieved that he had rashly judged her. "Can you tell the kids I'm not going to hell? I'm not, am I?"

"Stay here." She patted his arm and kissed him on his cheek.

Deb went out the patio door and Chris watched her with John; soon, with her arm around him they came into the living room; he avoided looking at his dad. Deb sent him upstairs to get his sister.

When both children came to the living room, Deb directed them to sit in the love seat facing the couch.

"Look at me," she said. "I know that today you heard some things that upset you. I want you to hear the truth from me."

John and Lori knew the drill when their mother demanded their attention. Their eyes focused on hers, they did not move a muscle.

"Every person is on a journey; we are all on our way to God. Some people have different names for God and that is o.k.. Now, God gave us a wonderful gift and that is free will."

Neither child moved; neither even blinked an eye. A tear trickled down Lori's left cheek; she brushed it away and continued to stare at her mother.

"And that means that God will keep waiting for us. So, you must believe that God loves your dad and your dad is on his journey. When he finds the answers he needs, God will be there for him."

Their shoulders relaxed; the eyes turned to their dad.

"Is that true, dad? Are you on a journey?"

Coleman looked at these children he loved so much; he always believed he would do anything for them, and his heart was breaking. *Oh, God, how I wish I could believe* he moaned inside, but with a forced smile to his son, he said, "Well, John, your mother is very smart; do you believe her?"

Both children ran to the couch and jumped on their dad, saying, "We're sorry, Dad. We love you."

Their hugs were so tight that Deb was sure they squeezed out the tear that was sliding down his cheek.

"I love you, too. Now, go outside and play. Remember, this afternoon we're going to that movie you both have been begging to see."

"O.k., Dad." Lori gave her dad another hug, and with her soft gentle hand, wiped away his tear, and then ran after her brother. After they went outside Chris looked at his wife with a quiet peace he had not known for a long time. "Thanks. Maybe you should tell me more about what is going on in the parish. Come over, here, beside me."

"First, I want you to understand that all those good things you heard about Father John at the funeral Mass were just part of the picture. What he really taught us to believe is that we are so special to God; you are the beloved of God, he used to say. And he made us believe that we all had a part to play in making St. Joseph's a welcoming community, where there was room for everyone. Now, this new group that asked for a meeting with the deacon thinks that God is punishing us for being too easy on ourselves; they are talking about a moral rebirth and a spiritual renewal."

"And you think that's bad?"

"It's not what it sounds like. They want to go back to an understanding of God as a judge, as the master, as a…"

"Maybe this world would be better if people could know a God that was a master. Maybe if people saw that the good are blessed and the evil are punished, they could understand a God like that. Then we would all know that there is a God in charge." Deb had snuggled close enough that he now felt her body tense. He kissed her cheek and said with a grin, "Maybe just a thunderbolt now and then to let us know who's the boss."

"Oh, Chris," she said with a playful punch to his arm. "I wish you could have heard how Father John explained the parables of Jesus, especially the one about the Prodigal Son; you would never again doubt how deep God's love is, even when we sin."

"What are you going to do?"

"I know what I'm not doing and that's attending that meeting on Tuesday. Those people are taking advantage of fear and see this as an opportunity to establish order and discipline in what they call a disorganized parish with too many parishioners doing their own thing."

Chris gathered her in his strapping arms; she always felt so protected by his embrace and he always enjoyed knowing that. They sat in silence for some time, each lost in thought.

Chris had not told her why he left so early every weekday morning. His visits to St. Joseph's had given him no answers to satisfy his soul's doubts, but he knew that something continued to draw him there.

He tried to block out the question his son and daughter asked—*are you on a journey, Dad.* Maybe Deb really was that smart; but he didn't feel as though he was on a journey; he felt as though he was in a fight; *and in a battle,* he told himself, *someone always has to surrender.*

Eight

Tuesday evening was sultry; the clouds in the night sky hid the summer stars. When Deacon Cummings looked up into that darkness he smiled. The light coming from the church hall had spread into the night; a sign for him of righteousness and God's approval. *Thank you God, I am your humble servant.* His chest swelled with satisfaction; *all things come to those who are patient*, he reminded himself.

Someone had opened all the windows and the animated clamor excited him. When he walked in, his eyes swept the gathering. He estimated that thirty people had already arrived and it was only 7:15.

He noticed that Mike Mahoney and Mike Anderson were there without their wives. When he saw Dan Salvage at the back door, he hurried to give him a special welcome. "I am so glad that you've come."

Dan enjoyed the warmth he felt from Deacon Cummings. He wanted to say something about God's justice, but decided it could wait.

Deacon Cummings felt the impatient zeal throbbing within the room. At 7:30, on the dot, he rapped on the wooden table placed at the front of the room. "Please, everyone, take your seats. He relished the few moments it took for them to move and prayed *Thank you, God, for this group of followers; we will give you the worship and service you demand.*

After a short prayer, he began with a brief overview of what he considered evidence of why God was calling them to repentance. When he mentioned the lack of respect shown by those who came to Mass dressed in shorts and tee shirts he looked around at all the heads nodding in agreement.

When he asked for input regarding the various groups and activities over the last two or three years, he was bombarded with loud complaints about the parish being too free and too open to all kinds of people.

Someone in the back shouted, "God is King! We should get down on our knees before the Almighty One."

Another person yelled, "He's right! Have you seen all the people who bow instead of kneeling when they come into church?"

Another voice erupted from the second row. "Even worse, what about standing during the most sacred parts of the Mass! No one fears God's punishment anymore."

The Deacon pounded on the table to get some quiet. "Listen to me," he said, "You do need to be patient. These abuses did not happen overnight; it will take time to return to the discipline you are asking for. However, there is truth in what you have said. Perhaps we can discuss a name for our group that will help us keep our focus. Any ideas?"

For a few moments all went silent as they began to consider how they wanted to be known. Mike Mahoney offered the first suggestion; others followed. Twenty minutes of debate ended with a unanimous vote for God's Troops, a name that satisfied everyone's desire for an accurate sign of their steadfastness and determination.

They applauded their choice; a recording secretary was chosen from several volunteers and priorities were decided upon; they expressed their gratitude for the deacon's reminder that they could not concentrate on every abuse in one meeting.

Reverence at Mass was decided upon for next week's topic. The people knelt for the deacon's blessing. Their exhilaration and confidence made for a noisy exit; no one noticed that an unseasonable chill had invaded this dark summer night.

During the following Saturday evening Mass Father Clarke paused in the middle of a prayer; he was confused when several people knelt down; he looked at the determined faces of those, most of the assembly in fact, that remained standing.

He remembered that years ago a group of ten or so had caused quite a stir by protesting a change that Father John had introduced. He recalled the delight he felt when Father John explained that they were changing their practice of kneeling during the Mass; from now on, he had said, we will stand to show that we are followers of a risen Savior; "Resurrection People," he had called them.

Father Jim continued his praying, his mind filled with questions: *where is the joy that I always loved in this parish? What is going on? Celebrating with the people here at St. Joseph's continues to be the highlight of my week; this heaviness I feel, is different from the grief of losing John; they are afraid of something. Oh, God, help me concentrate on what I am doing here.*

After Mass as he greeted people leaving the church, he tried to look in their eyes; he saw a smile as they shook his hand but it was the duty-smile; their eyes were fearful.

He was glad to see, near the end of the line, a group of women all talking at once as they approached him. He was even happier when they asked to speak with him in private. *I can always count on the women to let me know what's going on,* he laughed to himself.

He motioned for them to follow him to the sacristy away from the crowd. Once they reached the safety of the sacristy they broke out in unison, "Oh, Father, we need your help. Something awful happened last Tuesday." Several women in the group shoved Susan Mahoney to the front.

"My husband came here to a meeting on Tuesday night; when he got home he was all fired up about bringing obedience and discipline back to religion. He told me all the awful things they said about the good that Father John did in this parish."

Carol Anderson jumped in with, "They even named themselves God's Troops! We're so worried, Father. Can you help us?"

"Can you identify others who feel as you do?"

"Absolutely!"

"If you can get in touch with them this evening, I will be glad to meet with all of you tomorrow after the last Mass. Do you think that's feasible?"

"Absolutely!" They replied again.

Father Clarke already saw a little light coming back into those barren eyes. His smile reflected his gratitude as he said, "I'll see you tomorrow, then. And, thank you."

After the 12:00 Mass on Sunday, Father Clarke was eager to get to the cafeteria. His eyes swept across the group of fifty, most of whom were women.

Susan Mahoney noticed him first; as she walked over to welcome him, the group became very quiet. Father Clarke gave them a reassuring smile, and motioned for them to be seated.

He began in a calm voice. "God is here with you now; you must believe that and you must try to comfort yourselves with that truth. I know that the recent evil that we have endured has shaken us all, but I assure you, God is not punishing you. Yes, God always calls us to conversion, but neither the murder, nor the storm, not even the toppled tree on the rectory are signs of God's disapproval."

Glances and nods to each other, and attempts to smile encouraged a few to reach out to hold the hands of those next to them.

Deb Coleman spoke what was on everyone's mind. "Father, we are afraid of what may happen in our parish. What should we do about *God's Troops*?"

"For now, I would suggest that we wait and see. This may be merely a cry for security. Continue with your other groups, reach out to those who are worried and pray. Talk with those who are in the group and try to see if there is a way to reach out to them. Keep believing in a loving God and your faith will be contagious."

"It's very difficult," added Carol Anderson, "when your husband comes home and starts telling you what went on at their meeting. It scared me."

"And they may also be scared." The whole group turned to see a man in the back row. Noelle Russell smiled; she knew how Rick felt, but she thought he was with the kids. "They feel strong when they have rules to keep everyone in line. Fear can do strange things. We all like to feel safe, and like to think that if we follow the rules, everything will work out for us."

Murmurs of agreement swirled around the room.

"Life, however," reminded Father, "Obliges us to live with and ponder the questions that life hands us. Remember, how Mary did not understand everything that happened to her. We are told that she kept these things in her heart. Remember the words from Scripture? She pondered these things in her heart. Do you think Mary had answers when she stood at the cross watching her son die? Maybe she had the same questions we do—why, why, why is this happening to my son. He has done nothing to deserve such injustice. She couldn't do anything to change or stop the evil. But we know there was a resurrection, new life, after that."

"So you're saying that we have to be patient and wait for whatever?"

"That's right. Know that God is working with you right now. Support each other during this waiting time. I know you can do that and good things will come to pass, I promise you."

"Thank you, Father," the crowd replied in unison.

Most got up and headed for the door, spirited chatter accompaning them out the door and all the way to their cars. Noelle hurried back to her husband. "Thanks for your words of wisdom," she said. "I was so proud of you. Where are the kids?"

"Your mom and dad stopped in after their Mass, so I decided to rush here; I don't know where this is going, but I wanted to be here with you."

A few others lingered at the front of the hall, talking with Father Jim. He realized that he had become more than a weekend visitor; he was needed here, now.

He noticed Deacon Cummings and his wife as they left. *I didn't see them before,* he thought. *They are a strange couple; I guess it's true that opposites attract. I hope the deacon doesn't think I'm stepping on his toes.*

Nine

Another Tuesday; when Coleman looked at the calendar on his wall he noted that it was seven weeks since they found Father John murdered. Week after week the team of detectives met to discuss any additional clues and reviewed what they had so far. Two weeks ago, Coleman had gotten the group's enthusiastic approval for Matt and his Plumbers to set up a web site as another way people could give information to the police.

He canceled today's afternoon meeting of the task force. Each meeting reminded him how powerless he was; besides he did not want to tell them again that the pressure was mounting from the mayor as well as from several prominent people throughout the city and county. He, more than anyone, knew his team's persistence and determination to investigate any tip that came into the department.

He had anticipated solving this crime within a month. He had never felt so helpless before. He tried to quell the desperation in his heart as he envisioned this case ending up in the unsolved file. That would be a first for him; a failing he could not accept. He pounded his desk.

As they left their offices at 6:00 he complained to Russell. "Another long day; and nothing new." Knowing he should not say it, he nevertheless caved in to his exasperating question. "Are you praying that we solve this case?"

Russell's eyes bored straight into his partner's soul. If he admitted that he was praying, then he would have to come up with a defense for why it was taking so long. *God, I'm just too tired to defend you today.* He certainly can't say that he wasn't praying. He decided on the easy way out and ignored the bait. "Don't you worry; we will find the killer. We've never quit a case before; we're not quitting this time. I'll see you tomorrow." To himself he said, *Chris, neither God nor I will quit on you, either.*

Within three weeks, the members of God's Troops increased to seventy-five. The majority were men, but some twenty women were present every week; these women also began preparing coffee and cookies for each meeting. Dan Salvage realized that he looked forward with increasing enthusiasm to Tuesday evenings.

The deacon's welcoming attitude toward him had been contagious; others were now inviting him to sit with them; *they are not afraid of me anymore,* he told himself. *And I should do the same for someone else.*

With the deacon's encouragement, each meeting opened with the Act of Contrition, followed by some prayers and devotions linked to their desire for repentance and renewal.

Mike Mahoney, Mike Anderson and Dan Salvage were always the first to arrive. Tonight they shared with Deacon Cummings their conviction that before long they would bring their church to a place of clear definitions when it came to right and wrong.

He told them how pleased he was with their dedication and encouraged them to look forward to a time of great satisfaction and abundant blessing from a God who must be pleased with their efforts.

Dan announced that next week he would be bringing another new member to the group. For the first time since he had left prison, he told them, he felt his life had meaning. The deacon's praise so overwhelmed him that he set aside any worry that the person he was bringing was an ex-con like himself.

Wednesday morning Coleman and Russell were in Coleman's office having their usual morning coffee when the phone rang. "No, it can't be." Russell saw all the color drain from his partner's face.

With his coffee mug suspended in mid-air, his heart waited for his permission to continue beating. "What happened?" He called before Coleman had even put down the phone.

Coleman's face was blanched and his hands were shaking. "You're not going to believe this; that was a call from Holy Name parish; Father Bill Williams was just found murdered!"

Russell grabbed his trembling hand with his left one as he set down his special Dad-mug.

"Isn't he the one you introduced me to at Father John's service?"

Russell heard his heart pounding; he barely nodded his yes.

Holy Name Church was on the outskirts of the city. The siren blared and their wheels screeched; it took Coleman and Russell less then twenty minutes to get there.

They jumped out of their car and ran toward the officer at the front door. He repeated a similar story they heard more than seven weeks ago; two men went to check on why Father did not show up for Mass; this time the front door was unlocked, and they had gone upstairs. Officer Bailey led them to the priest's bedroom.

His room was not as large as Father John's, but Coleman listened to its silence clamoring for answers to the same why he heard in his soul every day.

He stared at Father Bill Williams; he remembered wondering if his good looks were a problem, considering his calling. Movie-star good looks and, he guessed, about ten years younger than Father John. He was dressed only in green shorts, which contributed to the raw appeal of his health-club body. *I'll bet more than a few women were captivated by that sexy lock of brown hair on your forehead—hair now matted with blood,* thought Coleman.

Russell had already counted the stab wounds. Twelve gashes, again. The muscled arms folded across the chest. And again, the open Bible; but when Russell picked it up, it was not Matthew; it was Mark, Chapter 14. He took a closer look; it was still the story of the Last Supper. *I hope there is no serial message here,* thought Russell.

Outdoors, Coleman pointed to the jagged edges of a broken window at ground level leading into the priest's study. They came across a partial footprint near the crushed hedge. Father Bill's bedroom on the second floor was in the back of the house. It was reasonable to suppose that he never heard the shattering glass.

This rectory had no alarm system; the back door was locked with its dead bolt and safety chain; the killer must have walked out the front door.

The people had not moved from the front of the church. As Coleman and Russell approached, every eye searched their faces for some kind of assurance. Coleman hated the truth inside him; he refused to let them know how helpless he felt. He struggled for a promise he could offer them. When he heard his own words about making progress, he hoped they believed him more than he did.

He detected a special affection for Father Bill, who lived alone in this house; he was impressed by the considerable support for this priest who had come to this parish only a year ago.

An attractive woman, with short dark brown hair and eyes of the same warm color, stepped forward and introduced herself as Marge Peterson, the parish council president. Her confident body language was in unmistakable contrast to the distress Coleman felt in her handshake and saw in her dark eyes. He sensed an instant bond with her. *She knows that there are things she should tell me and she should do it soon.* He asked her to wait with his partner. "Don't be afraid," he said.

He turned back to the crowd. He realized that the depression he felt had lifted. "You're free to go," he said. "I understand your anxiety, I really do. I promise you that we will not give up. As you leave, please give Officer Bailey your names and addresses; we'll have someone call on you, to try to help you through this."

Coleman watched as they lined up in front of Officer Bailey. His eyes followed them as they walked away, most headed back to the church. Deb's words about his journey came back to him; *I do not feel as if I am on a journey,* he thought, *more like stuck in a ditch.* So lost in thought, he forgot that Marge was waiting nearby; Russell called to him twice.

"Oh, right. I'm here."

Marge pointed to a wooden bench under the tree and when all three were seated, she bit her bottom lip and took a deep breath.

"I am aware of some information that the majority of people in the parish do not know."

Another deep breath. Coleman was spellbound by the blend of strength and vulnerability he saw in her. Sitting so near to her, he realized that her beauty was much more compelling than physical attractiveness.

She turned her face toward him and their eyes met; his made her strong; hers filled him with reverence. *I can to do this for Bill,* she told herself.

"Detectives, I was a member of Father Bill's support group; he was a recovering alcoholic and had come to Holy Name only a year ago from a treatment center in another state. That is where he went when he left St. Joseph's."

She could tell by their faces that they were making comparisons between Father John and Father Bill. *Please,* her eyes begged, *do not prejudge him.*

"I hope it won't be necessary to reveal Father Bill's past, but I know you will hear about it and I would rather you hear it from me. Bill, I mean, Father Bill met with us every week. He was so sincere in his recovery."

"Did anyone at St. Joseph's know about his problem?"

"I know he was well loved there, just like here. I don't know how many knew of his problem, but two of his former parishioners were part of the support group, Mike Anderson and Mike Mahoney."

"This is all very helpful. We're grateful for your openness." Coleman knew that Marge had more to tell them; he also saw how drained she was. He and Russell stood. "We will talk with you again."

She extended her hand to him; he held it just long enough for both of them to know that the fear was gone. "I'll do anything to help. Please, find out who did this."

"Can we walk you to your car?" asked Russell. Marge replied that she was going to stay there for a while. She lowered her head and closed her eyes as she caught sight of the coroner entering the rectory.

Back at the precinct, the task force had gathered and Coleman recounted the murder scene noting the same number of stab wounds but the different Bible selection. He went on to summarize the conversation he and Russell had with Marge Peterson.

As he glanced around the table Coleman tried to avoid the flicker of expectation he saw in the intense eyes focused on him. He could think of nothing else to add; his fingers drummed the edge of the table.

Russell jumped in. "We need to get into the mind of this person. He used a different Bible passage for a reason. Is his message related to the Last Supper? Or is he telling us that he plans to kill one priest for each Gospel?"

Coleman suggested that everybody spend some time comparing the two passages. Since they now knew that at least two men had a connection with both priests, he assigned two other detectives the job of going back to Holy Name to check through the parish files for any other former St. Joseph's parishioners.

"Russell and I will go through Father Bill's room again and talk with Marge Peterson; she is coming in this afternoon."

As he passed around the table the information he had in his hand, his typical thoroughness was even more intense.

"Here are the names and addresses of the other parishioners who were there this morning, plus the secretary and maintenance supervisor; try to meet with all these people in the next two days if at all possible; be sure to find out how many people knew Father Bill when he was at St. Joseph's."

Marge took her lunch hour to go to the precinct. Russell saw her first and waved her to a chair beside his desk. Coleman hurried to complete his phone call and they ushered her into one of the small conference rooms where they would not be interrupted.

"Thanks for coming," said Coleman. "How are you?"

Marge smiled at him; there was a spirit within him that spoke to her soul. *I will feel better telling him everything,* she decided.

"Detective Coleman, I'm not sure why I want to tell you things that even my mother did not know. When I was ready to tell her, she was too sick and she died before I ever had the chance."

She sighed. "Detective Russell, I don't mean to ignore you; I'm aware that while I'm talking it seems that I am speaking only to Detective Coleman, but…"

"Don't worry about it; I understand. Just tell your story."

"I guess the best thing is for me to go back to the beginning. I was a friend of Father Bill when he was at St. Joseph's. My ex-husband is an alcoholic and was very abusive. Father Bill had helped me leave our home several times and go to a shelter with my—our—daughter, who was then sixteen. Even though the police had been summoned to our home many times, I never had the courage to follow through by filing charges until Father Bill helped me see and accept my own worth."

She stopped to brush away the tears from her cheeks.

Now I understand what I saw in her, thought Coleman. *Did Father Bill see it too? Was her allure too much for him? Did his concern for her become the love and refuge she needed?*

The soul-mate connection between Marge and Coleman took a surprising turn when she looked him straight in the eye and said, "No, Detective Coleman, our relationship was never improper. I am not ashamed to say that I loved Father Bill; I loved him more than any man I ever knew, but it was not romantic; it was deeper than that, if that makes sense."

Coleman was too shocked to protest her assumption; *what could I say, anyway,* he thought; *she would know I'm lying.* "That's good to know," was all he could manage.

"My daughter is now away at college and Dave, that's my ex-husband, is on parole. He did six months in prison and he is forbidden to have any contact with me or our daughter. I don't know where he's living right now."

She stopped and Coleman was mesmerized by her splendor; *why did the violence she suffered not overcome her,* he wondered. *Who could have desecrated such goodness?*

He heard Russell's voice. "Please, take your time."

"Thank you, Detective Russell. I'm so sorry; I thought I was strong enough to do this."

Coleman ached to put his arm around her. He was stunned by the words of a prayer he heard in his soul. *O God, please help her.* Before he could scorn the absurdity, he was shocked when Marge said, "Thank you, I can go on now.

"After Dave was sent to prison, Father Bill helped me open my own business as a caterer." Her whole face brightened. "I often cater special celebrations both at St. Joseph's and at Holy Name."

Coleman could hold back no longer. "Marge, I have to ask you this; if it is too personal, I understand. How were you able to not only survive your husband's abuse but come to the place where you are now: strong, whole, and successful."

She blushed a light pink for merely a second. "It was a long and painful journey of healing. Father Bill was the one who helped me first, to believe that no evil is greater than God. Then, to take each day, each hour, really, to remember that I am the beloved of God. In God's eyes I am beautiful and God is in love with me. Even to this day, I remind myself of that truth many times during the day. The other thing he taught me was I would be stuck where Dave had left me until I could come to the point of forgiving him."

Coleman could only stammer his appreciation for her answer. *You have no idea,* he thought, *how beautiful you are.*

Suddenly, Marge began to sob. Coleman and Russell were beside themselves. With her sobs came fragments they strained to understand.

"O God, by helping me; and seeing the consequences I suffered; because of Dave's alcoholism; Bill finally admitted to his own problem with alcohol; that's why he went for help; that's why he asked me to be one of the members of his support group; he was doing so well; why did this have to happen?"

Coleman resisted the surge of anxiety that threatened him with the truth—he might never know that answer. He said "We hope to figure that out, soon."

He realized as soon as he heard his own words that he not only intended to solve this crime; he was also in a confrontation with God that would not end until he had an answer that made sense. Although he exhibited no external sign of anger, he felt every muscle in his body clenched in determination.

"Can you tell us how Anderson and Mahoney came to be in Father Bill's support group?"

"I had the impression they had been friends ever since he was at St. Joseph's. Both were very sympathetic and accepting of Father Bill; it was Mike Anderson, though, that spent more personal time with Father Bill; they went out a few times after the meeting, I would guess to a late movie. They also golfed on Saturday mornings. However, now that I'm telling you all this, I did notice something curious about a month ago."

"Why do say curious?"

"About a month ago Father Bill confessed he had been in a relationship with someone. I noticed that both of them became quite uncomfortable, sort of squirming in their seats and they made an effort not to look at each other. At the time, I laughed it off, because I thought, just like men, they find it so hard to talk about feelings. I think Father Bill noticed their uneasiness, too, because as soon as he said it, I sensed that he regretted it.

He tried to make light of it by saying that his mouth had gotten ahead of his brain; but he promised no secrets and said that after he prayed about it some more he would share the truth with us, even though it would be painful."

"Did he ever say who it was, that he was involved with?"

"No, but he told us that he kept a journal, and that he might bring it to our meeting one day after he had sorted out his feelings a little more."

"Did that ever happen?"

"No, I never saw it; I don't think anyone did."

"Did anyone ever bring it up?" asked Russell.

"No. We all trusted him and knew that when he was ready he would share it with us. Everyone in the group loved Father Bill. I don't know why I remembered that incident; I just have the feeling that maybe they already knew about it and were embarrassed for Bill."

She wiped her eyes. "Oh, I miss him so much. I will do anything to help you, as long as I trust you to protect Father Bill's reputation. If he once made a mistake, he was a redeemed man now. I would not tolerate any suggestion that his life was a sham."

Her devotion worried Coleman. "We will keep you informed. Marge, I can't tell you how grateful we are."

After she left, Russell said, "She sure gave us a lot to think about. Before we go to Holy Name, do you think we should call Anderson and Mahoney and have them come in here after work?"

Coleman's distracted nod and distanced look did not go unnoticed.

"What are you thinking? What's wrong?" asked Russell.

"Extraordinary woman. I hope we don't uncover anything to devastate her loyalty to him. Yes, go ahead make the calls. I'll meet you in the car in ten minutes."

Coleman picked up the phone to make a quick call home. *Why am I doing this,* he wondered. *Am I feeling guilty about Marge?* The answering machine came on. "Hi, Hon. Just wanted to say hi; I guess you're out shopping. Love you." Somehow, he felt a little better.

They drove to Holy Name parish in silence, each fighting his own troubling fears. After entering Father Bill's room, Coleman and Russell rummaged through every desk and drawer. They found nothing.

Looking towards the bed, they had the same thought at the same moment—was it really under the mattress?

Without a word, they lifted the top mattress and there tucked near the foot of the bed was a dark blue notebook.

Coleman gave it a firm yank; he held it with both hands clenched, alarmed by its strange heaviness.

Avoiding eye contact the two detectives settled themselves next to each other on the edge of the bed. Coleman stared at the cover and then opened to the first page.

He was shaken to see in Father Bill's own handwriting: *O God, have mercy on me, your sinful servant.* At the bottom of the page was last year's date. Coleman recalled Marge's words about redemption.

Russell reached over and turned the page.

An icy, harsh quiet closed in on them. They read paragraph after paragraph filled with anguish over his past sins and heartrending words of gratitude to God for being forgiven; he ended each session with a prayer for the strength to go on.

After reading several pages, Coleman and Russell looked at each other, speechless.

Russell turned another page.

He wrote every day and on the evenings following his support group meetings he always expressed appreciation for the acceptance that he received from them; these pages also made clear his hope for the future.

On one page he wrote, *Day by day I am being convinced that my fall from your grace, O God, was a happy fault because I am becoming a humble man. I live with the truth that I am powerless to do what is right and good. I thank you for the people who travel with me on this journey back to you and to the fullness of life. I promise to live each day in the joy of being forgiven. I hope that someday I will be able to ask and receive the forgiveness of those I hurt.*

On the very next page, Father Bill wrote about his possible unwise decision to open up to the group about his sinful relationship.

Russell pointed to the next sentence. *I realized that I had been too hasty when I noticed that both Mike Mahoney and Mike Anderson became very nervous. All of a sudden I became scared that Mahoney already knew. I need to speak with each of them before I make my confession.*

Coleman ripped the page in his haste to turn it.

Bill's writing turned into a conversation style. *Oh, Mickey, I'm so sorry. I was so confused; I was ready to give up my whole life for you. I sinned, I know that now, but I was so in love with you.*

Russell looked over at Coleman whose face had taken on a scowl; their eyes returned to the page.

I never had the chance to tell you. Why did you go away without saying a word? I know now that what we did was wrong, but I never blamed you; it was all my fault. I know it would have never worked, even though I tried to convince myself that we were strong enough to make it and that somehow we were different. Now, I have faced the truth and I'm sorry for the pain I caused you; I hope you can forgive me. I remember how lost I felt when you never called. Then I got angry thinking you had found someone else. Finally, I realized it was over. That's also when I knew I had to go for help. I know I was not the right one for you and I hope you have found that one now. Please forgive me.

Russell leapt to his feet. "That sounds like a rehearsal to me. Who do you think he was planning to meet? I'll bet a month's pay that if we find out who this is, we find a connection to the killer."

Coleman growled and shoved the journal into Russell's hands. He stood and stretched as he lumbered over to the window.

"O.k.; say it." said Russell.

"I'm not sure. I mean, I'm really sorry that he's dead, but, all this sex stuff; it just makes me so mad. I mean, all those people who respect them and look what goes on."

"I know; and I'm not saying it's all right, whatever this was with Father Bill, but it's different, you know; this wasn't about a sin *to* someone, it was about a sin *with* someone."

"He wasn't supposed to be doing it at all."

"That's true; this sounds like an excuse, but it's not; they're still human. By reading this, doesn't this prove that Father Bill was not only aware of his sin, but also sorry?"

"Is that enough?"

"Well, I think it's our background that makes us link justice to punishment. If it's a personal sin and this sounds like it was two people consenting to something, then maybe justice has to be between them and God. I think that's why he wrote earlier about a happy fault."

"Yeah, now, what's with that?"

"Well, I think what he was saying is that God is greater than any sin and so he can be grateful that his sin taught him that."

"You mean that God is o.k. with our sins? I mean, this is just one priest whose personal life we know was not what it was supposed to be. Don't you think this stuff is monstrous?"

"Try to calm down. Not every sexual sin is the same. We can't lump all the wrongs together. And just because God is forgiving, or when anyone forgives, it doesn't mean that the act was less wrong; even when there are consequences to be paid, there still comes a time for forgiveness. Going back to Father Bill, I think this was a wrong relationship, a sinful one, but—"

"Doesn't make it right."

"I know, but I try to imagine God like a parent; I don't want my kids to do the wrong thing, but it won't stop me from loving them. So, nothing we do can stop God from loving us."

"You make it all sound so simple. What if this has to come out? Marge will be devastated."

"Marge will be able to handle this; didn't you say she was extraordinary? She will find a way to understand what he did and continue to love who he was."

"It doesn't seem right that someone like her has to have so much pain in her life. Especially, when you know how much other bad stuff has happened to her. If I could be God, I would make sure that the bad stuff only happened to bad people."

"I'm sure you would, Chris. Life would be so much easier if the good people did not suffer; at least it would make sense. How often I wish God were interested in making bargains with me; I've learned it doesn't work that way. We've got to live with questions and with evil. We've got to admit that we are not in control."

"Not good enough, Rick. If I'm going to trust in a God, I want a God who is in control."

"God is in control; what you want is a controlling God. Anyway, we'd better get going. Mahoney and Anderson are due in an hour."

"You're right. You take Mahoney; I'll take Anderson. I think we should tell them that we know about Father Bill's support group and then push hard about why they were nervous. One or both of them knows something."

Mahoney and Anderson arrived within minutes of each other. They gave each other a worried look as Coleman explained that he wanted to talk with Anderson alone and Mahoney was to go with Russell.

Directing Anderson towards the conference room near his office, Coleman opened the door and told Anderson to make himself comfortable. "Want some coffee?"

"No, no, thanks."

Coleman observed that Anderson was clenching and unclenching both hands and his breathing was labored.

Without delay, hoping that the element of surprise would break him down, Coleman leaned over and snapped, "We know about Father Bill's support group; why were you so nervous when Father Bill told the group about his sexual relationship."

Even as the beads of sweat betrayed his humiliation, Anderson straightened his shoulders, put both hands in front of him on the table and leaned forward, "Who said I was nervous?"

"I'm asking the questions. Are you aware that Father Bill had a journal?"

"Yes, he told us he kept one."

"Well, we have it."

He tossed the journal on the table.

Anderson looked away, then lowered his eyes to the floor and grabbed the edge of the table.

Coleman studied the strong hands. A surgeon's hands. He sat down on the table, close to Anderson's face.

Anderson looked up, his dark eyes flared with hurt and anger; he opened his mouth but closed it again, and put his head down on the table.

"Just tell me what's wrong; what happened?"

"This isn't easy."

"Just tell me the truth. Then I can help."

He lifted his head; he ran both hands through his thick hair, once, twice; his fists landed on the table, and the words began. "Well, you have to understand; Father's confession reminded me of a personal problem that I don't care to discuss."

Coleman glanced at his watch. *Maybe bluntness will move this along,* he thought.

"We have enough to implicate you in both murders; the only way I can help you is for you to tell me the truth."

"O.k., o.k.."

Anderson lowered his eyes, inhaled and let the words stagger into the waiting air.

"Twenty-five years ago, when I was an altar boy I was molested."

He hit the table with his fist.

"The priest who did it died seven years ago. He was so popular; I knew that no one would believe me, so I pushed it out of my mind for years. I even tried to enter the seminary, thinking I could make up for whatever was wrong with me. I was so miserable, I left. Then I went into therapy for six long years. A year later I met Carol."

He looked straight at Coleman, his eyes fulfilling their function of soul-exposure.

"My wife doesn't know. She introduced me to Father Bill when he was at St. Joseph's; we talked a lot about many things, even went golfing together. We never talked about that. We became good friends and I decided that after all these years I could go back to church."

His words faded away as he stared into space.

Coleman broke in, his voice subdued, "Go on; tell me what happened."

"Well, when Father Bill left St. Joseph's we knew why, but we didn't talk about it with anyone. When he was assigned to Holy Name, he called me. He said he needed a favor and would I be part of his support group, so I thought, *Sure, I can do that.* Then, when he brought up this relationship thing, he reopened all those wounds. I wasn't sure I would be able to stay in the group."

Both men sat in silence for what seemed like a very long time to Anderson. The ramifications of what he had just confessed loomed before him. "Does this have to get out?"

"I hope not, but it's too early to say."

Anderson stared straight ahead. More silence. Regret. Panic.

"I should have asked for a lawyer. I'll deny everything I said here."

"Listen to me, if that's all there is to your relationship with Father Bill then I don't see any reason why anything has to be said. But," his tone increased in volume with each word, "if I find out you know more than what you're telling me, all hell's gonna break loose! Do you understand me?"

"Yes, I do. I don't know anything, honest. I was in the group because he asked me to be; I just figured it was because we were friends. I don't have anything else to say."

"O.k., then. You can go. We might want to talk with you again. As long as you're telling me the truth, you don't have anything to worry about."

As Coleman opened the door to usher out Anderson, he saw Russell saying his final words to Mahoney.

Coleman waved his partner over to the conference room. "Tell me, what did you get from Mahoney."

"First, he denied any embarrassment regarding Father Bill's revelation.

"Anderson, too."

"After I convinced him that his connection with Father John and Father Bill could result in the police putting him on the suspect list, he acknowledged that he had struggled with his own sexual identity as a teenager. And when Father Bill mentioned a sexual relationship, he was dealing with his own personal attraction to Father Bill. Since his marriage twenty years ago, he had never felt that way about another man and so he claimed this disturbed him a great deal. He had never shared this with his wife, or with anyone for that matter."

"Do you think he's covering up the fact that he and Father Bill did have a relationship?"

"Anything's possible, but I feel pretty sure he was telling me the truth; I don't think he would make up a story like that. He wouldn't take a chance on having his whole life ruined. I told him that the most I could promise was I won't reveal anything unless he becomes a suspect for some reason."

"Anderson's story was also personal; he said that he was molested many years ago and that priest is dead. After he became friends with Father Bill, he returned to the Church, but never discussed that part of his life. I told him he had nothing to worry about if he told the truth. "

"So where are we? How about the names of the other members of The Plumbers? Matt's the leader, but I think I remember two Michaels; one was called Mike; I'm not sure about the other one."

"Let's make a quick stop and see who's there now."

Each detective grabbed a coffee and they headed for The Plumbers. Matt was startled when he opened the door. "Gee, I wasn't expecting you again. We haven't gotten anything new at the web site."

"That's not why we're here," said Russell. "We need to talk with the two Michaels."

"Only one is here; he's asleep on the couch. He works nights at the 24-hour convenience store. He lives with his mother on the next block, so he comes over for lunch and hangs out until it's time to go to work at 11:00. Hey, Mike."

Mike opened his eyes and was on his feet in two seconds flat. "What the? Why do you want to talk to me?"

"Take it easy," said Coleman. "We just want to ask you some questions."

Both detectives walked toward the couch where Mike was sitting, dragged two chairs from the computer table and placed themselves face to face with him.

"How well did you know Father Bill?" asked Russell.

"We talked sometimes, that's all. And I think that he and Father John were good friends. When both priests were at St. Joseph's I sometimes saw Father John on Thursday mornings putting his golf bag in his car."

"How did you see that?"

"That's when I'd go over there to talk with Father Bill. Then two years ago Father Bill went away; I didn't know why, but I figured he must have done something wrong, because it was so hush-hush. Yeah, there were rumors all around, but I never found out if any of it was true. And even if it was…" His smile was condescending, "Father Bill was just being a man."

"What do you mean by that?" barked Coleman.

"You know, just doing things that men do. Never saw anything, so I can't say."

"Where's the other Mike?" asked Russell.

"You mean Mick," corrected Matt. "He should be coming in soon. He takes a class at the business school downtown; Father Bill helped him get in by writing a recommendation for him.

He usually comes here for a couple of hours and then goes to his job at the bar."

"Which one?" asked Russell.

"The Cobra Club."

"That's the gay bar," said Coleman.

"Yeah, so what? All of us know and it don't matter to us. So Mick, he's our friend and he knows he's accepted here and can be here as much as he wants."

"Did Father Bill know?" asked Coleman.

"Of course. He was a friend, and had helped Mick when he was trying to decide when and how to come out. Father Bill even went home with him the day he told his parents. Mick had said he would've never made it through all that without Father Bill."

Ten minutes later Mick came in. He nodded to the detectives and shot a questioning glance to Matt who said, "Mick, the detectives here want to talk to you."

"O.k.." Mick's demeanor was casual as he sauntered over to a chair.

"We know you and Father Bill were good friends," said Russell. "Can you tell us about that?"

"He helped me a lot, when I needed it."

Mick had been tapping his foot from the time he sat down; now he pressed it against the floor.

"Don't have nothing else to tell. We became friends when he was at St. Joseph's, that's all. In fact, I hadn't even seen him for two weeks. And I sure don't know why anyone would want to kill him."

He became more upset with each sentence and turned away from Coleman and Russell. The foot resumed its tapping.

When he turned back he avoided their scrutinizing eyes as he whispered, "I want to help you find who killed him, but I don't know nothing!"

His obvious distress moved Coleman to squeeze his shoulder. "Listen, Mick, we didn't mean to upset you. We just want this killer so bad. Take it easy, o.k.?"

Mick shook his head as he headed for the kitchen.

As they walked towards the door, Coleman said to Matt, "You said nothing new at the web site, right? Did you add Father Bill's murder to the page?"

"Yeah, but most of the e-mail we're getting is from people who are scared and worried about why it's taking you so long to solve this; we did get a few confessions, but they were so far off target, that we dismissed them as nut cases."

"Just in case, don't delete any; we may have to review even the craziest note, but we don't have time today. We'll be back."

Coleman looked back at the house after he heard the door close. "Mick is troubled about something and I don't think he was telling us everything. If he is the Mickey in Father Bill's journal, it is possible that he wanted to resume their relationship and when Father Bill refused, he killed him. What do you think?"

"Could happen, I guess, but somehow I got the feeling that his emotions were genuine and the grief is too personal to talk about. Besides, how would their relationship tie in with Father John?"

"What if Father John became aware of the relationship and convinced Mick to break it off; that would explain Father Bill's statement about never having the chance to explain. What if Mick felt betrayed by both priests and thought that if he killed Father John first no one would make the connection?"

"I hate to admit it, but that's a real possibility. However, my gut tells me, that Mick just felt safe with Father Bill; but we don't have much to go on either way."

"And you don't want to believe anything else. Don't let this get too personal, Rick."

Rick didn't say a word; Coleman's perception irritated him, but he had no defense at this point. The lateness of the day didn't help his mood, either. He was glad to get back to the office.

The messages from the other members of the task force were more of the same: no new leads. Both priests sure had a lot of admirers. *I guess being discreet worked for Father Bill,* thought Coleman. Immediately, he chided himself for being so callous.

One officer left a message about rumors when Father Bill was transferred out of St. Joseph's, but everyone seemed honest enough about being happy that he had returned to the area.

A note from Officer Kelly mentioned how some parishioners asserted that they had grown in their affection for him because of his failures. A few men said how much more comfortable they were with Father Bill than any other priest they had known and they firmly believed that the priest's own failures made him a better listener when they went to Confession.

After reading that last report, Coleman grinned and said to Russell "That sounds like more evidence for that happy fault idea."

Russell returned the grin. It had been a very long day. He was frustrated with Chris right now; a comment like that would ordinarily get him to talk more about his faith because he was so sure that his partner was close to conversion, but he was still irritated with that earlier remark. He needed his own answers tonight. "Good night, Chris."

Ten

Bishop Joseph Steele sat in his living room brooding over his options regarding the day-to-day situation at Holy Name. The drapes were closed because the housekeeper was intent on keeping out the afternoon sun and after dinner he was too tired to remember how pleasant the evening sky could be. "Every bone in this old body tells me I'm exhausted, but I can't go to bed this early," he muttered out loud. "Good grief, it's only 8:30 and I know I won't fall asleep anyway."

Holy Name had no deacon, the Sisters left five years ago; the lay leadership team of three women and two men was dedicated, but they had only begun their leadership training classes a few months ago. He doubted that anyone was yet qualified to carry out the administration of the parish.

Maybe I do need to watch a sunset, he thought as he dragged himself out of his recliner. Yanking open the drapes he was greeted by gold, pink and rose layers of clouds hovering over the sparkling beams of a retiring sun. The prayers of praise that would normally rise from his soul were replaced by a sigh so profound that he supposed it could be a prayer; he could not recall ever having so many nagging doubts before, but tonight he grappled with his faith in God's providence.

He shuddered as he heard again the wild scream of Father Bill's mother when he had to call her that morning. Mrs. Williams lived in Florida where she had moved ten years ago after her husband had died. He was grateful that he knew the pastor of her parish whom he had called first; because she lived five minutes away, Father Mark was able to be with her when the call came in. *Words are useless,* he had said to Mark, *but she will need your arms. Let her cry as much as she needs.* He had promised himself that he would call her every day until he would bring her son to her.

His thoughts went back to his afternoon conversation with Marge Peterson. She felt bound to tell him of her earlier meeting that day with Detectives Coleman and Russell; he assured her that he trusted her prudence and that she should feel free to cooperate with the police.

He appreciated her suggestion that the team members would be willing to take turns leading the daily communion service. Sundays were his main concern; what was he going to do about Mass on Sundays?

The diocese had been plagued with the priest shortage for years now. The nearest parish, St. Patrick's, had two priests, but the pastor would soon be 70 years old and was in poor health. *And I can't bring myself to relocating the not-much younger associate,* he mused.

He looked at a trace of pink in a sad blue sky; all that beauty had passed away so quietly. He glanced at his watch as he slumped back into his recliner. At 9:30, he sighed, *I should not put this off any longer.* He picked up the phone and called Father Joe Perry, knowing that dependable and trustworthy Joe would do whatever he was asked.

Joe picked up the phone on its second ring. When he heard the bishop's greeting, he gulped an anxious mouthful of air and said "Yes, Bishop. What can I do for you?"

"Joe, you know how difficult it is for me to add to your responsibilities. I need…"

"You need a priest at Holy Name. When do you want me there?"

"I'm not going to ask you to leave St. Pat's. I would like to ask you to say one Mass there beginning this Sunday. I know it will not be enough for the people, but I hope they will understand that I don't have another solution."

"I'm sure they will, Bishop. They are under such tension now, but they are also aware of the overall situation."

"Thank you, Joe. I knew I could depend on you."

The next morning at Holy Name the entire leadership team was on hand for the communion service. Less than ten minutes earlier Marge had received a call from Bishop Steele telling her about Father Joe.

When Marge went to the podium and made the announcement regarding the new Sunday schedule, she was not surprised by the audible dismay that came from the assembly.

One of the other women on the team seated in the first pew took that as her cue; she stood and faced the congregation. Appealing to their common sense she pointed out that having one Mass was preferred to the prospect of closing their parish altogether. Heads began to nod as the depressing reality sank deep into their communal heartbreak.

After talking with Marge, Bishop Steele remembered his promise and he slowly punched in the eleven digits. On the fourth ring, he heard a weak hello.

"Good morning, Mary. I hope you have been able to get some rest."

"Oh. Hello. Good morning, Bishop. You're so kind to call me. When I eventually fell asleep I dreamt of Bill, and I was so happy. Then I woke up, and remembered."

"I know, Mary. I wish I could say something to take away your pain, but we both know there is nothing we can do except drag this heavy cross. Even if we come to understand why this happened, the hole in our hearts will remain."

"That's so true, Bishop. My heart is broken. Bill's brother, the one who isn't married, who works at the stock exchange in New York, is coming in this afternoon. His other brother, the one in the Marines, is arriving tomorrow from North Carolina with his wife and their two children. I know they would also like to be at the services you are having up there, but I'm thankful that they will be here with me. I need them so much."

"Everything will be fine here, Mary. I don't want you to waste a minute worrying about anything. Bill had many people who loved him, so we are having a prayer service Monday evening and a Mass at 10:00 on Tuesday. Then I will be on the 5:00 evening flight to Orlando. I will bring your son to you. You must believe that God was very pleased with him."

He heard her stifled sob as she murmured her appreciation for his kindness.

His thoughts strayed to the other sorrows in her life. Father Bill's father, an alcoholic, had died in a drunken driving accident when Joe and Ed were in high school and Bill was in the sixth grade.

Now she was living through the singular anguish of a mother who must bury her son. He believed that her prayers had sustained her son through the most shameful days of his life as a priest and she needed to understand that she had not prayed in vain.

"I'll see you on Tuesday, Mary. My prayers are with you. And my love. Call me if you need anything. Goodbye now."

Monday evening the prayer vigil was scheduled for 7:00. Coleman was there with many other detectives standing along the rear wall. Though they came out of respect, the urgency to solve these murders kept them on the alert.

Numerous parishioners from St. Joseph's were also there. Coleman noticed that Mike and Carol Anderson and Mike and Susan Mahoney were in the last pew. Both Mikes were seated with their heads bowed.

He nudged Russell as he watched Mick and a few other Plumbers getting into a pew across the aisle.

As the solemn music began, Coleman observed the Bishop's rounded shoulders and his unsteady steps as he proceeded down the middle aisle.

After an introductory prayer Bishop Steele took one careful step at a time down the marble steps; the altar server reached out to steady him. The Bishop smiled at her. The strain in every line of his face broadcasted his desire to be very close to this congregation.

His tone was clear; his words were sincere as he tried to offer hope to the people of Holy Name without diminishing the pain they were enduring. Coleman listened intently as he heard the familiar theme of God's overwhelming love for them; his eyes searched the faces attentive to the bishop trying to evaluate the faith that was so palpable in this place.

What will happen to their faith, he asked himself, *if they find out that Father Bill was not who they thought he was?*

Coleman's desire for answers made sense and had him comparing the two priests. *One was, at least as far as we know,* he reminded himself, *the ideal picture of a good priest. The other had fallen through his own human weakness, yet people who knew him intimately, claimed that the forgiven sinner was also a good priest. What kind of God did these men serve? Did they regret they trusted a God so weak he could not save them?*

The bishop's words waned, but his face captured Coleman's attention. His words did not persuade him, but his faith was so real that Coleman battled the fascination that pulled at him. How could he dare surrender to the prodding in his heart? How could he walk with a God who demanded such total submission?

The following morning at the memorial Mass, Bishop Steele made a promise to improve the Mass situation at Holy Name. His anguish was apparent as he told the congregation that he would make time for everyone from both parishes if they desired to talk with him.

Worried questions scattered themselves throughout the assembled as he assured them that he would welcome any ideas they had in respect to the future of their parish as well as St. Joseph's.

Outside, after Mass Coleman and Russell waited off to the side; people clamoring to ask him questions surrounded the Bishop. He understood why the police wanted to meet with him; he gave them a brief nod, but returned his attention to the people.

Coleman and Russell edged themselves closer. Realizing he could not continue to ignore them, Bishop Steele excused himself from the group.

When Coleman asked to make an appointment to talk with him, the Bishop's reply was guarded. "I cannot imagine what I can add to your investigation, but I will cooperate in any way that I can. I have some time at 3:00 this afternoon; I can spare only a half hour because I have a flight to catch."

"We appreciate that, Bishop. We'll see you then."

Promptly at 3:00 Coleman and Russell were welcomed by the bishop's secretary and led to a small room; Coleman noted the simplicity of the dark wood paneling that provided a stark background to a light brown wooden cross that dominated the opposing wall. He glanced at three pictures of former bishops lined up on the left wall, with a large picture of the present pope above them.

They exchanged pleasantries, expressed their appreciation for the bishop's time and all sat down at a modest round table in the center of the room. Even though a large window made up most of the right wall, the room was dim; the candle-like lamps of the small chandelier above the table dared to overpower the shadows.

Coleman apologized in advance for some of the questions they would be asking. He had known this day would come; now he felt a nervous and lonely twitch in his stomach.

Bishop Steele's entire body stiffened. "I understand. Maybe I can spare you some discomfort by telling you that I encouraged Father Williams to acknowledge his problem and I helped get him accepted at the treatment center. I always firmly believed that he was a deeply spiritual man, but neither he nor I doubted that he required therapy. I was kept informed of Father's progress and I insisted on admitting him back into this diocese. I entrusted him with the growing parish of Holy Name; a large number of new parishioners had moved there in the last few years and so I felt he would have a little more flexibility there because he would not have to deal with entrenched ideas, the *we've always done it this way* arguments that customarily surface when a new pastor takes over. I am familiar with all the members of the support group and I took for granted that this would indeed be a success case."

Coleman found himself speechless for a moment; all his questions answered without one word coming out of his mouth.

Russell jumped in with "We appreciate your candor, Bishop. What can you tell us about Father John, anything that might suggest why the killer would have felt betrayed by both priests?"

"Father John made the title shepherd as real as it could be. He and Father Bill became true friends when they both served at St. Joseph's. When Father Bill's problems necessitated his departure, Father John treated him with such sensitivity and affection that Father Bill told me he knew Christ was talking to him; he never felt judged; he only encountered the compassion of a brother and a friend."

"Thank you, Bishop. We have to examine any connections." said Coleman.

Russell felt every nerve in his body tingling; *O God,* he prayed, *don't let him mention any of his repulsive theories.*

In a vain attempt to hide his angst Bishop Steele said, "I do want you to know that I will remain accessible to you throughout the investigation. However, if you unearth any salacious details please—" His words melted into the darkness of the room.

Russell was quick to smooth the tense air by telling him that he was a member of St. Joseph's and knew both priests. "Please be assured, bishop, that I love my faith and my church. We are bound to look at every possibility, but I promise you, that only what pertains to the case will be revealed."

In a tone that struggled with each word, the bishop said, "I am pleased to know that, Detective Russell. I trust that your partner feels the same way."

Feels like manipulation to me, said Coleman to himself, but he nodded in the affirmative. Russell was relieved.

The bishop himself walked them to the door and promised to continue to pray that their work would result in a swift solution.

Coleman mulled over the conflicting images he had of the bishop. Kind. Concerned for the people. Believed in a loving God. Defensive, too, that's for sure. And protective. *He isn't too crazy about us; I don't even think he bought all that we're-really-good-guys stuff Russell fed him.*

Coleman studied his partner for a minute or so. "Was I picking up vibes from you to go easy on him? I wanted to bring up the journal, but for some reason I couldn't. He seemed to know Father Bill pretty well, but he didn't hint at anything more that his alcohol problem."

"Maybe he just didn't want to give us something if he didn't have to; I think that's why he was so worried about, as he said salacious details. I assumed he was preparing himself for the worst when he asked us to safeguard their reputations. Besides, what could we say about the journal? We don't know much except that he had a relationship with someone; I thought the timing would be bad today; he said we can come back."

"Time will tell, I guess." Coleman swung into his parking space and turned off the ignition. "Time will tell."

After checking their messages and meeting with some other detectives, they both headed home.

As Coleman reviewed their conversation with the bishop, he speculated on the disgrace that might come to light in the next few weeks. He detected a vague irritation eating away inside. *Why am I so disappointed by the bishop? Was I conned by a phony sincerity? Was I beginning to believe all that stuff I heard him say about a loving God? Now, I see that his main concern is to protect the church and himself. Why does that make me sad? What if he is on a journey, too?* For some weird reason that thought consoled him.

Eleven

Flying home, Bishop Steele was glad to be sitting alone in a near empty plane; he reflected on the rituals he had celebrated with Father Bill's family and friends and the images soothed his grief. The pilot's announcement of twenty-five minutes until landing brought him back to thinking about his tormenting responsibilities.

How am I going to shepherd the congregation at Holy Name? With only one Mass on Sunday, what message am I giving to those faithful people? How many will turn to another church that offers them a better spiritual home?

Scenes of his meeting with the detectives kept interrupting his anxiety. *I was not as honest as I should have been with them; I know there were rumors about Bill that I avoided discussing with him. There was so much good in him I did not want to lose him; that's why I persuaded him to go for help. They could deal with it; they could help him and they did. O God, what will happen if what I was afraid to know is revealed? How do I protect the church? How will I prevent people from condemning Bill for his faults?*

That evening, his crushing worries drove him to phone Frank McCoy, his best friend and a brother bishop. He always found Frank's words of wisdom a balance between bureaucratic necessities and spiritual integrity.

Bishop Frank McCoy's diocese was somewhat larger, but he was also dealing with a priest shortage.

When his phone rang at 10:00pm Frank was snoozing in front of the TV; he fumbled for the mute button as he looked around for the receiver he had knocked to the floor.

He found it on the third ring, and when he heard Joe's voice, his first question was, "How are you?"

Because of some mutual health problems this was not the ordinary polite query; not only were they both on high blood pressure medicine and coumadin, but Joe had also undergone bypass surgery a year ago.

"Oh, I'm fine, physically. What I really want to talk about is how am I going to counter all this media hype. I'm worried about these investigations, Frank; I'm afraid that Bill's situation will become publicized and cause all kinds of bad press for the church. We both know Bill was genuine in his repentance, but you know what the media will do with his story. Plus, now I have two parishes without a priest. What am I going to do?"

Frank's answer was immediate, his tone filled with genuine concern for his friend. Joe and Frank had gone through the seminary together; they had become bishops at the same time. They both loved the Church and wanted to protect it; they did not always agree with the directives that came from Rome. Neither wanted to lead any reform movement, either.

"I don't think there's much you can do about the way the media decides to handle this; after all, the murder of two priests has everybody's interest and if you can add alcohol or sex to the mixture, why, that's all they need for a movie of the week. So all we can do is hope the killings were not personal and even then, it's asking too much to think they'll leave the other details out of the limelight. This one needs a lot of prayer, Joe."

"You're right, of course."

Frank heard the uneasy sigh of his friend flooding the line. Because they had been such good friends for years he knew he could vent his opinions to a sympathetic ear.

"On the other hand, the priest shortage—you already know my sentiments on that. Hell, Mike Rogers and Dick Quinn are still living in this diocese; they were damn good priests; but now they're married priests and I can't use them. They would be ready to take over a parish with two weeks notice. What a waste! And then there's Sr. Emily Murphy and Ann Thompson—both have completed their theology studies. Hell, they know more than some of my priests; there are days, Joe, when I just feel like saying, to hell with all this crap; I'm going to ordain them!"

Joe heard in his own sigh a mix of amusement and surrender because they had talked about this so many times before.

"Do you ever imagine what would happen if we did that? Or if we call back a married priest? Every time I see Larry Strong, his wife and their two daughters at Mass, my heart just aches for everything that's been lost to us as a church. However, you bring up a splendid possibility with Sister Emily and Ann Thompson; I know Emily from somewhere; she must have worked in this diocese at one time; I met Ann at that awards dinner you had last fall. I can't ordain them but would they be interested in being a pastoral administrator? That way I would have someone responsive to the people who could do everything except say Mass and give absolution in Confession. How much to you know about their circumstances?"

"I know Emily is looking for a job. Ann has a family, so I'm not sure she'd be ready to move. If you want, I'll call both of them tomorrow and tell them to get in touch with you."

"Yes, do that." A thrill surged into the secret center of his being. He had not felt this alive for a long time.

"My faith tells me, Joe, that we will learn a lesson from all this. Besides, don't we always preach that God never abandons us?"

"I firmly believe that." So much heaviness had vanished from his heart. "Well, it's getting late, Frank; time for my medicine and then I'll watch the news. Have a good night. Let's get together soon."

"Try to take it easy, Joe. I'll talk to you soon. Good night."

At the 8:00 Mass the next morning Bishop Steele smiled as he gave the final blessing. He slept quite well last night. His energy level was soaring; he listened to a new song in his heart.

Bishop McCoy finished his Mass with a smile too. At 8:45, before even thinking of breakfast, he called Ann Thompson first and told her about his conversation with Bishop Steele.

Ann was delighted to hear that Bishop Steele was choosing to go in that direction. "However," she said with an obvious longing in her voice, "My husband has just been promoted and our children are so involved in their school programs and activities I just can't ask them to move for me. I want so much to minister in that capacity and I hope that I can someday do so here in this diocese."

Bishop McCoy made a mental note, telling Ann she would receive the first call because he was sure that a similar decision would be his to make in the not so distant future. He remembered what caught his attention when he first met her— the fire of the Spirit in her deep brown eyes. She was not very tall, but when she spoke it seemed that the glow from within lifted her from the floor. *O God, when will the powers that beg for vocations, recognize your gifts?*

Next he dialed Sister Emily. With the final word of explanation out of his mouth, her jubilant voice pulsed through the phone with "This is an answer to prayer!"

Continuing with unfeigned enthusiasm she told him, "I've been discerning my next direction in ministry and I'm confident that this is the confirmation I'm seeking. I am most eager to call Bishop Steele to set up an appointment: Thank you so much! Thank you! Thank you!"

Bishop McCoy could not remember smiling so often in the morning. He relaxed in his deep satisfaction for his friend, and relished the harmony and calm welling up within as he hung up the phone. Even his wheat toast and decaf coffee tasted better this morning.

Twelve

At the precinct that morning Russell's coffee spilled over the Dad-word on his mug as he came to a standstill in front of Coleman, who was yawning and had dark circles and bags under his eyes. *Did he even comb his hair this morning?*

"You look awful! What kept you up all night?"

Coleman yawned again, rubbed his forehead and ran his hand through his hair.

"I couldn't get Father Bill's journal out of my mind. Something kept nagging me; we were concentrating on the Michaels from The Plumbers because we or at least, I was thinking Michael was a teenaged boy."

"And now?"

"What if this was an adult relationship? Then it hit me— Mike Anderson and Mike Mahoney! What if either or both were lying about why they felt uncomfortable with Father Bill's disclosure? What if either was actually involved in a—"

"But, I thought you believed what Anderson told you about being molested. So why would he be in a relationship with Father Bill?"

"I know; that's what kept me awake. But how about this: what if Anderson was molested and still harbored so much hate or anger toward the priest who did it, that he pretended to be interested in having an intimate relationship, just to get close to Father Bill? And then to make him feel vulnerable and powerless, he breaks off the relationship. That would also give Anderson the satisfaction of having control over someone else. Maybe that's all he intended to do and thought he had accomplished his purpose, so to speak, when Father Bill was sent away. But when he returned, and when it seemed that he might tell the support group everything, Anderson was so scared of being embarrassed that he figured the only solution was to kill him. Plus, he could have persuaded himself that murdering a priest with a sexual problem somehow balanced the scales."

"How would that explain Father John's murder?"

"I wrestled with that, too. Let's assume that Father John knew about the relationship; remember what Bishop Steele told us: that Father Bill never felt judged by Father John, that he treated him like a brother. Anderson could have assumed the same thing. So to be safe, Anderson kills him first, a priest with a great reputation, who knows Anderson's secret. If he had killed Father Bill first, what would keep Father John from telling what he knew?"

"O.k., I'm not sure there's enough there, but, hell, I hate to agree with you, it's a possibility. What's your theory for Mahoney?"

"Again, what if the sexual identity story is a lie, that he was upset when he realized his attraction for Father Bill; what if they had in fact been lovers? Think of the guilt he would feel when he would come home each night. Then when he broke it off and Father Bill was sent away, he thought that was the end of it. When Father Bill returned and asked him to be in his support group, he thinks this is the only way he can be sure that their secret is never revealed. Imagine the panic when Father Bill started to talk about his past sexual sins."

"Wait a minute. Remember the line in Father Bill's journal that says he noticed both Anderson and Mahoney being uncomfortable, and that he was scared that Mahoney knew? That gives some credence to your theory about Anderson; Father Bill thought that Mahoney knew about him and Anderson. Since both of them became agitated..."

"Maybe Father Bill thought that Anderson had shared his terrible secret with Mahoney. Maybe he wanted to reassure them that he was not going to reveal names or details, just his own sinfulness and would ask the group for forgiveness. We don't know if Father Bill ever had the opportunity to explain his intentions to either of them. But even if he did, maybe even the remote possibility of exposure was just too risky for either of them. Furthermore, maybe they decided to do this together or be each other's alibi."

"Damn it all, I hate to see where this is headed. Can you picture the people's reaction if either man, one of their own parishioners, becomes a suspect? And for a reason like that?"

Coleman and Russell discussed how they should proceed; they needed a plan; they both had promised no revelations unless there was a direct connection to the murders. They had only their own suspicions, ugly and probable, but still only suspicions.

"Both wives," said Coleman "knew their husbands were in Father Bill's support group; which means they all knew he had a problem."

"An alcohol problem."

"Right. But we could use that as a way to ask if either one was aware of others who knew; maybe someone who saw a drunk priest as a sinner, unworthy, so to speak, to be at the Last Supper."

"What if someone, even in the group, thought that Father Bill should not have returned to the ministry?"

"O.k., these are good; hell, if we're lucky, we might even learn that both of them are innocent and find a whole new direction."

"The Anderson's will be at the big fancy fundraiser tonight at the Marriott. Let's aim to be at the Mahoney's by 5:30; that's usually when Mike gets home. Maybe you can grab a nap before then; you do look like hell!"

"I'll feel better after lunch. We both need to be very prepared for the meeting with the task force this afternoon; we can tell them about our plans to meet with the Anderson's and Mahoney's but I don't think it's necessary to reveal the reasons behind our suspicions."

"Right. See you at 2:00."

During the task force meeting, four detectives shared information and stories of the rumors that surfaced after Father Bill's departure from St. John's.

One woman was certain that Father Bill was having an affair, but had to admit it was only her intuition.

Several rumors involved alcohol and sexual abuse but again no one could offer any tangible proof.

Supporters for Father Bill's return to ministry outweighed the doubters.

No other former St. Joseph parishioners were at Holy Name; nor was anyone else from St. Joseph's in Father Bill's support group.

Coleman and Russell's decision to revisit the Anderson's and Mahoney's raised no questions.

Sitting across the street from the Mahoney's house, Coleman checked his watch again. Mike was running late today. "Must have been caught in traffic," Coleman said.

Finally at 6:00 he pulled into the driveway. As Mike got out of his car, he noticed Coleman and Russell crossing the street.

Mike waited for them to get closer, moved towards them with a pasted-on smile and asked if they had any news.

"No, but we want to talk a little more with both you and Susan.

"You're not going to bring up, you know, what we talked about?"

"Don't see any need to do that at this point. We just want to see if there is anything that you may have forgotten or thought was not important, anything that might give us a clue as to why someone would want both priests dead."

Mike winced. "O.k.; Sure thing." He took a deep breath. "Anything we can do to help." As he pushed open the front door, he called for Susan. "The detectives are here, Hon. They want to talk with both of us a little more."

Susan answered from the kitchen, "I'll be right there." She dried her hands, patted her hair and smiled as she walked into the living room; those sapphire eyes sparkled as she welcomed them into the living room and invited them all to sit down. "How about something cold to drink?" she asked as Mike went over to the bar to fix something for himself. She turned as she heard several ice cubes fall to the floor.

"Just ice, Hon. Sorry."

"Thanks, but we're fine," replied Russell. "We just want to take a few minutes to go over some details."

"Since you knew both priests," Coleman said as he made direct eye contact with Mike and then moved his eyes toward Susan, "could you tell us a little more about your relationship with each of them? For example, were you close enough to, say, go golfing with them, ever have an evening out for dinner, or…"

Mike's knee jerked when the phone rang; Susan excused herself and went into the kitchen to answer it. She called Mike to come to the phone. "It's Mickey," she said.

The high-gear commotion that took off in their heads was so loud that Coleman and Russell dared not look at each other as Susan came back into the living room.

Russell hoped that his nonchalance rang true when he said, "Something made you happy."

"Oh, yes," said Susan, "That's our daughter, Michelle; we've always called her Mickey. She wants to know if she can come over this evening; she has something important to tell us, and she wanted to be sure her dad would be here."

The phrase, timing is everything, repeated itself over and over in Coleman's now raring-to-go mind.

He had to find a way out. "Listen, Susan we don't want to disturb your evening with your daughter; we'll come back another time."

"Oh, o.k.. You are so kind. Mike and I want to help in any way that we can, you must believe that. We loved both Father John and Father Bill."

"We know. Tell Mike we said good-bye and thanks so much for all your cooperation."

In their car, Russell stifled a low whistle. "That was pure gift," he said to Coleman as if he needed to underline their unexpected bargain. Michelle and Father Bill. Now they had a whole new set of questions.

Did Father Bill know Michelle was pregnant?

Did he know she had an abortion?

How much had Father John known?

And had Mike Mahoney figured it out?

They recalled that Susan had stated that he was furious when Father John told them Michelle was not obliged to reveal the father's name.

"No wonder Father Bill was scared. What was he thinking, having Mike Mahoney in his group? Having sex was bad enough, but with the daughter of someone in your support group?"

Russell struggled to find some words. "Maybe," he began, "maybe, he thought he would try a confession to the group first and if they were forgiving and understanding, he planned to ask forgiveness of Mike."

"When he saw Mike's reaction, he figured it was too late."

"Bill must have never made a connection, though, to Father John."

"Probably never dreamed that Mike would hurt anyone but him. After all, he was the sinner."

Coleman moved their car in front of a house further down the street and under a large oak tree. They waited for Michelle to arrive.

Within twenty minutes, a red Toyota Corolla pulled into the Mahoney driveway. With her blond hair pulled back in a ponytail, dressed in white slacks and a navy top, Michelle skipped up the steps and onto the porch.

Must be very good news thought both detectives as their eyes followed her bouncing entrance through the opened door.

Thirty minutes later Russell said, "They must have a lot to talk about." He sighed and checked his watch again. "Oh, finally, here they come."

All three Mahoney's came down the sidewalk, looking like the perfect picture of family harmony. *Susan must be thrilled with this,* thought Coleman. *I'd love to see those sapphire eyes now; I bet they're dancing.* Mike had one arm around Michelle and was holding Susan's hand.

When they got to the car, he hugged Michelle and held her close for a long time; then Susan took her turn and also gave her a kiss on the cheek.

Her happiness skipped all the way down the street to Coleman and Russell as she hopped into her car. She backed out of the driveway and with her arm out the window waved goodbye to her parents.

Mike was still holding Susan's hand as they turned and walked back to the house. Coleman watched as he entwined his fingers around hers; even from this distance, he could see the tender squeeze. He kissed her cheek as they reached the porch.

Coleman and Russell followed Michelle to her apartment. She waved to another woman coming out of the building and squeezed the arm of an older gentleman who held the door open for her. *Who could not see that she's in love,* thought Coleman. *And we're the ones to bring her back to earth, or even worse, back to her past.* He sighed as he punched in her number. "Ms. Mahoney, I am Detective Coleman, here with my partner Detective Russell. May we come up to your apartment? We need to ask you some questions."

Her voice quivered as she told them that she had a date at 9:00. "But, yes, I'll talk to you. My apartment is 914."

Coleman and Russell knew how close they might be to solving the case. The usual exhilaration that pumped through their bodies at times like this was absent. They headed for the apartment lobby.

When the elevator door opened a crowd tumbled out and pushed past them. Coleman was glad that he and Russell were the only ones waiting to get on.

Once the door closed, Russell moved his finger over the numbers looking for the ninth floor button. With their eyes fixed on the numbers as they lit up one by one, neither spoke.

When the door opened they came face to face with Michelle. Coleman blinked away his stare; *I knew she would have her mother's eyes.* Michelle nodded and produced the obligatory smile as she motioned them to follow her.

Inside her apartment, both detectives were impressed as they took a quick glance at the uncluttered living room.

Both were stunned when Michelle said she was wondering how long it was going to take before they questioned her.

Coleman asked "And why is that?"

"My parents told me of the investigation including what they said about the abortion and how Father John had been counseling me and my parents. I suppose you want to know who the father was."

Russell hoped that his voice showed the compassion he felt inside when he informed her that they knew who the father was.

Michelle's entire body stiffened as she directed them toward the couch.

When all were seated, Coleman and Russell looked at her flushed cheeks; the eyes became clouded and her hands were folded on her lap. "How did you find out?"

When Coleman told her about Father Bill's journal Michelle gulped a moan and dropped her head into her hands.

Coleman and Russell remained silent and watched her, aware at the same time of the mixture of emotions swirling inside of them.

A few moments later, she lifted her head just long enough to inhale a long drawn-out breath and covered her face with her trembling hands.

Michelle allowed the tears she had repressed for so long to be released. With sobs that rocked her whole body, she stumbled towards her bedroom.

Coleman and Russell waited, each lost in his own web of contradictions and conflict.

The crying became hushed and then there was silence.

Raising an eyebrow at each other, they were ready to check on her when Michelle returned to the room. Her eyes were red, but she managed a feeble smile and thanked them for their patience.

In a whisper, both Coleman and Russell apologized for upsetting her.

Coleman cleared his throat and said, "We won't take too much more of your time today. We just want to know if you had talked with Father Bill recently."

Michelle shook her head no. "Can I explain?"

Both detectives nodded a silent yes.

"We had not seen each other or even talked on the phone since he had become pastor at Holy Name. He never knew about the baby. When I found out I was pregnant, I never told him. In fact, I began dating one of the guys from my class, two or three times a week, hoping that if he saw me with someone else, he'd realize it was over. I didn't want to hurt him, but I was so confused and didn't know what to do."

With an explosive rush of words grateful to be released from their hiding place, she quickly went on.

"I didn't want him to know about the baby because I was sure he would insist that I have it. He would have even left the priesthood for me, but I knew that would be a mistake. I was too young; Bill was 14 years older and although I thought I was in love, I knew it would never work. I was so torn between my religious beliefs and my fear of telling my parents, that I didn't sleep for weeks. Finally, I made up my mind about the abortion by talking with one of my girlfriends, who also went to the clinic with me. I will never forget how awful I felt when it was over—how dreadfully empty I felt. That's why I went to Father John. I couldn't handle the guilt by myself any more. I even thought of killing myself."

Coleman reached over to touch her hand. "I'm glad you went for help. Did you ever tell anyone who the father was?"

"No, no one, not my friend, definitely not my parents. Father John helped me realize that some things are better left unsaid. My father had a hard time dealing with it; he was so angry."

"Did Father John know who the father was?"

"I never told him, but sometimes when he talked with me, I was sure that he knew. Maybe it was just my own guilt or my feminine intuition."

She gave in to a fleeting and halfhearted smile.

"But we never spoke about the father, just about how I was handling the guilt. Even though Father John had assured me that God had forgiven me, I still have nightmares every so often."

"Are you seeing anyone now?"

Coleman was relieved to see that her face brightened up; *I can understand the magnetism of those eyes,* he thought. The tears had made them even more transparent. He could forgive her anything.

"I just came from my parents' home; my boyfriend, Tom, proposed to me last evening. I wanted to tell them in person because our relationship over these past few years has been somewhat strained, to say the least—but they had met Tom and seemed to like him. Tom knows about the abortion, but said that it all happened before he met me, so he doesn't want to know who the father was. Tom's a software design genius, and works in the same office as I do."

"You said you had plans for the evening, but we have more questions. We'll come back tomorrow." Coleman's words said tomorrow, but his eyes told her he hoped she would keep talking.

"No, let's get it all out tonight."

"O.k., we appreciate that, Michelle. We know this is difficult, but we really do need your cooperation. Would you tell us how you know that your affair with Father Bill was a secret?"

Her cheeks smoldered with her shame as she glanced away from both detectives and began her confession.

"It all started after one of the youth group dances at St. Joseph's when I was a senior. I noticed that he was watching me when I was dancing; I had seen that look before and knew exactly what it meant. So, when he invited anyone who wanted to talk to come over to the rectory after the dance, I went with five others, boys and girls. We talked and sang; Bill played the guitar; it was so much fun. At 12:00 when everyone was leaving, I pretended I couldn't find my keys; Father Bill offered to take me home, but after the others drove off, we went back into the rectory and I stayed until 1:30.

"Did anyone question you the next day?"

"No, we weren't in the same classes. Besides, Bill and I only talked that time; I was captivated by his charisma and I enjoyed the thrill of fantasizing what might happen. It wasn't all his fault; I knew what I was doing, but I wanted him so much. I would have slept with him that night if he had given me the chance."

"Didn't your parents question you when you came home so late?"

"Oh yes. I told them that my girlfriend, Liz and I had gone for pizza because Liz had broken up with her boyfriend and wanted to talk. The part about the boyfriend was true, but nothing else. I was grounded for two weeks, so I called Father Bill and told him what happened."

"But he wanted to see you again?"

"I wanted to see him. After that, we met once a week at the rectory on Thursday afternoons on my way home from school. Thursday was Father John's day off and Bill was always waiting for me at the back door so that the secretary never saw me. And his room was upstairs at the back of the house, so we felt safe that she couldn't hear us. And by the time I left, she had gone home."

Coleman was all set to ask another question, but hardly taking a breath, Michelle continued.

"It took a month before we made love for the first time. The week before I thought it was never going to happen; but I was sure he could tell from everything I said and did that I was ready."

Coleman wondered if he was too interested in all these details. She needed to talk, he convinced himself and she might end up telling them something useful. At the same time, his outrage was confusing him; *why am I so angry at Father Bill and why does she insist on taking the blame?* His mind was filled with excuses for her when Russell's words about a *sin with* popped up before him.

"One time we weren't being very careful about the time; we heard Father John's car in the driveway and I wasn't even dressed yet. Bill ran down to his study and I grabbed my clothes and ran into the bathroom; when I heard the two of them talking I could make out that Bill was telling Father John that I was in the bathroom, that he and I had been working on the next youth group meeting. After checking in the mirror that I looked all right, I came out and greeted Father John as I was coming down the stairs. Bill thanked me for all my help and walked me to the door. I was so scared I dropped my books and when Bill helped me pick them up, he made some humorous comment that even made Father John laugh. Bill was so calm about the whole charade that it made me smile that we had pulled it off."

"Is that why you think that Father John figured it out?"

"I hadn't remembered that until now; I was so certain at the time that Father John didn't suspect anything that I forgot about it."

"So, how long did this go on?"

"Five months and two weeks, until I found out I was pregnant. I knew he wouldn't call our house and I realized he would be tormented by a breakup, but I just couldn't have a baby and I was too upset to tell him. Besides, the prom was coming up in a month and one of the boys in my class, Danny, had asked me to go. I had always liked Danny, but going to the prom just made me feel worse. That's when I decided that my only solution was to have an abortion. But I continued to date Danny through the summer, just to let Liz think that he might be the father."

"And she's the one who went to the abortion clinic with you?"

"Yes. And by the end of summer, Father Bill had left the parish and I was so relieved; I had stopped going to Mass with my parents, because I felt so guilty, and weeks after Father Bill left, I told them about the abortion but not who the father was. We were fighting so much, so I moved out after graduation. I got this job and enrolled in night classes at the university."

"But Father John never asked you about Father Bill?"

"No. When I told him about the abortion, he promised me that God still loved me, plus he encouraged me to join a group called Project Rachel, named for the Rachel in the Bible who mourned the children killed by Herod. They help you to believe and accept God's forgiveness; and we talked about how to go on living after realizing what we had done."

She choked and wiped her eyes. There was no denying how captivating she was. Coleman's heart and mind were battling to find something to say. For a fleeting instant he was caught up in an image of a loving parent; he remembered something Russell had said about unconditional love; he felt a strange peace holding him and then the vision evaporated. Michelle was still speaking.

"I stayed with them for more than two years, meeting every week and even now I'm in touch with several women but I'm not a regular at the group meetings anymore."

The burden had been shared. She bowed her head; quiet settled in, but only for a moment. Raging alarms clanged throughout her shaking body. *What have I done,* she screamed in silence.

She fell to her knees in front of Coleman. She clutched his hands, and sobbed. "Please don't tell; please don't tell my parents. This would kill them."

Coleman took her head in his hands; her tears spilled over his fingers. He stared at the storm clouding her eyes. He wrenched an oath from his soul. "I promise; I promise; I will do all I can to keep your secret."

Russell spoke. "We will do all we can, Michelle, to keep it that way unless it has a direct connection to the murders."

Michelle suddenly realized she was on her knees. She released her grip on Coleman, quickly wiped away her tears and stood up.

"How could that be?"

Coleman clenched his fists. He tore his eyes away from Michelle's and looked at Russell who was startled at the message he saw there. *Find the right words, my partner, like never before.*

"Someone may have found out what was going on back then and decided to keep the secret until now. Maybe someone wanted money to keep quiet; maybe someone was outraged that Father Bill had returned to the ministry."

Her eyes froze the same way her mother's did when it was suggested that someone might have judged Father Bill unworthy as a priest. Coleman argued with himself; *O.k., o.k., if I want to forgive her, then I have to forgive him, too. At least, she seems to have regained her composure.*

"We'd better leave now and give you time to get ready for your date. Try not to worry, please; you have been a great help. We promise that if your story does have to be revealed, we will accompany you to your parents first."

"I don't know if I could handle that!" She began to wring her hands.

Coleman grabbed them. He looked again at Russell.

"Michelle, you will have whatever strength you need when you need it. I promise you."

His words came from a source so intense that she caught the comfort they were intended to bring. With her teary eyes shimmering, she murmured her thank you.

Coleman held her hands for a moment longer.

She offered to walk them to the elevator, but both detectives assured her that it was not necessary.

"Are you o.k. now? We didn't want to upset you so much," said Russell.

"Tom's a lucky guy." Coleman winked and pointed to the engagement ring as Michelle closed the door. He was grateful to see her smile.

"How many more secrets do you think we're going to be asked to keep?"

Russell shook his head. "I'm hoping no more."

"But it's better knowing at least this much truth, don't you think? After all, some of the other scenarios were even more embarrassing."

"That's true, but this is still going to be devastating if this has to come out. I really hate this."

"At the risk of shocking you, by saying something spiritual, couldn't this all fit in with that happy fault thing we were talking about?"

Russell's smile could not have been bigger. "Well, I do thank you for that reminder. You are right, of course, but it's going to be tough on people if they learn about all this stuff. On the other hand, the real reason for the murders might be even worse, if that's possible."

"By the way, what you said to Michelle really seemed to convince her. How can you be so sure?"

"What? That she would have the strength? Because I've seen the power."

"Huh? Is it something you would tell me?"

"When I was eleven years old, my older brother was killed by a drunk driver. I thought my mother would never stop crying and my dad would never laugh again. But what I remember most is that neither one stopped praying. I couldn't understand it. I was so angry because I thought God should have saved my brother."

"So then you do understand where I'm coming from?"

"We probably have more in common that we realize. Anyway, my mother said God was all she could hold on to. My father wouldn't even talk about Josh, but I would see him sometimes sitting in his chair and somehow I knew he was praying, too. Then one day my father smiled; it was different from before, but it was the most beautiful smile I had seen. I knew he had seen something true and beautiful, and he could go on now."

"Did he ever tell you what happened?"

"No, but I overheard him one night in the kitchen with my mother; they were both talking about Josh and I thought I even heard them sharing a laugh, something that had been missing from our home for so long. My mother still cried sometimes, but I could sense a peace all around her. I never put it into words before, but it was like there was always a tear in the background; our life was changed and yet somehow it still was good."

"When did you stop being angry with God?"

"That year, at Easter, when I heard the words again that Jesus is risen, I could feel Josh standing beside me and I knew that God was real and lived with our family. That's when I knew that whatever you think you cannot do, or if you think you cannot go on, there's a power stronger than anything on earth to help you."

"My father was killed; murdered; the killer was never found. My mother, like yours, kept praying and I guess she found that same power you're talking about. But I never did. When I got older I decided she just couldn't accept the fact that God really couldn't help her."

"Is your mother still living?"

"Yes. We used to fight all the time; now it's easier to just ignore the whole thing. I love my mom, so I made up my mind to accept her and her beliefs, and she accepts me. But who knows, if there is a power out there, maybe—Deb says I'm on a journey; maybe she's right."

They rode the rest of the way in silence. When they reached the station, Coleman glanced over at Russell, who was lost in thought, and whispered, "Thanks."

Russell managed a slight smile and a quick nod.

Once inside they checked their messages from the task force. Nothing new, as they had expected.

Both detectives realized that if Mike Mahoney was the killer, then no other priest was in danger. Coleman thought about his promise to Michelle; his eyes stung as he remembered hers. Never before had he been desperate to find another suspect.

Thirteen

Monday evening, 11:00 pm in the rectory of Our Lady of Guadalupe parish, Father Andy Sanchez tapped his foot under the desk, hoping to figure out a way to end the babbling coming out of the man sitting in his office.

The evening began with eager anticipation. Ed, as he had identified himself, had asked to talk with Father Andy about the parish plans for a broader outreach into the community. On the phone he said that he was aware that most of the parishioners were Hispanic and he knew that Father Sanchez was aware of other ethnic groups nearby.

He was very interested, he said, in helping the church prepare for its annual Culture Appreciation Day. As a caterer, he was willing to donate his time and some food, and had many ideas he wished to discuss including several new study and prayer groups that were being formed in the parish.

When Ed did not show up at the appointed time of 8:00, Father Andy was disappointed and chided himself for not getting an address or phone number. By 9:15 he dismissed the whole idea and promised that he would not allow himself to be so easily conned next time.

The sound of the doorbell at 9:20 suggested he may have misjudged Ed; *something must have detained him,* he thought.

But maybe I should not be so quick to forgive, he warned himself.

He seemed pleasant enough in the beginning; he described various ethnic dishes that he would gladly prepare and donate. A half hour later he began quoting Bible passages using them to criticize Bishop Steele.

Father Andy at first thought he would have no problems showing Ed the folly behind his conclusions, but soon realized how useless it would be to continue. He found himself staring at this man and prayed to God to help him find a polite way to end the evening as soon as possible.

Maybe if I stand up, he'll get the hint, thought Father Andy. "I thank you for your ideas, but I do not think we will be able to use your services."

He moved around the desk to shake Ed's hand. That's when he saw what he did not believe. *A knife; its coming right at me. Oh my God, please help me.*

He clutched at his chest, gasped as the knife made its first painful jab, and fell to his knees. With all his strength, he fought the second thrust as the piercing blare of the security system startled and stopped his attacker.

The killer dashed to the front door where he collided with a bumbling man. *Who is this drunk? He won't remember a thing,* he told himself, as he hurled him against the wall; he dragged the dazed man into the office and as he passed out cold, shoved the bloody knife into his limp hand. The alarm was still ringing; he raced to his car and roared out the opposite end of the parking lot behind the parish center.

In less than five minutes the police arrived. They found the unconscious man in the entrance to the office and a bleeding lifeless Father Andy near the desk.

One officer checked the priest's vital signs and called 911 followed at once by calls to Coleman and Russell. Both reached the scene within seconds of each other where they learned that Father Andy had been rushed to St. Mary's hospital.

The first officers on the scene described what they observed; one of them held up an evidence bag containing the knife.

"Make sure nothing happens to that." Coleman was afraid to allow himself too much hope, but this could be the break they needed. He tried to dismiss the satisfaction that seeped into his consciousness.

Coleman and Russell looked down on the drunk as he was regaining consciousness. They ignored his pitiable condition seeing instead his value to them. *We've seen him before,* thought both detectives. *Who is he?*

Russell asked his name, and why he had come to the rectory that evening. The man on the floor tried to focus his eyes, gawked up at all the police and then stared down at his hands; he noticed the blood and moaned.

Coleman reached out and grabbed the dazed man's hand; he pulled him up and helped him into a chair. The man stammered a feeble thank you. He looked over to Russell and told him that his name was Charlie Sullivan; he came to beg for some money so he could get a room to sleep in tonight.

"Why did you have a fight with Father?" Coleman's eyes searched Charlie's face and bloodshot eyes.

Charlie was adamant. "We didn't fight. I didn't even have a chance to see the Father."

Russell pointed to the blood on Charlie's hands and sleeve; he stared at the blood, shook his head back and forth, and mumbled, "I don't know how that happened. Wait a minute; I remember something; someone ran into me and knocked me down. He threw me against the wall."

"How did you get inside?"

"I don't know. I only remember that the alarm went off."

Giving the area a swift once-over inspection, Coleman said to Russell, "He must have tripped and fallen into the door smashing the glass; that would have triggered the alarm."

"Stay right here," ordered Russell.

He and Coleman moved toward Father's office. They caught sight of a yellow Post-it pad on the floor near a chair that had been shoved aside. A black pen had rolled to a stop by the leg of the desk.

With meticulous care, Coleman picked up the note pad and Russell pointed to three printed letters smudged by blood. They could make out an M, an O, and an N.

Russell scanned the desk and noticed a Bible with a bookmark peeking out of its pages. He opened the Bible to Matthew, Chapter 26. *Wonder why he didn't use Luke this time?* He signaled Coleman to come and take a look.

"I think Charlie may be telling us the truth. Someone else was here, someone who brought this Bible. Take Charlie down to the station so he can sleep it off tonight and we'll talk with him in the morning."

"Hey, now I remember; that's where we've seen Charlie. He's been in before, always drunk; he gets a bed for the night and he's always released in the morning."

"I recognize him now, too. If we're lucky he'll remember something after he sobers up. Meanwhile, let's hope that Father Andy survives and can identify his assailant."

"Amen, to that."

Bishop Steele fell into a restless sleep in his recliner before the 11:00 news ended. When the phone jarred him out of a disturbing dream he thrashed the air attempting to turn off his alarm. On the third ring he awakened. He groped for the receiver he had knocked to the floor.

Detective Coleman expressed regret for the lateness of his call and explained the situation concerning Father Andy. The bishop bolted to his feet, thanked him for the call and gasped for air; he fell back into the chair. "Oh, God, I can hardly breathe, help me, please," he said aloud.

Seizing his keys, he turned his eyes away from his trembling hands. Speeding along the deserted streets, he uttered a grateful "Thank you, Jesus" at each green light.

The hospital entrance was just a few feet ahead.

Inside the hospital, Father Andy was rushed into surgery; the first stab wound had punctured his lung, but had missed his heart by less than an inch. The second had scraped a jagged gash in his arm.

A two-hour operation left him in a coma. Knowing that the next forty-eight hours were the most critical, the doctor shook his head as he pulled off his bloody surgical gown, on his way to the waiting room.

He greeted Bishop Steele, Detectives Coleman and Russell, and announced what everyone hoped would turn into better news: "We did our best; now all we can do is wait."

"And pray," added Bishop Steele. Doctor Brady nodded in agreement.

"He's being taken to intensive care. You may go there and wait, Bishop. You'll be permitted to go in and anoint him."

When he was ushered into Father Andy's unit, Bishop Steele, choked back the anguish in his heart, wet his thumb with oil and made the sign of the cross on Father Andy's forehead, his eyes, ears, mouth and hands.

He pressed his hand against his own chest; nothing blocked the invasion of fear and heartache in his soul. He slumped down in the chair next to the bed, massaged his head with both hands and wept.

He lifted his head in the dimly lit room. His tears washed the creases in his face. He whispered, "Oh, God help me. I commend to your loving care this young servant of yours; please heal him and restore him to us and to your church."

Knowing his five minute limit was nearly over; Bishop Steele wiped his wet face and straightened his clothes. His bleary eyes rested on the still body; he made the sign of the cross and opened the door into the hallway.

The detectives were waiting. Exhaustion tugged at his eyes and mouth, and hung on every word. "I'll contact Andy's parents in the morning."

"Where is his home?" asked Coleman.

"Father Andy came to us from Texas. Both his parents are living and he has a younger sister."

"That's going to be a tough call," said Russell aching for something significant to say. "But there's nothing else you can do here. Would you like us to take you home?"

"No, I'll be fine. Thank you for your concern."

As the bishop turned to leave, Coleman blurted out, "Bishop, how do you—Never mind, we can talk about this some other time."

Bishop Steele gave his complete attention to Coleman; his eyes were serene but the trench lines in his face were hollow. "If you were going to ask me how I continue to pray to a God who seems not to be listening, I'm not sure I could say anything meaningful tonight. But do ask me again some day soon."

Coleman's jaw dropped as he realized that the bishop had again read his mind.

Fourteen

When the phone rang at 7:30 am in the Sanchez home, Andy's little sister, Corita, ran to grab it. She smiled to herself when Bishop Steele identified himself, remembering how kind he was to her at her brother's ordination eight years ago.

He asked her how she was enjoying school and she reminded him with a giggle that she was now 18, graduated in June and was working part time to help pay for college which she would start in the fall.

She chattered on about becoming a nurse, but how she'd really like to go on someday to become a doctor.

All of a sudden her pounding heart told her how unusual it was for the bishop to call their home at this time of the day. Her voice cracked. "Bishop, why are you calling so early? What has happened to my brother?"

"Corita." The bishop hesitated; he had to calm his voice. "Corita, let me speak to your father."

The phone slipped from her hand; she caught it as she turned to call her father and saw that he was standing in the kitchen doorway. She stiffened her arm to hand him the phone, unaware that her whole face was preparing her father for dire news. Her voice was a whisper as she identified Bishop Steele.

Mr. Sanchez seized the phone. "Bishop, what's wrong?"

"Jorge, I have some bad news." He gave him the most important facts first emphasizing his firm belief that Andy would recover.

Jorge tried unsuccessfully to still his shaking hands; he rubbed his hand over his heart working to massage the terror thumping inside. His questions staggered out one after the other.

"Tell me what happened, Bishop. Did someone try to kill him? Is it the same one that killed those other two priests? Did the police catch him? When can we come to see Andy?"

"I wish I had all those answers, Jorge. I will tell you what I know. The police suspect it is the same person, although there was no break-in this time; it seems that the killer was visiting or had a meeting with Andy. When a drunken man came to the rectory, he accidentally set off the alarm and the killer was gone by the time the police got there. The man was too intoxicated to be able to give the police anything to go on."

Mrs. Sanchez and Corita tried to piece together the bits of the conversation they overheard. They cried and clung to one another. Each one trembled with her own memories. Corita pulled out a kitchen chair; she eased her mother down to its thin soft cushion.

Bishop Steele continued. "I've already made plane reservations for all three of you; there's a plane leaving at 11:00 your time; I'll meet you at the airport and take you to the hospital. I know how useless it is to tell you not to worry; but pray and thank God that Andy is still with us and that he may be able to help us bring an end to this horror. Now, give my love to Anna and Corita. I'll see you at the airport in a few hours."

"Thank you, Bishop."

Jorge missed the phone cradle twice as he tried to hang up the phone. He absorbed his wife and daughter into his arms. "He's alive," he sobbed, "but hurt really bad."

All that the bishop had told him spilled out in partial sentences.

"But now we must hurry, we must pack quickly and leave for the airport in a half hour. I will call my boss and explain what happened; Corita, you do the same with your boss. Hurry, hurry."

All kinds of thoughts somersaulted in Anna's mind; she remembered going to sleep last night worried about the murders. She shared her concerns with her husband earlier that evening. She said she wanted to call Andy; he told her she fretted too much.

She detected the torment in his eyes as she headed to their bedroom. She grabbed his hand, noticed a tear and patted his arm. "It's o.k. He is going to be all right."

As she pulled down their suitcase from the top shelf, she tried to recall the dream she had last night; she remembered there was darkness all around and she knew her son was in danger; she screamed his name, but there was no sound and he did not hear her.

She saw her mouth opened and felt her hysterical cries. A dazzling light appeared in the night sky where she gazed on a brilliant chalice. She remembered the immense calm that came over her. When she awoke that morning, she dismissed the dream as typical of a worried mother.

Now she thanked God for preparing her for this trial. She believed, or so she tried to convince herself, that the radiant chalice was a sign that her son would live. Her lips quivered in prayer as she pulled clothes off their hangers. She heard her husband talking to his boss and glanced across the hall to Corita who was on her cell phone.

Mr. Sanchez worked at the local restaurant as a maitre d' during the dinner hour. When his boss heard the news his reply was instantaneous. "Do not even think about us, Jorge. I will take care of everything. Go and be with your son."

Corita was a receptionist at the health clinic; her boss was always stressed out. As Corita heard the phone ring, her finger twirled a strand of her shiny black hair into a tight knot.

Maria Cortez said hello. Before Corita ended her sentence, she heard, "Oh, Corita, I am so sorry. Don't you worry; we'll manage somehow. Call me when you get back. I'll pray for your brother."

Her heart still pounding Corita swallowed hard as she looked over her clothes. "I really need to get this closet organized," she murmured to herself. As she folded a blouse and placed it in her suitcase, she broke into sobs.

Corita's mother ran into her room, wrapped her daughter tightly to her breast and kissed her hair. "Come now, Corita. God is here. Andy is not going to leave us; there is still work for him to do."

Her words quieted Corita's tears just as her father approached her room. He walked over to both of them; he opened his mouth, but not a word made its way out. He gathered them close, held them tight and then whispered, "Let's be ready to go in five minutes."

~ * ~

At the precinct that morning Coleman and Russell arrived early. Even the off chance that Charlie, now awake and sober, might be able to tell them something useful energized both men.

Their steps quickened as they heard humming from Charlie's cell; he was buttering his toast as they got to his door. Recognizing them this morning, he waved and said "Mornin', Officers."

145

A shadow tramped across his face as a vague recollection from last night reminded him that this time something was different.

He saluted the detectives as they opened his cell door and sat down on the bed with him.

Coleman asked, "How are you feeling this morning, Charlie? How's your breakfast?"

Charlie squinted and grinned. "Fine, fine, everything's fine."

Coleman leaned closer. "Charlie, do you remember what happened to you last night?"

Charlie leaned close to Coleman's eyes and shook his head yes. "I got hurt."

"That's right, Charlie. Do you remember how you got hurt?"

Charlie squinted his eyes again and wrinkled his nose. "I remember bumping into something before going up the sidewalk."

"Could it have been a car? Did you see a car parked in front of Father's house?"

"I think so. Yeah, there must have been a car there 'cause, I always just walk right straight up to the door. It was dark, you know."

"Did you hear any noise when you got to the door?"

"The alarm! It was so loud."

"Did you hear anything before the alarm went off? Try to think, Charlie. What did you do when you got to the door? What did you hear?"

"I was pounding on the door, but no one was coming. I tried to see through the window because the light was on in the office; sometimes I can see Father coming to answer the door. Something ran past me; a squirrel, I think. I turned to see what it was and when I turned back that's when I tripped and fell right into the window and then I heard the alarm." Charlie shuddered.

"Then what happened?"

"Somebody shoved me against the wall. He really hit me hard."

"Did you see what he looked like? Can you remember his face?"

Charlie shook his head no. "Must have been pretty strong, though, cause he really pushed me hard."

Dismayed and frowning, Coleman and Russell stood up. They thanked him and told him to finish his breakfast.

"And then you can go." said Russell. "If you think of anything else you come back here to the station and tell us, o.k.?"

"O.k."

They left Charlie's cell and moved on to their desks. Russell wondered if Charlie might be in danger if the killer supposed he could identify him. "Let's keep surveillance on Charlie, at least for a couple of days."

"That's a good idea. We might want to think about publicizing the fact of having a witness but then we would need to bring Charlie in for protection before releasing a statement to the press. Let's hope we won't have to go that far."

When the task force gathered later that morning, they had reservations about Father Andy's attacker being the same person who murdered the other two priests. No break-in this time; and it happened in the office, so Father Andy either knew the person or was expecting him to come for a meeting.

Niggling questions popped up around the table. If all three priests knew the person, why did he break into the other two rectories? Or did he? Remember Dan Salvage had been hired to do some maintenance work by Father John; do we know if had a key to the rectory? And if he did, maybe he made it look like a break-in as he left. Or is this someone in Father Andy's parish who thought he could count on the police figuring it was the other killer?

Coleman reminded them that the presence of a Bible is one piece of information that was never made public. "So I think that indicates that it is the same person. And now we have a murder weapon. Forensics may be able to tell us if it's the same weapon. What we need to do is establish a connection among the three priests."

Coleman and Russell decided it would be helpful to call again on the bishop. Coleman picked up the phone and dialed; when the bishop got on the line he updated him on their progress and then requested an appointment at his earliest convenience.

Bishop Steele said he could see them at 2:00 that afternoon. Coleman informed the task force, "We'll meet again tomorrow. Keep up the good work; I know it doesn't look like we're making any headway, but it will all come together, sooner than later, I hope."

Driving to the bishop's residence, Russell rehearsed his thoughts over and over before clearing his throat and swallowing hard.

"I've been thinking about what you said the other day about your father's death and how your mother found her strength. You didn't mention what religion your mother belonged to. Would she object if you came with Noelle and me and the kids to Mass on Sunday?"

Coleman laughed out loud. "Actually, she'd be thrilled. She's Catholic; I was raised Catholic."

"Oh, I didn't know. I shouldn't have presumed."

"It's o.k.; I haven't been to Mass in years. Deb and our kids go to St. Joseph's. Remember when I told you that Deb said I was on a journey? Well, that's because the kids overheard someone at Mass talking about hell and they got upset."

"I guess I don't pay much attention to people when I'm there; I never noticed Deb or your kids, except at Father John's service, but there were so many people there that belong to other churches I didn't give it a second thought."

"Well, you probably go to different Masses. Deb takes the kids to the early Mass so that we can have some family time when they get home. I know she wants me to go back and now I worry even more about what my kids think about me, and about what's right and what's wrong."

By this time they were nearing the parking lot at the cathedral. "Maybe we can talk more about this sometime."

After ringing the doorbell, they allowed their eyes to enjoy the variety of shrubs and flowers around the bishop's residence. A tangible peace enveloped them.

The secretary walked quickly in front of them; she smiled and extended her arm towards Bishop's Steele's open office. Coleman was glad to see a much brighter room than the one they met in last time. On his large cherry desk, the eighteen inch square space in front of the bishop was the one empty spot; all around were files, letters and books stacked in neat piles.

The bishop welcomed them as he motioned for them to sit and asked if they would like coffee or iced tea. Both opted for the cold drink as did the bishop; the receptionist smiled at both detectives and left.

A few minutes later the housekeeper carried in three tall frosted glasses filled to the top, sliced lemons on a small glass plate, and a plate of chocolate chip cookies. She pushed aside some files to make room for her tray and put it right in front of Coleman. *Tastes like homemade*, thought Coleman, with his first bite.

Coleman and Russell reviewed with the Bishop what they knew so far about Father John and Father Bill. They spoke first in general about the possibility that because both priests served at St. Joseph's at the same time, the killer may have killed Father John first because he assumed that Father John was covering up for Father Bill.

Coleman continued, "Father Andy was the same age as Father Bill but he had not served at St. Joseph's or at Holy Name. And he didn't seem to share either man's enthusiasm for golf so we can assume they didn't spend time together socially. They had not even attended the same seminary."

The bishop confirmed that all their information was correct.

"Bishop," Coleman said, "you told us that you were familiar with all the members of Father Bill's support group. What can you tell us about Mike Mahoney?"

"Is he a suspect?"

Coleman glanced at Russell and then at the bishop. He sipped his ice tea trying to find the right words. "We have reason to suspect that he found out about Father Bill and... and his daughter."

The bishop sighed; he pushed back his chair. "They were intimate?"

Coleman divulged as few details as necessary about the affair, and why it ended."

"Did her parents know? Did she ever get counseling?"

"Her guilt drove her to Father John, but she never told him or her parents who the father was, but she thinks Father John might have figured it out."

"So, you think that her father found out about Father Bill. Do you think he blamed Father John for keeping it quiet?"

"Maybe, or else he might have been angry because Father John helped Michelle find forgiveness."

"But how does that connect to Father Andy?"

"We were hoping that you might have an idea."

"Now that you've told me about the abortion, the one thing that I can think of that all three parishes have in common is Project Rachel. Did the Mahoney girl ever tell you which abortion support group she joined? I know for certain that John, Bill and Andy had them in their parishes."

"Well, it's worth an inquiry." Coleman scribbled a reminder in his notebook. Michelle's sapphire eyes flashed in his mind.

Russell said, "We have other problems, too. We haven't figured out why the killer is leaving the Last Supper passage with each victim and why he might use only the Gospel passages from Matthew and Mark relating to the Last Supper when all four Gospels recount the story of the Last Supper. When we found the Bible in Father Andy's office I expected the bookmark to be in Luke's gospel, but it was Matthew; the same one he used in Father John's murder. So far the task force interpretation has focused on some kind of betrayal, but we can't figure out why the killer went back to Matthew."

"You are right that all four Gospels tell the story of the Last Supper and the betrayal by Judas. Matthew, Mark and Luke are called the Synoptic Gospels because they are similar; John's Gospel is different. If you do a little study of your Bible, you'll see what I mean."

Coleman caught the hint, but his smile was hidden inside, as was his changed perspective on the bishop. *I'm glad that he has become so easy to talk to; we've come a long way since that first meeting.*

"However, if you compare Matthew and Mark to Luke, there's an incident missing in Luke and that's the story of the woman who anointed Jesus with expensive perfume. That story is also in John but not in the same chapter as the Last Supper. Judas complains because he thinks that the money is wasted on perfume used to anoint Jesus and should have been given to the poor. So it's possible that the killer considers himself Judas."

"I don't understand, Bishop," said Coleman. "Judas betrayed Jesus for money; we were concentrating on the killer judging the priests as being Judas."

"Detectives, think about this; you know, better than I, that people who commit crimes often have twisted reasons for their actions. What if the killer sees Judas as condemning riches; then he could be telling us that priests waste money on themselves. People sometimes do see priests who are as consumed as unbelievers in their quest for the good and temporal things that life has to offer: priests in expensive cars, living in luxury, enjoying the very good life, so to speak. The killer may have lived with great resentment for years. Priests, and bishops, too, are struggling humans and sinful ones; often we make mistakes, sometimes horrendous ones. And often the people blame us because they think we should be better than what they see; and many times we should be."

"That's a big help, Bishop, Thank you. Of course, that would leave Mahoney out of the equation; money would not be a motive for him."

"Not that I want Mike Mahoney to be the guilty one, but another angle does occur to me. Rather than money wasted on perfume, maybe he is telling us about the woman; Jesus said that by pouring the perfume on him, she had prepared him for burial; he praised her even though the others, including Judas, condemned her."

"I see what you might be saying here. Jesus protected the woman from criticism and embarrassment. Father Bill, in Mike Mahoney's opinion, had taken advantage of his daughter, brought shame on his family. So he didn't deserve to be one of the apostles."

"Very good, Detective."

Coleman's satisfaction with himself was transparent. Russell was impressed.

The bishop took a quick look at his watch and apologized that he had to leave soon to go to the airport to meet Father Andy's family. They were scheduled to land in 90 minutes.

Coleman and Russell thanked the bishop and asked him to call them if he thought of anything else that might help. "And, I'm sure we'll want to talk with you again, Bishop."

"Please, do come again. Remember," he shook a friendly finger at Coleman, "We still have that why-doesn't-God-do-something problem to discuss."

Coleman's mouth dropped open; he never expected the bishop to remember his question.

By the time they reached the car Coleman had recovered a bit, but he told Russell that he was even more impressed with the bishop's honesty about the church and priests. He grew up thinking they were always right; he never heard any priest let alone a bishop, say they were sinful human beings.

"I know what you mean. I'm glad we can talk about these things. I can't say much at home and Noelle knows I can't discuss cases with her, but the kids keep asking questions every night when I get home."

"I understand. Deb is the same way; every day she wants to know if we're any closer to the answer. Of course, she knows I can't give her any real information. By the way Lori is having her thirteenth birthday party next Saturday; she's been talking about it for months; she can't wait to be a teen. And I'm dreading it! She had planned to invite Father John; I'm sure it was Deb's idea. She hoped if I saw him in our home for a fun time, that maybe I would get into a conversation with him. Do you want to come and bring Noelle and your kids?"

"I'd like that. Let me check with Noelle; I don't think Sharon or Bobby have anything special coming up."

"Let's stop at the hospital before heading back to the station and see how Father Andy is doing. I know Operation Soul Search is meeting this afternoon, but we have time."

When they checked in at the nurses' station, they learned that nothing had changed; Father Andy remained stable but non-responsive. His family was expected within the hour.

The nurse confirmed that a guard had been placed at Father's door and that visitors were limited to family, other priests, the bishop and police. In addition, the switchboard operators were instructed to keep a record of anyone calling to find out about Father Andy's condition. The two detectives decided to come back tomorrow to meet the Sanchez family.

Back at the station, the task force was already gathering when Coleman and Russell appeared. Captain Randolph motioned them to hurry in; he told the group the mayor was putting even more pressure on the chief to resolve this case. "Have you followed up on all the tips?"

Officer Kelly reported that five parishioners from St. Joseph's mentioned a homeless man that seemed to be at the church on a regular basis; someone at Holy Name described a similar person. Everyone knew that the priests would always give out money for a meal and a night or two at a motel.

Officer Collins told the story she heard of another man who came around to St. Joseph's by the name of Pete; this man had been in a mental institution, but everyone who mentioned Pete also told her about the stories that had circulated around the parish for years: that Pete had studied to be a priest, but had been dismissed from the seminary just two years before ordination. He often called himself "The Last Pope" because he said the first Peter was at the beginning of the church and he would be at the end. He lived in a group home now, but was often seen walking around in the neighborhood. Sometimes he would show up on Sunday and cause a commotion during Mass telling them that you're doing it wrong.

"What did he mean by that?"

"No one had figured it out. Also, a few neighborhood kids used to make fun of him; Pete's last name is Nowell, but the kids would taunt him by saying: 'His name's Nowell, but he's not swell; he's in our 'hood, but he's no good.' Pete would chase them and try to scare them, but he never did any harm. Yet, he did frighten some of the children at St. Joseph's School a few years ago when he came into the school office yelling that they were not teaching the children the truth about Jesus. Sister Ann talked with him and calmed him down; then she brought him to Father John and he never appeared at the school again."

Officer Sweeney added that no one she had spoken to at Holy Name recalled seeing Pete at their church. However, several were acquainted with him and had heard what happened at St. Joseph's. He would have to take a bus to get to Holy Name, they had told her.

Captain Randolph reminded them about the blood stained note pad that was picked up in Father Andy's office with the three letters, M, O, and N. Maybe it means money, said one of the team members; maybe Father Andy was trying to tell them the man wanted money.

Coleman related how the bishop gave them some unusual insights into the killer's motive. The money angle could link the three parishes: Our Lady of Guadalupe is a new church; St. Joseph's is a big church and looks rich; Holy Name just had a big fund-raiser for a new building; the killer could be someone who protested all this money being spent on buildings.

The other interpretation about the woman and the perfume, giving them Mahoney as a suspect, met with much more enthusiasm.

While listening to these theories, the bloody note from Father Andy's office kept bugging Russell. *We're missing something,* he told himself.

Russell doodled when something bothered him as much as this did. On his note pad, he had printed M-O-N; he tried adding other letters to come up with a word; e-y made the only word that suggested a motive, but it didn't satisfy him. Was it too much of a stretch to think he was trying to write Mahoney?

He spun the pad around; *now there's something else to think about*, he said to himself.

"What if the letters aren't M-O-N but N-O-W? Didn't you say that Pete's last name was Nowell? I think we should find this Pete and see if he knew all three priests. Having been in the seminary, he certainly would know his Bible."

Russell got a resounding confirmation from everybody.

"Maybe," said Coleman, "It means both money and Nowell; maybe it's Pete who feels that those who are living the life he had planned to live, are doing it all wrong!"

A surge of anticipation lifted everyone's spirits. Finally, they had some real clues to follow. They pushed aside the nagging warning that slinked into the back of their minds: only Father Andy will be able to verify their interpretation of the bloody note.

Fifteen

The next morning Coleman and Russell headed to Madison House at 304 Market Street. At the light brown circular desk in the center of the sun-bright lobby, they showed their badges and introduced themselves to Lisa, the resident nurse. Her attentive blue eyes focused on Coleman as he rattled off several questions about Pete Nowell—when was he permitted out alone, how often did he go to St. Joseph's, how did he get to his destinations other than by walking and could she tell them what priests visited him.

Lisa's brief smile preceded her efficient response: "Pete is allowed out any time of the day on his own after he has eaten breakfast and taken his medication; he is permitted to go to the rectory at St. Joseph's only during the week, and never the school; Pete has not been anywhere near the school for over two years; he goes by bus or in a car with a volunteer; Father John used to come for a visit from time to time and take him to the movies in the afternoon."

Coleman smiled. "Thank you."

"I'm not Catholic," she said suddenly; for some reason she assumed they needed to know that. "But, I feel so bad about all this; I saw the picture of Father Bill in the paper. He came here, too, but I don't remember if he visited Pete or someone else."

Coleman asked if Pete had any family members who ever visited.

"He has one older brother, named Ed, who comes with his wife to visit once a month now." She told how they didn't come as often when their children were young, because they were afraid of Pete. Now that the children were in high school, they came with their parents and seemed to be learning how to interact with him. Lisa admired the oldest daughter because she was very compassionate with him. The behavior of the two boys implied that they had a difficult time tolerating the visit, but they came more or less willingly every month.

"We would like to talk with Pete, now, if possible," said Coleman.

"He had a bad spell yesterday. He lost his Bible and by the time we found it, he was shaking all over; he could hardly breathe. He is resting today, but you can visit with him in the commons room."

She went on to explain that in the commons room he could be monitored more easily than inside his apartment and yet they could still have a private conversation. When the doors were closed, that was a signal to the other residents not to enter.

Lisa walked them to the room across from her desk; she invited them to find a comfortable corner while she sent for an attendant to bring Pete to them.

Coleman and Russell paused for a moment in the doorway. On the wall to the right were three outdoor peaceful scenes done in pastels. The wall that faced them was mostly a window. As they walked towards a comfortable looking peach colored couch Coleman reflected on the contrast; all this light and peace while the person they were waiting for lived in darkness and confusion.

Just as Russell was ready to make an observation about Lisa, an attendant holding Pete's right arm to steady him, walked into the room. In his other arm he cradled a Bible. She placed both her hands on his shoulders and turned him toward the couch where he saw Coleman and Russell.

He slid his feet slowly across the dark blue carpet until he was standing in front of them. His pale face highlighted his midnight blue eyes; on his chin and above his lip were a few gray whiskers that had been missed by the razor that morning.

Coleman and Russell stood; Coleman extended his hand as he said, "Good Morning, Pete; I'm Detective Coleman." As he shook Pete's hand, "And this is my partner, Detective Rick Russell." Russell smiled as he took Pete's hand. Pete returned the smile and steadied himself on Russell's arm as he lowered himself to the couch. Coleman sat down at Pete's right and Russell on his left.

When Coleman told him they would like to talk with him about his friend, Father John, Pete murmured a weak o.k.. He gripped his Bible with both hands and leaned forward. He began rocking his entire body back and forth while saying how much he missed him. Coleman urged him to relax and try to remember when he last saw Father John.

Pete froze his swaying while he closed his eyes and thought; after he squeezed his eyes open and shut several times, he reopened them and spoke in a staccato rhythm. "I—am—not—sure." He continued in the same rhythm saying that it was definitely an afternoon because they went to see a movie and then had pizza. After they ate Father John drove him back here to his home. He repeated three times how good Father John was to him.

"Did you and Father John read the Bible together?"

"Sometimes. Mostly we talked."

"Do you have a favorite story in the Bible?"

"I like the stories that Jesus told, especially the one about the prodigal son. But that's not what Father John and I talked about. We talked about the Last Supper."

He bit his lower lip and became silent. Tears began to flow; he wiped them away. Resuming his unsteady rocking movements he moaned, in a low steady voice. "He was my friend even when he did it wrong."

"What did he do wrong?" asked Coleman.

Suddenly Pete sat up straight and tall. His eyes were clear. His words flowed in an unbroken stream.

"He didn't tell them about the women at the Last Supper. I know he believed me when we talked about it. He told me so. They had to be there. It was a Jewish feast; women and children were there. Everyone was invited to the meal; no one was thrown away."

Then he broke down sobbing with "Jesus never threw anyone away."

Coleman and Russell were beside themselves.

"Please, Pete." Russell massaged Pete's arm. "Take it easy, you want to help us find who hurt your friend, right? Just settle down now and talk with us, o.k.?"

As if his words poured healing balm into Pete's soul, he raised his head. "I'm fine. How else can I help you?"

Astounded Coleman and Russell asked in unison. "Did anyone else do it wrong?"

"They all do it wrong."

The conversation became natural and smooth after that. Russell asked Pete if he knew Father Bill and Father Andy. Pete replied that he liked Father Bill when he was at St. Joseph's but he had not seen him for a while. He heard that he went to Holy Name.

"I was glad that he came back," said Pete. "Father Andy had a big picnic at his parish last summer. Joe, one of the volunteers, took me there; I liked all the food; there was so much and you could have anything you wanted. That was the last time I saw Father Andy; I hope he's going to have that picnic again this summer."

Coleman told Pete that Father Andy was in the hospital because someone had tried to hurt him.

A shadow clouded his face as Pete began again to rock back and forth repeating his mantra. "Did it wrong! Did it wrong, wrong, wrong!"

Coleman and Russell each took an arm and offered to walk Pete back to his apartment. But he declined. "No, I'd like to go outside and think for a little while."

As they reached the hall, Lisa noticed them and signaled for an attendant.

After watching Pete walk down the hall, Coleman and Russell stopped at Lisa's desk and asked if there were a log of the days and times that volunteers took the residents out. She reached into the file cabinet beside her computer and pulled out a blue notebook.

Russell flipped through the pages to the Monday of Father John's murder; Pete was out with Father John that afternoon. He was also signed out on the dates of the other two attacks, but he had been out most days during the summer. Always he was signed back in by 9:30 or 10:00.

"Was it possible that he left at night unnoticed?" asked Coleman.

"That would not be possible." Lisa pointed out how everyone must pass by the front desk and there was an alarm system on the door. Coleman and Russell thanked her and went on their way.

"Pete is a mystery," said Russell. "Do you think he's capable of murder?"

"I really don't know. What if he experiences psychotic episodes relating to his interpretation of the Last Supper? If he believes that they all do it wrong, then he could be a serial killer who may murder any priest he sees."

They shared their concerns with the chief and set up a consultation with Pete's doctor for tomorrow morning.

When they met Dr. Barbara Lewis at 10:00 am in her office, both detectives scanned quickly the diplomas and certificates on her wall; nine of them framed in wood and placed three by three. A fresh bouquet of flowers added a touch of softness to a very organized desk. She greeted them with an easy smile; her short white hair framed a delicate face that made her sky-blue eyes sparkle.

She had been treating Pete Nowell for several years now. She reminded them, at the same time motioning for them to sit in two chairs facing her desk, that what she was willing to share with them was limited by doctor-patient confidentiality. Her eyes were fixed on Coleman as she stated her conviction that Pete was incapable of murder.

"Can you tell us what he means when he says that they all do it wrong?"

Coleman saw a slight twinkle in her eyes. "He's talking about the Last Supper; he thinks that everyone should know that there were not only twelve men present. Women sat at the table, too. And their children." Her eyes danced as she smiled and said, "And I agree with him."

"Does it make him angry that the priests don't talk about that?"

"Not angry, sad. The only thing that makes him angry is his dependence on the medication. The only time I have seen him become physically disruptive is when he forgot to take his medicine. Sometimes he refuses to take it because he becomes angry or frustrated about his need for it. Then he is so contrite about the trouble he caused and he goes back on his schedule."

She went on to tell them that even when he was angry, she never observed any break with reality that would be severe enough to make her think he was prone to commit injury of any kind.

Coleman appealed to her discretion to notify him if she perceived any modification in Pete's behavior that spelled remorse or violence.

Her silence and the unflinching eyes reminded him that she could only do that if she suspected that he was about to commit a crime. It was also a signal, confirmed by her smile, that she had nothing more to tell. "My next appointment is in ten minutes, Detectives."

That evening, when he answered the phone, Bishop Steele was glad to hear the voice of Bishop McCoy.

Although Bishop Steele had expressed his gratitude to his friend after hiring Sister Emily, he reiterated his appreciation this evening.

"Frank, I can't say enough about her. She traveled to Holy Name every day even before she secured an apartment for herself; I was so impressed with her resourcefulness in designing a temporary office in the parish hall. I have been hearing such superb things about her that I promised myself a morning, soon, to attend one of her communion services. But now I have another parish without a priest, but thanks be to God, I don't have to find a permanent replacement this time."

"Any idea when Andy will be back?"

"No. In the meantime, what do you think about arranging for Mass every other week at Holy Name and Our Lady of Guadalupe? One week I would say Mass at Holy Name and ask Emily if she would hold two or three communion services at our Lady of Guadalupe, and the next week, she would have the communion services at Holy Name and I would say Mass at Guadalupe."

"Well, it certainly isn't ideal, but what else can you do? You have no one to spare. I had no doubts Emily would do a bang-up job and I'm sure she'd be eager to work with you on this adjustment."

"And what a plus, that she's bilingual; that will endear her to the Guadalupe parishioners, too. But, I pray, that I don't lose anyone else."

"How's the investigation going? Do you think any of our dirty laundry is going to come out?"

"The two detectives that I have been dealing with seem sincere in their promises to reveal nothing except what is relevant to the case. Of course, I know they have to share this information with all the other detectives and there must be someone there looking for a great story for one of the tabloids. For the time being though, I don't think anyone will jeopardize this case. They just called me today to ask about Pete Nowell; do you remember him?"

"I do. Poor fellow. He was forced to leave the seminary. Didn't he have a breakdown not long after? I always felt so sorry for him. What would make them think he could do something like this?"

"Well, he told the detectives his version of the Last Supper. You remember how he first got into trouble because he demanded that the seminary remove that picture of the Last Supper. Most of us never thought much about it in those days, but now with all we've learned through biblical research, there's no doubt he was right. But what scares the police is that he keeps saying that all the priests are doing it wrong. They're concerned that he disconnects with reality and they don't know if he went after John, Bill and Andy because he knew them, or if they were the most convenient ones."

"If that's the case, then you could be in danger, too."

"I don't think his obsession with the Last Supper is the explanation. All three of those guys opened up all the authorized roles for women that are allowed. As a result, women in each of those parishes held approved leadership positions. Beyond that, a rather new study/prayer group, Magdalene Witnesses is active in each of those parishes."

"I heard about that group. Has that caused any trouble?"

"Just the opposite. Since those groups came into existence a year ago, studying the story of Mary Magdalene, becoming aware of the fact that she was the first to proclaim the good news of the resurrection—this has energized people. Their desire to evangelize has matured along with their interest in the place of women in the church. I know it's a risky matter because I know they discuss ordination, but this issue of Jesus' inclusive behavior is not going to go away."

"I have to admire you, Joe, for your courage. Several priests have come to me about forming these groups and I've been avoiding the topic, but maybe, I should follow your lead. I have a meeting with two of my priests tomorrow; do you mind if I suggest that they contact you?"

"I'll be glad to talk with them. But, be careful; I also might try to influence them to switch dioceses; I need priests, you know."

With a good-natured chuckle between friends, they said goodnight. Hanging up the phone, both were haunted by the foreboding of a future church deprived of the Eucharist due to an insufficient number of celibate male priests. And each prayed for perseverance and valor for his friend and for himself.

Sixteen

Thursday morning an obliging sunrise dared to advertise a new day. Bishop Steele chose this morning to drive to Holy Name to participate in Sister Emily's communion service. *In a few days she will have been there a month already; even though these days have been filled with sadness they have passed by too fast,* he thought; *I owe her my gratitude and I want her to know that she has my support.*

When he arrived he slipped into a pew near the back of the church behind several women. The dance of the morning sun through the stained glass windows lifted his spirits.

A pale blue cloth covered the altar; a gentle breeze caused it to flutter and become still again. It reminded him of the prophet Elijah who found God, not in a mighty wind, or an earthquake, but in a tiny whispering sound.

At 8:00 Sister Emily walked to the altar. Shimmers of silver accented her short black hair; the glow from her dark eyes dissolved her slight crows feet; the warmth of her smile distracted any notice of her less that perfect teeth.

She extended her arms their full length as she welcomed everyone to this day celebrating the feast of St. Mary Magdalene. Her opening prayer thanked Jesus for entrusting the good news of his resurrection first to Mary Magdalene.

As Sister Emily sat down, a small round woman stood and walked to the podium to proclaim the first reading from Corinthians. In spite of the fact that Bishop Steele could recite this passage from memory, the words seared his soul as though he was hearing them for the first time.

"We no longer look on anyone in terms of mere human judgment."

What a burden is human law, he thought, *when it is not open to the message of Jesus. How often I have made judgments based on law rather than faith. Help me, O God, to be ready to hear your truth.*

The gospel recounted the familiar story of Mary Magdalene meeting Jesus in the garden. This story fascinated him every time he read it. Sister Emily looked out at the congregation; the bishop looked around; what was that tingling delight he felt in the air?

"We hear today that if we believe that Jesus died so that all might live, then we can no longer judge people by mere human standards. If we try to get inside the mind of Jesus as we reflect on these words, what could that mean for us in today's church? To faithfully honor today's celebration of Mary Magdalene, let's candidly imagine Jesus deciding on who would tell his followers that he was alive. Close your eyes for a moment. Behold Jesus walking around near the tomb, excited about revealing himself to his friends. See the smile and the brilliance in his face. Watch him coming upon Mary Magdalene. Can you picture him saying to himself, 'Curses! Why is this woman here so early? I can't let her tell everyone my good news. I'll have to wait for Peter or John to show up.'"

Everyone laughed and opened their eyes. Bishop Steele mused to himself that Jesus might have had a very long wait.

"Jesus is still asking women today, 'Why are you weeping?' We know the answer to that question. Though we shed tears, we listen to Jesus who is still bidding us to go and tell the good news. Let us delight in today's feast reminding ourselves that we—both women and men—we all are created in God's image and that Jesus has entrusted us with the good news of resurrection. Therefore, we have every right to anticipate that the inclusive vision of Jesus will be accepted and recognized soon. Enjoy this day in hope."

The bishop had to hold his own hands to keep them from applauding. *Some day, O God,* he prayed, *someday soon, weeping will turn into joy.* His exhilaration came to a screeching halt as his own words came back to him; something good will come out of this evil. This date, July 22; a gift and a promise; he had recognized the gift; *will I be ready for the promise,* he wondered.

At the peace rite, as people shook hands and hugged each other, those near the bishop now recognized him. Questions fluttered around in their hearts and stomachs. *What did he think of Sister Emily's preaching? Why is he here?*

This was the first time Sister Emily had a clear view of the bishop and she too felt a few flutters inside. *I spoke what I have come to know as truth, she told herself. Your power, O God, is always directed toward love. I believe you are here with me.*

After the final Amen Bishop Steele walked outside with several people, chatting about the lovely weather, when Sister Emily joined them. He gave her a hug and said how pleased he was to have this opportunity to experience her refreshing and inspiring service.

All the faces around him relaxed into smiles; wide smiles, grateful smiles, hopeful smiles. As if someone had given them a cue, they spoke as one, told him of their admiration for Sister Emily and invited him to come again.

Sister Emily invited Bishop Steele to her apartment for breakfast; it was only a block that way, she pointed. On this clear and fresh summer morning a walk seemed like the perfect thing to do.

As their steps fell into a relaxed pace along the tree-lined sidewalk, Emily asked him about Father Andy.

"That's another reason, I came." The Bishop told her of his plan to ask her to do some Sunday communion services at our Lady of Guadalupe until Father Andy recovered.

As they were nearing her apartment, the white stone front of the high rise gleamed in the morning sun. "Do you like your apartment?"

"Yes, I do. The first time I lived in an apartment was when I left St. Joseph's."

Emily steered the bishop towards the parking lot and the entrance.

"I'm ashamed to admit this; I forgot that you had been the principal there."

"Oh, that's understandable, Bishop. We had more than twenty schools in this diocese; and besides, that was five years ago."

"So you knew Father John and Father Bill."

"I knew Father Andy, too. We had taken a summer seminar together two years ago."

Emily's apartment was on the fourteenth floor. "You have a great view; you must see some majestic thunderstorms."

"And beautiful sunrises. Would you like an English muffin with your coffee?"

"Sounds great. You know, the police are trying to find something connecting John, Bill, and Frank. You must know Pete Nowell, too."

"I do. When I started Magdalene's Witnesses at St. Joseph's, Pete came to the meetings. He was so happy when he heard that Father Andy introduced the group too. And I was the one who had convinced Andy to do that; we had talked a lot about Magdalene's Witnesses during that seminar. You don't think Pete's the…"

"No, but I'll have to share this information with the police."

After a second cup of coffee, the bishop decided to take a little walk through the neighborhood before he went back to his office. He told Emily he would be in touch, with a schedule for Sundays.

She walked him to the elevator and as the door closed, Emily praised God for this bishop and his courage. *He will become an inspiration for his brothers, I'm sure.*

Seventeen

Sitting beside his bed with her head bowed, Father Andy's mother caressed his hand and whispered to him in between her many prayers. She brushed away the black strands of hair that curled around her face. The creases in her still youthful face betrayed the worry that she insisted on praying away.

What was that she just felt? Her world stood still; she caught her breath and loosened her grip. He had moved his fingers; she was sure of it.

She screamed for her husband to call the nurse. A flash of white rushed to the priest's bedside. She checked all his vital signs and patted Mrs. Sanchez's hand as she rushed to call the doctor.

Every line and wrinkle in the doctor's face bulged with concentration. He listened to his heartbeat, he tapped here and there, he lifted his eyelids and shined into them his tiny light; then he turned to the family and his lips relaxed into a smile.

"It will only be a matter of time. I am optimistic that he will make a full recovery, but I can't say how long till that happens. Keep talking to him, about family, about work, anything. Hearing you will help."

Mr. and Mrs. Sanchez and Corita hugged and cried and laughed, all at the same time. Their exhilaration stole into the corridor as Coleman and Russell got off the elevator. Quickened steps got them to Father Andy's room.

The doctor closed the door as they approached and he stopped long enough to give them the news. Tapping on the door, the detectives were swept into the celebration.

Coleman waved his arms and twice tried to call for their attention. "You must understand why this news has to be restricted to the police; we will inform the bishop but we will tell him also that Father's Andy's condition must remain a secret. His confirmation of the killer's identity is vital to our case so we do not want to provoke a jumpy killer into an unwelcome visit here."

Everyone nodded in agreement, their smiles faded into worry.

"Thank you, Detective," said Mr. Sanchez.

Coleman and Russell gave a thumbs up as they opened the door to leave. "We'll be looking forward to more good news soon!"

Three days later it was his mother's voice that tugged at Father Andy; his eyelids twitched and little by little his eyes focused on a familiar head bowed.

"Mother!"

His whisper was so very faint, but to Anna it was a shout. She lifted her head at once with "Praise God!"

His weak smile was the most exquisite gift Anna could imagine. The tears began to roll down her puffy cheeks as she stood and leaned over him to kiss his forehead.

Corita bolted from her chair and clutched his hand. Then she raced to the cafeteria for her father.

Huffing as he raced along the corridor to his son's room, Corita's father stopped dead at the entrance to watch as the doctor peered again into his son's eyes.

Corita clutched at her father's arm and the doctor waved them in.

When he completed his check-up, he cautioned them to be patient. "He needs to rest, but to all appearances he will fully recover. For now he will be able to respond to simple yes or no questions, no long conversations."

In unison they responded, "God bless you, Doctor. Thank you. Thank you!" Corita quietly clapped her hands.

Jorge Sanchez followed the doctor out of the room. His disheveled black hair confirmed his inner struggle. He glanced up and down the hall, as he hung on to the doctor's white sleeve. His questions were hushed: "Should they wait until Andy is better before they inform the police? Will Andy's progress be slowed down if the police question him too soon? What if the memory of that night never returns? Will he ever be safe?"

Doctor Brady patted Jorge's arm. "It's o.k. to let the detectives know; but be sure to emphasize that Father Andy can only tolerate simple questions, and that their visits are limited to five minutes. I think his memory will return, but when, I can't say."

Jorge tried to smile his gratitude; he nodded as he let go of the doctor's sleeve. He reached for his phone and it slipped out of his hand. He wiped a lone tear away as he picked it up and called the bishop and then the detectives.

Bishop Steele was so overjoyed that he promised a visit immediately after his 4:00 meeting.

Coleman was ecstatic. "We're on our way; we'll be there in ten.

Both detectives ran down the steps to the evidence room; Russell scribbled his signature for the envelope containing the piece of paper Father Andy had written on.

Winding in and out and around the traffic Coleman found himself distracted by his inner calm; the exact opposite of the excitement he felt only a minute ago.

What's happening to me, he wondered. *I've never felt this way before.* Moments later it was gone; he wanted to tell Russell about it, but how would he describe it? He saw the hospital looming into sight and soon forgot everything in his eagerness to hear Father Andy's story.

As Coleman and Russell dashed off the elevator they saw Mr. Sanchez with the guard outside his son's room. Their expectations shrank as they listened to Jorge reiterate what the doctor had said about simple questions and only five minutes. Both detectives patted him on the shoulder as they promised to follow the doctor's orders.

They turned the doorknob and inched their way to Father Andy's side.

Coleman leaned over to Anna, and whispered, "May we have some time alone with your son?"

She nodded without saying a word; her dark shimmering eyes fixed themselves on him and silently pleaded for patience. She clutched Corita by the hand and joined her husband in the hall.

Russell hid the bloody note sealed in its clear envelope behind his back.

Father Andy scrutinized the faces of Coleman and Russell; he smiled and raised his hand in blessing. Coleman and Russell blessed themselves.

Coleman whispered "Welcome back! We are only going to ask you a few simple questions for now, Father. Just nod if your answer is yes, or move your head left or right if it's no. O.k.?"

Father Andy nodded. Coleman asked if he knew why he was in the hospital. Father shook his head no.

Russell showed him the bloody slip of paper and asked if he remembered writing those three letters. Again, they watched as his head signaled a no.

Coleman detected a trace of bewilderment in his face and hoped that a simple recounting would stimulate his memory. He spoke slowly, recited how the alarm had sounded, how the police had found him on the floor of his office bleeding from a stab wound and how they found that piece of paper near his hand.

Father Andy continued staring at them, his dark brown eyes vacant except for an intense glimmer. Coleman quit talking. *We're pushing too hard too soon; he's not ready,* he told himself. Coleman gently placed his hand on top of Father Andy's and encouraged him to get some rest.

When they rejoined the anxious family outside the door, they thanked Jorge for getting in touch with them. Coleman put his arm around Anna. "He was not able to tell us anything today."

She grabbed his hand. Her eyes said *thank you for your kindness; I'm sorry and please, help me to believe that this will soon end.* Coleman rested his other hand on hers; she read in his eyes a determination that filled her with hope; her face was brightened by a quick fading smile.

Her voice trembled with worry as she said, "The doctor says it could be a long time."

Coleman stared into her faith-filled eyes, and thought of his mother. *If you are a God who cares, care now,* he thought. He promised they would stop by again in a day or so. As they walked away, Coleman, Russell, Jorge, Anna and Corita silently pleaded in different ways for the same miracle.

At 5:30 that evening Bishop Steele tapped on the door as he poked his head into the room. With a grateful smile, he walked with surprising speed first to Father Andy and raised his hand in blessing. He seized his hand and held onto it as he cried, "Welcome back."

Andy smiled his fragile smile and Anna whispered to the bishop to ask Andy if he knew who he was.

Bishop Steele turned back to Father Andy, and said, "Andy, do you know who I am?"

Andy pointed to the bishops' ring. A tear glistened in the corner of his eye; Bishop Steele laughed and repeated "Good, good."

For fifteen minutes he visited with the family, cheered their spirits and prayed with them. When he noticed that Andy was resisting sleep, he bid them all a good night. He walked over to Andy again, gave him another blessing, squeezed his hand and said goodbye.

As Mr. Sanchez walked with the bishop to the parking lot, Bishop Steele sensed there was more to his burden and heartache than the obvious.

The bishop suggested they sit in his car for a while and talk. Jorge found it difficult to express his fears, but finally admitted that he felt so weak and was trying so hard to be strong for Anna.

The bishop gazed on this gentle hard-working man, faithful husband and kind father. With words he used often before with many husbands and wives he helped Jorge discover that Anna ached to share his grief and that their love for each other was intended to sustain both.

After they prayed together, Bishop Steele blessed him. Jorge opened the car door and stepped out into the night air with a new lightness in his step. He hummed to himself and enjoyed the image of embracing his devoted Anna and confessing how much he needed her.

Early the next morning Bishop Steele woke from the most restful sleep he had for months. As he was getting dressed he was surprised by a phone call from Father Jim Clarke who apologized for calling so early.

"I'm on my way to school, but I was hoping, Bishop, that you would have some time this afternoon; I would like very much to meet with you today, or at your earliest convenience."

"Hold on, a minute, Jim. Let me check."

Father Jim scribbled on a note pad watching the minutes go by; he breathed a sigh of relief when he heard, "Any time after 2:00 today will be fine."

"Thanks so much: I'll be there as close to 2:00 as I can."

At 2:05, Fr. Jim was ushered into the bishop's office. Even before he sat down his high energy lit up his face.

"Bishop, I want you to know how much I have welcomed the opportunity to serve at St. Joseph's. Having ministered in schools most of my ordained life, it has been a refreshing change to be immersed in a parish situation. Even though I was at St. Joseph's on weekends for two years, I think the people considered me a convenient Sunday visitor. But now, many of them have come to discuss their concerns, or problems and their faith."

He took a short, hasty breath. "Now, usually at this time of the year I take a two-week vacation before school reopens, but this year I'd like to delay that until the Christmas season. Summer school was over last Friday and so I have more time during the week; in addition to saying weekday Mass I would like to be a part of the parish activities, especially the weekly meetings. Two groups have caught my interest: the Magdalene Witnesses and God's Troops."

The bishop savored his exuberance. "I admire your generosity, Jim. But I don't want you to overextend yourself. After all, you render a singular service to the students at the high school. And I would not want that compromised in any way. This has been a terrible trial, but something good will prevail, I honestly believe that. However, I am also interested in learning more about that new group, God's Troops. The stories I've heard trouble me. I didn't want to put Deacon Cummings on the spot in public and I haven't had the opportunity to call him in for a private dialogue. I have the impression that being thrust into a leadership role after Father John's death may have engendered some inflated ideas of influence. I know he means well, but even when he entered the deaconate program, he was somewhat overzealous. We had to do quite of bit of exegesis and clarification for him to come to terms with the changes brought about by the Vatican Council; and what confounded me was that the deaconate program he was so adamant about entering was itself a product of the Council."

"Yes, I remember because I taught some of the classes. He is very dedicated but somewhat narrow in his views. In fact, I was surprised to learn that his wife belongs to the Magdalene Witnesses. That must cause some spirited table conversations!"

"Well, Jim, again I do appreciate your generosity. I am sure the parishioners will appreciate daily Masses again, too. And at Christmas time I want to hear that you're taking a great vacation. Thanks for coming to talk. Keep me informed. Did you know that John, Bill, and Frank all had Magdalene Witnesses groups in their parishes?"

"Yes. Is that significant?"

"I'm not sure; that and Project Rachel are the only connections the police have discovered so far."

Eighteen

A whisper from one boy became an uproar from the three planted in front of the computer. Matt zoomed his chair from across the room to see what had them glued to the screen.

Another message from *The Herald*, but this one was too scary to ignore. For a week The Plumbers scrutinized his messages; so far they judged his threats as fanatic rubbish not worth passing on to the police even though he had named the parishes of St. Joseph's, Holy Name and our Lady of Guadalupe.

Today's message claimed that the three priests were a sacrifice for their flocks. It continued that until the message was heard, there would be more sacrifices because God would not be mocked. If the members of the flock do not repent, they would also be sacrificed. The message ended with screaming capital letters: THE HERALD ANNOUNCES: "SOON ALL WILL KNOW THAT GOD IS THE MASTER OF HEAVEN AND EARTH."

"This time I think we should call Detective Coleman," said Matt. "Glad I have him on speed dial."

In less than twenty minutes Coleman and Russell tore up the sidewalk; Matt stood at the door holding it open for them.

When they read the message Coleman advised Matt and his friends that one of their experts would meet with them. "With your help and his expertise, we'll find this Herald. This is good, guys. We appreciate this a great deal."

"Great job," added Russell. The boys gave each other a jubilant thumbs up.

Back at the station, Russell spoke with the tech people and arranged for one of them to meet with The Plumbers. Passing by Coleman's desk, he noticed a far-away stare in his eyes as he tapped a pencil. "What's up?" he asked.

Coleman jerked back to reality. "Just remembering something. But I have something else to ask you. If this Herald guy has some deep-seated divine delusion do you think Bishop Steele could help us again?"

"I think you find the bishop an interesting person, don't you?"

"I admit he impresses me. I'd like to talk more with him. Would you call him?"

"Sure. Besides, we should update him anyway. Maybe he can see us today."

Eager to help in any way the bishop shuffled a few appointments so that he could meet with Coleman and Russell that afternoon. On the way, Russell picked up their earlier conversation. "Tell me what impresses you about Bishop Steele."

"He comes across like the genuine article. He gave Father Bill a second chance and when we told him about the affair, he still did not condemn him. He was even concerned about Michelle, and whether she had gotten counseling. He seems to understand weakness and accept the human condition rather than play the judge."

"I agree. I think we're fortunate to have him as a bishop."

"Here we are. I'm curious to hear what he'll say about this Herald person."

As the bishop leaned forward, his eyes appeared to widen as he listened to Coleman describing the message from the Web site. The conversation yesterday with Father Jim Clarke kept running around in his head. *What is this gnawing panic overtaking me?*

"Officers, have you heard about the new group at St. Joseph's called God's Troops?"

"We did," replied Coleman. "From our wives. Why?"

"Well, Father Jim Clarke and I just discussed them yesterday. Given the rumors I heard, I thought they were merely a sincere but misguided group concentrating on a God of punishment. But with what you've told me, I'm afraid that someone in that group is the Judas we talked about: someone who judged these priests as wrongdoers."

"When we talked about Michelle's abortion, you thought it was because all three priests had Project Rachel in their parishes, helping women find forgiveness."

"That's true, but if my fears are right, I think you will find your connection at the God's Troops meeting."

"Today is Wednesday. When is their next meeting?"

"Tuesday. You can confirm the time with the secretary at St. Joseph's, but I think the meetings are scheduled for 7:30."

While still with the bishop they set up a meeting with Deacon Cummings. "As soon as we can get there," said Coleman.

"Your help has been invaluable, Bishop" said Russell as they left his office.

One ring of the doorbell and the deacon welcomed Coleman and Russell into his home. He was taller than Coleman remembered; *leadership must agree with him,* he thought.

They noticed that his wife was putting a casserole in the oven; she checked the temperature, and smiling, joined them in the foyer.

"This is my wife, Sarah; these are the detectives who called; Detective Coleman and this is Detective Russell."

Sarah was much shorter then her husband and looked a few years younger. Coleman remembered seeing her in the front pew the day of the service; Sarah's buoyant attitude contradicted her husband's rigid posture. *I've heard that opposites attract; seems to be the case here,* he thought. The light-heartedness in her eyes told Coleman she enjoyed the challenge of living; on the other hand, the deacon's eyes were jaded. *Some Atlas-like burden he is carrying,* thought Coleman.

The deacon insisted that Sarah be included in their conversation, so all four went into a modest sized living room. On the coffee table were a Bible and several religious magazines. A three-foot large wooden crucifix dominated the wall above the television set. Photographs of their three grown children with their families were proudly displayed on the mantel above the fireplace.

Sarah offered the detectives coffee or a cold drink. They both declined.

Coleman explained why the police received a call from The Plumbers. Both the deacon and his wife were aware of the web site, but confessed they had not checked it for more than a month now.

Coleman told them how concerned the police became because of the recent message from a person calling himself The Herald.

At this point, Coleman took great pains to be discreet and mentioned the bishop's motive for alerting them to the group called God's Troops.

The deacon's back became even more erect; his smile disappeared; his face lost all trace of warmth.

"I can assure you that the group's singular cause is to restore the cherished and forgotten values to our church. I understand that some individuals dismiss us as ultraconservatives, or they become nervous because we want to restore discipline. It's a heavy responsibility the Lord has asked us to carry."

Both Coleman and Russell detected a slight grin on Sarah's face as she subtly nodded a yes. Her green eyes danced to her own melody as she gave her a husband a loving tap on the hand and let her palm rest there.

The silent communication between husband and wife softened every line in the deacon's face. He smiled at Sarah before continuing.

"We have no intention of using any kind of force; our purpose is to educate, to show people how far we have fallen from obeying the law." Sarah patted his hand again. "Besides revenge is from the Lord, not us; we are simple weak instruments of God."

"What do you do at your meetings?"

183

"We pray prayers of contrition for sins, our own and others, prayers of petition for reform and renewal of the church, and we discuss various ways that families can reclaim values in their lives, and how the church could help them do that."

Sarah slid closer to her husband, slipped her hand into his. Coleman was aware of an intense bond holding them together. "My husband and I have different viewpoints; I belong to the Magdalene Witnesses but we share the same zeal for the church." The spark in her eyes showed her admiration for what they had accomplished together. "I feel that our relationship is a visible proof to others that people with opposite opinions can learn from each other."

Russell responded that he was familiar with that group because his wife was a member and attended every Monday meeting. He conceded, with an embarrassed flinch, that he had not paid close attention to what it was all about.

Coleman said that he thought his wife must belong too, because she went to church every Monday evening. He looked into Sarah's exciting eyes and admitted that he had never asked her about it.

Sarah teased both detectives about getting more involved. The deacon even got into the banter suggesting they might join his group instead. "Think what lively discussions we could all have," he laughed.

Fat chance Deb and I would get along like the two of you, Coleman said to himself. He grinned and said to Sarah, "What goes on at your meetings?"

"The Magdalene Witnesses are a group of women and men who study and reflect on the role of women in the church. Sometimes a priest presents a talk on recent developments; other times we discuss church documents associated with the issue and once a year we pay for a noted woman theologian to come for a daylong seminar."

Sarah was stunned at Russell's question, "Are there any members in your group who could be so frustrated with the church's decisions regarding women that they would find justification for killing the priests?"

Coleman stared at Russell and then at Sarah.

She soon regained her composure. "The most appropriate answer I can give to that question is an invitation for both of you to attend our next meeting."

The deacon also extended an invitation to the detectives to attend his group's meeting on Tuesday. Coleman and Russell expressed their satisfaction for the openness from Ray and Sarah and told them that they would attend both meetings next week.

On Saturday Deb got up when she heard Chris in the shower; *even today,* she thought, *does he have to go in even today!* Lori's party was scheduled for 2:00 to 5:00.

Coleman knew Deb wanted him home that morning to help her decorate the back yard. He also had to pick up the balloons, the cake and the ice cream. He almost decided to tell her where he really went at that time of the morning. *She'd forgive me real quick, if she knew that,* he thought. Deb was already running down the stairs. "This house is a mess," she grumbled loud enough for his benefit.

"I'll be back before you know it," Coleman said. "We'll get it all done, I promise," he said as he playfully grabbed for and missed her arm.

"I won't hold my breath," shouted Deb. Something in his tone, caught her busy spirit and she turned to look into his eyes.

She remembered her own words about his journey and suddenly knew she couldn't remain irritated.

Lori appeared at the top of the stairs. "Why are you guys making so much noise," she complained.

"Hi, sweetheart. Happy birthday. Mom and I just want everything to be perfect today. By the way, I hope it's o.k. with you that I have invited my partner and his family to your party.

"Oh, Daddy, Sharon and I are in the same class; I already invited her."

Deb gave him that good-natured glare that said, *you really should pay more attention to your kid's friends.* He also saw in her eyes the love and acceptance that he knew he could not live without. *I should tell her more often how beautiful they are,* he thought; *how beautiful she is; she never asks me to prove I love her, she takes me as I am.*

Coleman's distractions at church were more than usual, but the peace was deeper than he ever experienced. The longing to stay in this presence was more powerful than ever and so was the fear. *I've gotta leave, now,* he said to himself; *I know I've only been here twenty minutes, but, I can't stay; I just can't stay.* He ran to his car, noticing his breathing was quite good today. He screeched to a stop at the grocery store. *Thank goodness*, he thought, *they're open for twenty-four hours.* Within minutes he headed home with balloons, cake and ice cream in the back seat.

Deb was just starting on back yard decorations. They worked together in silence, but kept glancing at each other with smiles that wiped away all the tensions of the morning. By 1:00 the back yard had been transformed.

Russell and his family were the first to arrive. Noelle ran over to help Deb finish setting the tables; Rick joined Chris near the barbecue grill. "Did you know our kids go to the same school?"

"I found that out when I told Lori I had invited you. Does your wife think you don't listen, too?"

"What can I say? She's right." Both men laughed, each one enjoying the comfort of their wives' unconditional love.

Soon thirty some guests had assembled. The dads all gathered around the grill giving Chris advice about the hot dogs and hamburgers while the mothers helped Deb make sure all the children had as much food as they could handle. When all that was left of the cake was crumbs and the gallons of ice cream were empty, the kids put their high-level energy into a Frisbee game.

As the women cleaned up the tables, their conversation turned to the Magdalene Witnesses; they all belonged. Their animated voices as well as their laughter filled the air; Coleman was dying to hear what they were saying and considered asking if any of the guys attended the meetings. He decided it would be wiser to continue talking about sports.

Nineteen

Monday evening at 7:15 Coleman and Russell headed for St. Joseph's church with their wives. Both husbands amazed their wives with their after dinner announcement that they would accompany them to the meeting.

Each wife, for her own reasons, decided to relish this rare event. Sarah had told Coleman and Russell that there would be no pressure for them to sign up as members. With no public introduction of visitors, they had no reason to feel uncomfortable.

Coleman followed Deb into a seat in the second row; he would have preferred being in the back. He glanced across the room and noticed that Russell and Noelle were sitting at the end of the third row.

Sarah opened the meeting with a prayer; Coleman realized she was the president, a fact she never mentioned in their conversation.

Coleman had not anticipated the genuineness of their prayers for blessing on the pope, the bishops and the priests. He grinned to himself as he realized he had indeed presumed their prayers would be more along the lines of *How long, O Lord, how long must we continue to suffer!*

He directed his wandering attention back to the prayer as Sarah begged the Holy Spirit to enlighten the hearts of all people so that God would be recognized in all women and men. She closed by calling upon God as both Father and Mother to help us see and listen to each other as sisters and brothers.

The primary topic of the evening was an article from a national newspaper pertaining to the Vatican's disapproval of inclusive language. The subject mystified both Coleman and Russell but soon they found themselves intrigued by the interaction and substance of the dialogue.

They listened especially as several women, in clear and calm voices, explained the pain they experienced at Mass when the readings were addressed to brothers instead of brothers and sisters, and when they heard that portion of the Creed "for us men and for our salvation he came down from heaven."

"And," another woman in the front row raised her hand and said, "Don't give in when a man tries to justify that language by saying men equals mankind."

She stood and turned toward the group, her eyes locked on to the men in the audience. "If I would ask you to name the two or three most important men in your life how many of you would name your wife?" The men roared. She smiled and sat down.

As they continued to listen it dawned on Coleman and Russell that they agreed with what was being voiced. They were amazed to realize that they actually understood why their wives found these meetings so important. *Enlightened* is how their wives would describe them later.

As more comments were made three or four women expressed their anger and frustration, but there was not a hint of violence to solve a problem. Coleman and Russell came to the same conclusion: Sarah was right; no one here was The Herald.

The meeting ended with prayer, asking for the strength to persevere in loyalty to their faith, while tirelessly doing all in their power to bring about change in the church. *You're going to need a whole lot of patience for that,* thought Coleman. Their final prayers were for Father John, Father Bill and their families, for the return to good health for Father Andy and for the police to be successful in their investigation.

On the way home that evening, Deb and Noelle were so elated with their husbands' new and improved attitudes that any suspicions they had earlier dissipated into the cloudless night.

When husband and wife held each other that night, a new closeness throbbed within them. Both wives initiated a night of such tenderness and intensity that surprised both husbands. Each one decided that next Monday he would become a permanent member of the Magdalene Witnesses.

Tuesday morning Coleman awoke before the alarm went off. For a moment he gazed at the sleeping gift that was his. He softly brushed away the hair that had fallen over her right cheek. *I love you so much,* he said silently. *O God, thank you.*

On his knees at St. Joseph's he remembered that peace that almost overpowered him. Now he felt it mushrooming within him again. *How can I ask anyone about this when I don't know how to describe it; it is inside and also around me.* He wanted to surrender to whatever it was. *What are you? Who are you? I'm falling into... into...* All of a sudden its power terrified him. *No, No, I can't; go away! Leave me alone!* Coleman stood and felt the wet warmth of tears rolling down his face. He had to leave; he couldn't stay there any longer.

He ran out the door; when he got outside he stopped and turned around; something was pulling him back. *No!* He heard the shout burst in his head; *leave me alone.*

He ran to his car. He dropped his keys; he picked them up; they fell from his hands again. He grabbed them and punched the button to unlock the door. Gasping for breath, he turned on the ignition and snapped on his seatbelt. His breathing slowed down and returned to normal. He waited; *whatever that was*, he shuddered, *it's gone.* He tried to recall what he had heard about panic attacks; could stress bring them on? That would be enough explanation for him. He turned the wheel and drove away.

This car must know its own way, Coleman smiled to himself, as he realized he was pulling into his parking space. He snapped into the present as he opened his door. Operation Soul Search was meeting again this afternoon; he would be so relieved when this case was done. *I guess I'm more stressed out than I want to admit. I need to talk to Russell about last night; so much to do today. We also need to check back with The Plumbers.*

As they talked Russell sensed a mysterious agitation and a strange sense of calm in his partner. Something in Coleman's eyes stopped him from asking the obvious question.

Russell kept a concerned eye on his partner during the task force meeting. *He's handling everything with perfect competence, but there's something different about him. Maybe we'll have a chance to talk after tonight's meeting.* Walking out the door at the same time on their way home for dinner, Russell said, "Are you worried about tonight's meeting?"

"No, I'm looking forward to it. See you later."

He didn't ask why, why would I think he was worried. Something's going on; what doesn't he want to talk about? Looking at his watch, he knew he would not have much time for dinner this evening. He hoped Noelle had everything on the table when he got home.

At 7:20 Coleman and Russell arrived in their own cars at St. Joseph's. Both were dressed in casual khaki pants and short-sleeved shirts. The deacon promised that they could slip unnoticed into the meeting. They took a quick count of the cars; at least fifty.

Coleman went in first; eight to ten men were standing near the coffee urn; Coleman filled a cup for himself and blended into the group.

When one of the men asked if he belonged to the parish, he said that his wife did and introduced himself using his first name only; he prolonged the conversation by stating that he had recently thought about returning to the church and was looking to get more involved in the church's activities. He got nods of approval and his eyes wandered over to Russell who approached a small gathering of four men and two women who seemed to know him.

Coleman walked to a seat in the back row and watched Russell being invited to sit with the group that welcomed him. That's when he saw Dan Salvage, sitting behind Russell, but he was not alone.

The deacon began the meeting with the Act of Contrition followed by The Lord's Prayer. Subsequent prayers were for the Pope, bishops and priests; similar to those said last night. Then they sang a hymn that Coleman had not heard since he was a child and he was charmed by a bit of nostalgia. This group was unquestionably larger than the Magdalene Witnesses and was predominately men; Coleman estimated sixty men and twenty women.

He heard Deacon Cummings call attention to the first item on the agenda: a petition opposing anti-Catholic bias in the TV and film industry. There was swift agreement from everyone present that they would sign the petition tonight and take copies with them.

Next item: a boycott of a local theater.

Next: a report on the mail campaign seeking financial support. Members were reminded that money for their cause was not only needed but would bring more blessings on them because it would be used for good.

That money angle got Coleman's attention, but before he had time to think about it, he was startled by the Deacon's announcement of the Bible passage for the evening: Mark Chapter 14.

He deliberately relaxed his demeanor; *I'm just a guy here for information,* he reminded himself. He glanced in Russell's direction and could read his partner's mind.

The deacon guided their attention to verse 27 where Jesus told his apostles that their faith in him would be shaken for Scripture stated *"I will strike the shepherd and the sheep will be dispersed."*

Coleman was taken aback by the clamor that erupted as soon as that sentence was completed. The deacon pounded on the table with his hand and rapped on his microphone three times; people who were standing looked around and then sat; the commotion dwindled to a mutter. Deacon Cummings called on Joe, a tall, well-dressed man in the second row.

Joe's imposing height and commanding voice demanded attention. He voice was strident. "Father John was our shepherd here at St. Joseph's. He was struck down like Jesus Christ and we have witnessed how the inadequate faith of the people in this parish has been shaken. However, instead of returning to the practices that we grew up with, we have multitudes persisting in their sinful ways. I propose we should be..."

"Stop!" Suddenly a man sitting only two seats away from Coleman jumped to his feet. "I condemn your cowardice and lies; we should be asking why the shepherd was struck down!"

From every corner of the room rose the shouts. "He's right! He's right!"

Another man shot up right in front of Coleman. "Look what's been going on for years now; Catholic used to mean no meat on Friday, no missing Mass on Sunday; when I was growing up Mass was in Latin, altar boys served at Mass, the thought of altar girls never entered our minds!"

The man beside Dan Salvage, right behind Russell shouted, "All this nonsense about women's roles in the church; read your Bible! Listen to what St. Paul said about women in his letter to the Corinthians: that women should keep silent in such gatherings and that they should be submissive. And again in Ephesians he says that wives should be submissive to their husbands because he is the head just as Christ is head of the church."

Coleman's eyes darted from one man to another. Russell leaned over and whispered to the man next to him.

Again, the deacon rapped the table; again people sat down and quiet returned. Deacon Cummings, his voice shaky, reminded the gathering that St. Paul was addressing people of a different time and place and that not every instruction was to be taken literally. He mentioned some recent writings by the Pope expanding the proper roles for women in the church.

To that, the man who had interrupted Joe retorted that even the Pope was yielding to the pressures of today's society. "Perhaps that was why the shepherds were being struck down," he shouted.

At that moment, a voice from the back wall where the lights were not on, yelled, "You're all wrong!"

Everyone spun around to find the face that belonged with the words. When they made out that it was Pete Nowell they all, without exception, groaned and turned their attention back to the deacon.

Their callous dismissal of Nowell gave the deacon a space of silence and he pressed on. "Pete, tell us why you think we're all wrong."

Pete remained where he was, resolute in his position near the back wall. He straightened his shoulders, raised his head and spoke, every word distinct and clear. "The shepherds were not struck down because they were wrong; they were struck down because they had learned the truth. Each of us is equal in God's sight; God is not held hostage by gender; God can and will call anyone to priesthood."

Pete's courage and composure in this hostile atmosphere astounded Coleman. Not only did he admire his self-assurance, he was amazed at Pete's calm conviction that he was speaking a truth they would all have to acknowledge at some future date.

Deacon Cummings' voice was gentle as he counseled Pete to heed the pope's ruling, but Pete alleged, with the same gentle voice, that the pope was wrong, too.

When they heard that, several men leapt to their feet. Deacon Cummings loudly thumped his microphone and yelled, "Let us pray; let us pray!"

The men looked at him and then at Pete; one by one they sat down.

"O God, look upon your dedicated servants and enlighten us. Help us to see our sins so that we may beg forgiveness."

As the flood of words spilled into the background, Coleman's attention reverted to last night's meeting. Frustration and anger in the women and even the men in Magdalene's Witnesses was molded into hope; here he watched anger swell from bitterness to intolerance.

He squirmed in his seat; his desperation to leave this place was getting the upper hand, however, his characteristic sense of duty enabled him to regain his perspective. He could hardly wait to hear Russell's take on this.

The group's deafening "Amen" shifted his concentration back to the room. A fleeting glimpse toward the back wall confirmed his suspicion that Pete had disappeared.

Deacon Cummings' prayer tempered the emotional tone in the room. He now moved the discussion to practical ways that the group might encourage a recovery of Catholic values that appeared to have been lost.

One of the women proposed a committee to review the religion books being used in the parish school and the parish religious education program. She protested with vigorous finger-pointing to pages in her child's third grade religion book; there's no doctrine here, no lessons about sin, she complained. Just stories about loving everybody.

Fervent nodding of heads and groans of agreement encouraged her husband to volunteer to head the committee and to notify Sister Ann of their verdict.

One mother mustered all her courage to remark that Sister Ann already had a textbook review committee. *She will think twice before saying another word here,* thought Coleman, as she was showered by charges that the committee was evidently not qualified to make the proper choice.

A hurried vote signaled approval for notifying Sister Ann of their verdict. Russell's wife was on that committee and he had always had a high regard for Sister Ann; he wished he could warn her about what she would be facing tomorrow.

Coleman glanced at his watch; *how can it be only 9:00?* He covered his mouth as he felt a yawn coming on. *I wonder when we will get out of here.*

At that moment, the man who had previously quoted St. Paul revitalized the group by asking how many were regular watchers of *The Enduring Message*, the program that was on cable television seven days a week.

Several enthused hands flew into the air. Another half-hour of opinions closed with a strategy for promoting *The Enduring Message* throughout the parish. The applause was thunderous.

At long last, the deacon called for a closing prayer. Afterwards, the group gathered around the table for coffee and cookies.

Coleman headed straight for the door; he was counting on Russell's immediate departure. Just as he reached the door he felt a strong hand on his arm; he turned to look directly into the eyes of Joe. "You're new, aren't you?"

"I—just—this—this was my first meeting."

"What did you think? Real dedication, don't you agree?"

"Zealous opinions, all right." His eyes searched for Russell.

"Will you be joining us next week?"

"You all gave me a lot to think about. Long meetings," He slid closer to the door. "I really can't stay any longer tonight."

"O.k., then. Hope to see you next week."

Coleman gave him a beleaguered smile and moved outdoors as fast as he could.

Watching to see Russell head for his car he fidgeted with his keys and the windshield wipers. When he finally saw that bald head coming out the side door, Coleman turned his ignition key and began pulling out of his parking space.

Russell scrambled into his car and before he drove off Coleman phoned him; they arranged to meet in the shopping center lot two blocks away.

Russell dashed over to Coleman's car; his first words were "I'm positive The Herald was there. And I think its Dave Monroe."

"Who's Dave Monroe?"

"The one who made all the hullabaloo about St. Paul; wasn't he something else!"

"You know him? What connection does he have with all three priests?"

"That I don't know. And, no, I don't know him either; I didn't even know his name but the guy sitting next to me told me. I literally felt like I was being choked, didn't you? That guy is sure pissed off about something."

"He was disgusting. But did you notice who was beside him?"

"Yes. Dan Salvage, but he didn't say a word. Do you think they came together?"

"Just a hunch. What do you think Pete Nowell meant when he said they were murdered because they learned the truth?"

"I'm not sure; that sort of threw me off track. If you remember when we talked with him, he said they all did it wrong. I don't know if we'll ever figure out what goes on in his mind. But at this point I don't think he's our killer."

"Did you see Mike Mahoney and Mike Anderson in the last row?"

"But they didn't say anything either. And both their wives are in Magdalene Witnesses. I wonder if their wives are as accepting as Sarah."

"Good question. Well, it's late, we'd better get home. Tomorrow we'll see if we can find out more about Dave Monroe. Are you going to tell Noelle what we heard here tonight?"

"I don't think so; it would only upset her."

"I agree; I'm not going to tell Deb, either. By the way, I'm going to join the Magdalene Witnesses."

"Me, too. Is that what was bothering you today?"

"No, not at all. When I figure it out, I'll tell you."

Twenty

The next morning Deb got up at the same time as her husband. She sensed that something significant must have happened last night, and she was beginning to question why he was getting up so early every day.

In the pit of her stomach she recognized an ominous churning; every morning she wrestled with her fear of not seeing him that evening, but today, this feeling was unlike any fear she had before. She realized that she had an uncanny ability that prepared her for troubled days ahead of the actual event. She often complained about it, and although some might call it a gift, to her it only gave her more days to be afraid.

Chris gave her an affectionate peck on the cheek as he orbited the kitchen; since Monday's meeting, it was as if his soul was singing some new song that she could not hear but its joy seeped into her soul.

She pulled him back to her; she did not want to let him go. *Oh, please,* she cried within, *please don't ever leave me.* She felt his arms surround her and she relaxed into their protection.

"I've gotta go, Hon; I love you so much."

Her pounding heart followed him to his car. *Oh God, please be with him, please be with him.*

Russell rose earlier than usual and Noelle knew he would not be having breakfast that morning. She smiled as she recalled yesterday morning when they first woke up and he told her he was going to join the Magdalene Witnesses. *I am so lucky; thank you God.* She giggled as Rick took her in his arms and gave her an extra squeeze, with, "Thanks for understanding."

She held open the door as he rushed by, giving her a wink, holding in his hand his Dad-mug half-filled with coffee and his teeth holding a slice of buttered toast while he ran to the car.

Both men pulled up to the precinct within seconds of each other. They chuckled and shook their heads, relishing the satisfaction of how well they knew each other.

Coleman typed Dave Monroe's name into the computer and waited; within seconds his record filled up the screen. Coleman and Russell were blown away by what they saw. Dave Monroe's record for domestic abuse named former wife, Marge Monroe, maiden name: Peterson!

The task force would be meeting at 9:00. Coleman and Russell looked at the clock; they had forty-five minutes to prepare their case, tying motive, opportunity, background, and circumstances together. Would it be enough to convince the entire task force that Operation Soul Search would soon yield the answer they all sought?

On the dot at 9:00 Chief Flannery entered the room; the entire force was seated around the table engrossed in studying the clues Coleman had printed on the board. With the Chief's o.k. Coleman summarized the factors leading him and Russell to their theory. He mentioned how The Plumbers' web site steered them to attend the meeting at St. Joseph's last evening. Without going into extensive details, he outlined the foundation upon which he and his partner believed they could construct a strong case leading to the arrest of Dave Monroe.

He pointed to number 1 on the board: Monroe's attitude toward women. Coleman summed up the essence of Monroe's statements at the meeting that demonstrated, without a doubt, his difficulty with women holding any sort of power or leadership position.

Number 2: Monroe's record for twelve domestic violence incidents. His fury had erupted twelve times; twelve times the police had been summoned to his home and he had been detained each time, but always released because his wife refused to press charges—except after the twelfth time.

Number 3: His wife was Marge Peterson; she finally left Monroe and filed charges by virtue of the help she received from Father Bill when he was at St. Joseph's with Father John.

Number 4: All three parishes have groups named the Magdalene Witnesses who promote the role of women in the church.

Number 5. Father Andy's note. The uncertainty about whether the letters were N-O-W or M-O-N seemed indisputable. When Father Andy was strong enough to talk they were confident that he would identify his attacker as Monroe.

Coleman concluded with what he considered obvious. All they had to do now was connect the dates and times to Dave Monroe and they had their killer. Both the Chief and the Captain congratulated the partners and the rest of the task force applauded. Chief Flannery admonished them to be careful; it was clear that this man considered himself on a mission and he would not let anyone stop him.

Eight task force members were assigned rotating duty to keep Monroe under surveillance; twelve more were given the daunting task of canvassing respective neighborhoods seeking out neighbors and friends, anyone who might have information about Monroe's whereabouts on the dates of the murders and the attempted murder of Father Andy. Coleman and Russell, as well as the whole task force, could all but taste victory. Their ebullience tempted them to go to the hospital to inform Father Andy and his family, but they decided it might be prudent to postpone broadcasting their excitement.

Deb watched the clock as the time for dinner approached. *You know, nothing happened today,* she argued with herself. She caught herself biting her nails again, after all these months. Finally she heard Chris coming into the driveway.

She called upstairs to the kids that dad was home and to get washed up for dinner. Her morning fear had stayed with her all day, but she brushed it aside for now; tonight he was home.

When he walked in, he smelled steak. *What day is it,* his eyes asked. Deb smiled as he kissed her cheek. "I just wanted to surprise you with your favorites. I'm glad you're home."

The next two days were filled with the monotonous and the tedious. The task force found that matching Monroe with the times of the attacks was a frustrating assignment. Several neighbors provided a name of a club that he frequented: the Main Night Club.

Coleman and Russell followed up with the bartender who confirmed that Dave Monroe stopped by two or three nights a week. He never missed a Monday until a few weeks ago. He still came on Mondays, but not every week; besides his behavior had become very weird; now he drank only soda, no beer, no hard liquor. The bartender added that Monroe had not been in for two weeks.

~ * ~

On Saturday at dinner Chris Coleman made a surprise announcement to his family. "I'm going to go to church with you guys on Sunday."

Lori and John jumped out of their chairs and fell all over him as they hugged him with the tightest embrace ever. Deb reached over and squeezed his hand. Her happiness tried to smother the fear that refused to go away. She held on to his hand for a long time.

That night, after the kids were in bed, he confessed to Deb that he was not sure why he made that promise to them. "Oh, I'm still going with you on Sunday," he said. "I just don't know what made me say it." He wondered if she could explain what had been happening to him, but he could not find the right words. *Right words? I can't find any words. I haven't even told her about my morning visits to St. Joseph's.*

Deb's silky soft hand turned his face to hers as she said, "I told you that you are on a journey." She kissed him, a long, adoring kiss. "Hold me; I need you to hold me."

Twenty-one

Monday night Coleman and Russell headed for the Main Night Club. By 10:00 they decided Monroe was not going to show. "Do you think he might be at the Magdalene Witnesses meeting?" asked Coleman. "I wish we were there."

"So do I. I hate to think of how many Mondays we might have to waste here."

They were sliding out of their booth, as Monroe opened the door. Wasting no time they slid back into their places. They had picked a booth along the back wall where they could sit facing the rest of the bar. Only five men sat at the bar; at two other tables Coleman and Russell saw a man and woman, but both couples were so intrigued with each other they were oblivious to anyone else.

Monroe strolled over to a booth along the side wall where two women were sitting together when Coleman and Russell had arrived at 9:00.

One was a blonde who had not removed her sunglasses all evening. The other one, a bit taller with chestnut hair, got up to let Monroe slide in between them.

The blonde repeatedly brushed her cheek against Monroe's, pointing to the dance floor, but he kept pushing her away. The other one continuously giggled and ran her fingers through his dirty blonde hair.

Two hours later Monroe pulled both women closer to him; the blonde knocked over an empty bottle as she pushed herself into his chest and wrapped her one leg around his. The other one leaned on his shoulder and tucked her arm under his shirt.

"What do you think is going on?" said Coleman.

Their jaws hung open as Coleman and Russell watched the crude performance displayed before them. First Monroe smooched the blonde, then he turned to the other one; back and forth he went, nuzzled his face into their breasts, kissed their necks, bit the ear of one and then the other. When he had enough he unlocked their hold on him with an arrogant sneer, shoved the blonde out of the booth, and slithered off the bench. He threw some bills on the table, leaned over, gripped the face of the blonde, pulled it up to his and mashed his lips to hers. He repeated the same routine with the other one; then swaggered alone out the door.

Holding their breath until the door swung shut, Coleman and Russell dashed to the table; Coleman sat down across from the blonde; Russell slipped into the seat facing the other one. Their badges were in front of their faces before either woman could protest their presence. They introduced themselves immediately.

Coleman directed each one to state her name; the blonde laid her slim hand with its decorated finger nails on Coleman's and mouthed "I'm Sheila" as her tongue licked her top lip.

The other offered a limp handshake to Russell with "I'm Kathy."

Both women verified that Monroe spent several nights a week there. He always stayed until close to midnight; both said they had never spent the night with him. Coleman and Sheila moved to a separate table; Coleman suspected each woman would reveal a secret or two that neither would tell in the presence of the other.

Coleman asked Sheila why she had not taken off her glasses. She tossed her head and ignored his question. She made it known that she was obsessed with Monroe and confessed that she lied earlier about never sleeping with him because she did not want Kathy to know.

As he got up to leave, she teased Coleman that she might remember more if he would dance with her. He declined, but when he looked over at Russell and saw he was engaged in a serious conversation with Kathy he said, "O.k."

As they danced, Sheila confided to him that Monroe was a fabulous dancer, but for the past two weeks he preached religion to her and Kathy. Then she removed her glasses to reveal a bruise; Monroe hit her two weeks ago, when she laughed at his "conversion."

He apologized over and over for hurting her, protested that he loved her so much it made him crazy, and then lectured her about her place as a woman, which was to satisfy him and to listen when he spoke.

Coleman asked why she chose to continue her unusual relationship with him. Sheila shrugged and said she was terrified she would lose him to Kathy, and she would rather share him than be alone. She knew he was in prison for abusing his ex-wife, but Sheila tried to sort out her mixed-up feelings by explaining that a part of her felt sorry for him and he could be such a charmer, plus sometimes she fantasized about a man who took charge and controlled her.

She pushed herself closer in to Coleman as he tried to back away. "What's the matter, Detective? Don't you find me attractive?" Coleman noticed that Russell was getting ready to leave.

"I have to go." He thanked Sheila for her honesty and joined his partner. Inside the car, Russell related a similar story from his conversation with Kathy.

She had also lied about sleeping with Monroe because he had convinced her that he only saw Sheila at the club; she put up with his bizarre behavior because she believed him when he said that he was only playing games with Sheila, that she didn't mean anything to him. He had never hit her, but he had gotten very angry and once he threatened her when he was ranting on about religion and she called him a hypocrite.

Russell said, "He sure did not act like the religious fanatic we saw last week. How do you think he reconciles his sleazy actions with membership in God's Troops?"

"Who can explain nutty? He sure sounds crazy to me."

In spite of gaining ample proof that he was despicable, Coleman and Russell were not sure they had learned anything of value. Neither the bartender nor the women were reliable witnesses concerning the nights when the murders were committed. Even so, if on the dates of the attacks, Dave Monroe left the club at midnight he would have had enough time to go to St. Joseph's and Holy Name. But then there's the discrepancy with Father Andy's attack; why did he set up a meeting with him instead of following the same pattern?

And where was he now going on those Mondays when he did not come to the club? Had he really infiltrated the Magdalene Witness meetings?

Exasperated by the inadequate proof they have gleaned this evening, both detectives conceded that Father Andy's corroboration was going to be indispensable. As they left the bar, Coleman said, "You drive."

As he got into the passenger side seat, Coleman experienced again that same strange comforting calm. Again it was inside and all around him. This time he had no terror; all too soon it was gone.

Glad that he's not driving, he took a quick glimpse at Russell, who was absorbed in his own thoughts. *I need to ask him about this; I wonder what he will think.* He opened his mouth, immediately closed it and swallowed hard; his throat was so dry. As he opened his mouth again, Russell said, "Remember, we have Phil working with The Plumbers tracing The Herald's e-mail."

"Right; we'll check in with him tomorrow. Tomorrow's only a few hours away," Coleman laughed.

"You sound very calm; I thought you'd be all wound up tonight."

"You think? Maybe I'm just too tired. Besides, I still think we're so close to the end. We didn't get very far tonight, but it won't be long, now."

"I hope you're right. By the way, I was thinking, just to make sure she is safe, we should visit Marge Peterson tomorrow. She has a right to know what we've found out."

Twenty-two

Marge Peterson was in her kitchen decorating a wedding cake when Coleman and Russell knocked on her screen door. She took special pleasure in their compliments but it did not take long for her to question their real reason for coming so early in the morning.

When Coleman asked if she heard from her ex-husband in the past few weeks her lips quivered and both hands tightened into fists. She shook her head no; when he informed her that her husband was living in the same city and was now a member of St. Joseph's, Marge's whole body shuddered. Coleman was saddened by the dark fear he saw in her eyes; a fear that she had convinced herself she had conquered.

She gripped the back of a kitchen chair and sat down. Russell offered to get her a glass of water, but she insisted she was feeling better and pushed herself to stand up. She glanced at Coleman; their connection was still real and gave her the strength she needed. He noticed that her face muscles relaxed and a stillness replaced the fear in her eyes.

"What have you heard about God's Troops?" He asked.

"Not much, but enough to know such a group would not exist at Holy Name."

She was so glad that Coleman and Russell were with her; she wanted them to stay for a while. "How about a piece of cake?" she asked. "Oh yes, I know it is too early for dessert." She heard herself rambling on and on about how she missed Father Bill so much and how God was so good to them; how fortunate they were to have Sr. Emily at Holy Name; how those who had objected to the bishop's appointment of her as the parish administrator had all been won over, except for a very few.

"A few, just a very few had transferred their membership to St. Joseph's." She finally stopped for a breath. "Now you can tell me about Dave," she said.

Coleman remembered virtually every word Dave Monroe had said at the meeting. He took Marge's hand and encouraged her to sit down. As she heard her husband's words she covered her face with her hands; her mouth was parched. She thought how ironic it was that when they were married she and Dave often fought because he thought she was spending too much time at church.

Remembering how much pleasure he found in controlling her, she began to understand how God's Troops would gratify his need for power. Believing he was a killer did not require any big leap in her imagination.

Suddenly she broke into body-shaking sobs. Coleman and Russell were taken off guard. Before either one asked, her sobs were broken with gasping words. "If I hadn't gone for help; if I had not gone to Father Bill; if he had had not helped me; this would never have happened. Oh, Bill, I am so sorry."

Coleman placed one gentle firm hand on her shoulder and another on her arm. He wanted so much to take away her pain. "Marge, you are not to blame in any way! You must believe that."

Both detectives hoped she did not remember how many times she had called the police. She must be so frightened, Coleman thought. "Marge, we have him under constant surveillance. We want you to be aware, but we are confident that he will not take the risk of contacting you. Continue to go about your life and work as usual, knowing that we are watching his every move."

Marge rested her hand on Coleman's arm; his need to make her feel safe had the desired effect. She expressed her appreciation to both of them and insisted that she was all right now. Coleman enclosed her in a warm hug before they left, reminding her to call even if she only wanted to talk.

When they got back to their office they found a message to come as soon as possible to The Plumbers; Phil was close to identifying The Herald's computer. As soon as they entered the driveway The Plumber's door swung open. Matt waved his arms wildly for them to hurry. "Phil traced The Herald's e-mail to the local public high school! We even know when it was used."

Russell's head was swimming with denials and contradictions. "A high school kid?"

"No, No" explained Matt "the computer lab is used at night for adult classes."

Phil followed Coleman and Russell to the school, where they enlisted the principal's cooperation. Without a moment's delay, Mr. Horan accompanied them to the lab.

The computer coordinator, Mrs. Lee, was at her desk preparing for her adult classes scheduled for the following evening. Mr. Horan made swift introductions and directed her to assist the police with whatever they needed. The first item they requested was a roster of her adult attendees. Mrs. Lee opened her top desk drawer and handed them four pages of names and addresses.

On the second page Russell pointed to Dave Monroe's name. He asked her to show them which computer he used and wanted to know when he would have time to write and send personal e-mail.

Mrs. Lee informed them that adults can remain for up to two hours any night after the formal class is over. She often saw Dave Monroe remain after most students left. She was impressed with his involvement and eagerness to learn.

When Phil logged on to Dave's computer, he worked for more than an hour attempting to retrieve the messages received at The Plumbers. Much of the personal work had been deleted, or so Dave thought.

Coleman paced while Russell talked with Mrs. Lee, advising her on the necessity to carry on her class as usual the next day. When she told him how nervous that made her, he gave her some helpful hints on remaining cool and composed. "You'll do just fine," he assured her.

Finally, Phil ejected a disk with all the information he needed to tie Dave Monroe to The Herald.

Twenty-three

The task force met every morning now; the information on Dave Monroe was mounting; if only they could make it add up to the conclusion they needed.

Coleman and Russell first had Phil explain the evidence recovered at the computer lab. Although there was no doubt that Dave Monroe and The Herald were the same person, none of the computer evidence amounted to a confession of any kind. None of the task force members found any information that could place him at any of the three parishes at the times of the assaults.

"Now," said Coleman, "Beginning on my right let's go around the table giving whatever information you have on Monroe up to this point."

"Monroe's neighbors, aware of his record, have monitored his comings and goings. When he first moved in he hung out at the bar every night; then his pattern changed to Mondays, Fridays and Saturdays."

"Recently a few of the men heard he had found religion and attended church on Tuesday evenings."

"One neighbor, a woman, attended the same computer class on Wednesday. No one had figured out where he went on Thursdays."

"Weekends were the most difficult to tie down, but two elderly women, one who lived across the street, the other next door, had often seen him bringing a woman home late in the evenings on Saturdays and Sundays, but they described two different women."

Coleman and Russell exchanged a calculated glance wondering if Sheila was the Saturday girl and Kathy the Sunday one.

Two officers had interviewed Monroe's boss. They had quite a story to tell. Officer Susan Richards began.

"During the day Monroe works at Ernie's Body Shop. The owner is Frank Scott, an ex-con. Ernie Ballwin, the original owner, had given him a second chance when he returned from prison. When Ernie retired, he sold the business to Frank so now he tries to do his part rehabilitating former inmates. He was fully aware of Monroe's background and told us that in the beginning Monroe was obstinate and seemed determined to screw up because he was drunk so many times, but recently had turned himself around."

Her partner picked up the next part of the story. "Two or three weeks ago Frank warned Monroe he was giving him one final break; the message seemed to have finally sunk in. Monroe went to his first AA meeting that week and now attends two or three meetings a week. Monroe has been on time every day since and now he tried to preach sermons to Frank, and ideas about women that Frank considered too weird! But he always treated the women customers with respect and that was all Frank demanded of him."

Russell asked if Frank knew where Monroe attended the AA meetings. Officer Richards said she had questioned him about that. He could not say for sure, but knew that there were meetings at several Catholic churches.

Coleman asked if anyone had inquired about Dan Salvage. Susan again said she mentioned his name to Frank and he told her that Salvage had been there several weeks ago, but not for a job; he wanted to see Monroe about something. He never expected that Dan would come job-hunting, because Dan had been a professional fund-raiser, an idea man, not a get-your hands-dirty type.

An idea man, right, thought Coleman; he was sure Salvage had brought Monroe to the God's Troops' meeting. He remembered his first suspicions of Salvage. Disturbing ideas marched into his mind like soldiers in a parade. He decided to throw them out to the group. "Is it possible that he and Monroe are in this together? Salvage could have gotten his revenge for Father John's testimony and Monroe has every reason to hate Father Bill. They must have met at prison. Put together Salvage's anger with Monroe's ideas about women, and you have a perfect combination for murder. And now they both have joined God's Troops; if they're on a mission, Father Andy is not safe and who else might be on their list?"

"Frank did mention that Salvage and Monroe had been in the same prison." said Richards. She added that they had advised Frank they were merely doing a routine follow-up and considering Monroe's recent change in behavior, thought it best that Frank not even mention their visit.

"Good thinking," said Coleman. "If we get Monroe tied to the killings, he'll give up Salvage, I know."

An awkward quiet settled around him; as the task force members waited for Coleman's closing remarks, he found himself distracted by the story of Frank Scott's generosity with former offenders; he wrestled with an unsettling invitation in his soul. A discreet kick under the table from Russell brought him back. He coughed, cleared his throat, thanked everyone for the good work and put forward a proposal to bring in Dave Monroe. "Tomorrow marks three months since Father John's murder. I think we have enough to build a case."

Chief Flannery was hesitant. "I don't want to lose this one by being too hasty. What kind of scenario could you use to get a confession out of him?"

Coleman turned to Russell. "Remember what we discussed when we had Charlie Sullivan in here after Father Andy's attack. Even though he couldn't give us a description, the killer doesn't know that."

"So, what are you saying?" asked the Chief. "You want Charlie here when you bring in Monroe?"

"We could tell Monroe we have a witness; Charlie could be in your office when we bring in Monroe."

"I sure wouldn't want to put Charlie in any danger, especially if you think that Salvage could also be connected. But your instincts are usually right on target. I'll trust you on this. Go ahead and talk with Charlie about this; make sure he understands what you want him to do and that he stays sober!"

"We might want him to act drunk, in case Monroe doesn't recognize him sober!"

That night, Coleman and Russell arrived at the high school at 8:45. A few minutes after 9:00 they saw the first few students coming out the door.

Coleman and Russell scrambled out of their car; as they got to the front door, a woman on her way out smiled at both of them and held open the door.

In the hallway Coleman paced and Russell leaned against the wall; it was a very long fifteen minutes; finally the classroom was empty except for Monroe and Ms. Lee. Monroe was so preoccupied he didn't notice them until they were standing on either side of him. He hit a key, the screen went dark, but he knew it was too late.

Coleman and Russell pulled their badges, as they read him his rights and ordered him to stand. He hit his fist on the table, barked several curses and shoved back his chair. Russell handcuffed him; Coleman and Russell nodded a thank you to a rigid Ms. Lee holding on to her desk.

Coleman smiled with satisfaction as they walked into the station with Monroe between him and Russell; there, in full view, was Charlie tripping over his own two feet, being led down the hall and into the Chief's office. Monroe scowled and twisted his head back towards Coleman.

Shoving Monroe into the interrogation room, he took off the handcuffs and pushed him into a chair. Coleman wasted no time telling him that they had traced The Herald's messages to his computer. Monroe gave no answer but a so-what shrug. Then Coleman recited to him the remarks he and Russell heard him speak at last week's meeting of God's Troops. Monroe shrugged again and grinned, his eyes glared first at Coleman then at Russell.

Such narrow eyes, thought Coleman, *yet incapable of hiding their hatred.* A flash of Marge under this man's wrath forced Coleman to strangle the delight in his stomach that urged him to pounce like a raging lion.

The pitch in Coleman's voice rose as he rattled off the attack dates demanding a where-were-you answer to each. Monroe shrugged and said he didn't remember.

Twenty futile minutes brought Coleman to the edge. He promised himself he would use Charlie only as a last resort. *Oh, hell, I guess I have no choice.* "We have a witness." His fist hit the table so hard Monroe's hands flew up to shield himself. "We're going to arrest you for the murders of Father John Martin and Father Bill Williams and for the attempted murder of Father Andy Sanchez."

Now Monroe sat straight up. "Whoa! What witness? I never killed nobody!"

"When you tried to kill Father Andy Sanchez, you were interrupted. Remember? You shoved the guy against the wall and put the knife in his hand. Remember that? He remembers you!"

"You're crazy! I don't know what you're talking about."

"Plus, Father Andy had enough time to write the first three letters of your name on a note; we have the note with M-O-N in blood!"

"That don't prove nothing! M-O-N- could mean anything! You're just nuts. You don't have anything on me."

"You made threats! We have them all!"

"Yeah, so what." His whole body seethed as he leaned close to Coleman; frenzy burned in his eyes. "I am The Herald! But I didn't do anything. All I tried to do was scare people; people need to fear, to be afraid again of God. No one is afraid anymore. Everybody is making selfish choices to please themselves. People are going to be damned for their pride and wickedness. The wrath of God is here. If you keep me here, it won't matter; your power is useless to stop God's wrath from accomplishing its purpose."

Coleman slammed his fist again on the table and turned away. *God's wrath; yeah, like I believe that,* Coleman thought. *Sometimes, I wish it were that simple.*

Russell got in Monroe's face. He grabbed his shirt and lifted him a full six inches off the chair and dropped him back into it. "Were you afraid of God when you beat your wife? Were you afraid of God then? Huh? You expect us to believe this garbage?"

Monroe pounded the desk again and again with his fist "You don't understand. All that stuff with my wife. That was before I believed. I'm different now."

Russell's face was a mixture of anger, anguish and loathing; he clenched his fist in front of Monroe's nose. "Really! What about the black eye you gave Sheila?"

"Did that bitch tell you I hit her? She's crazy. She's just trying to get back at me 'cause she thinks I lied to her."

Russell's fist moved closer. "You know what I think? I think you killed those priests and this bit about being The Herald is a set-up; maybe you knew we'd find you sooner or later, so this so-called conversion is just a plan to make you look like you're insane."

Coleman pulled Russell away, placed himself on the table and leaned over to Monroe. His voice was low and dogged. "Look, Monroe, if you did it while you were drunk, you can go for diminished capacity; you'll dodge the death penalty. Remember, we have two witnesses; not only do we have the witness you shoved against the wall, as well as Father Andy's bloody note but now that Father Andy is recovering, he'll be able to identify you."

As soon as he said it, Coleman regretted letting out that information. He heard Russell gasp. But he argued with himself, *Father Andy is safe now; we have this creep and I have to get his confession.*

"Monroe, listen, it will go better for you if you just tell us the truth."

"I'm telling you I didn't kill nobody. But I'm not saying another word until I have a lawyer."

"O.k.," says Coleman. "Do you have a lawyer?"

"Of course not; I can't afford a lawyer. But I know my rights; you can't force me to say anything else."

Russell hurled a chair across the room. "Get him outta here!"

Coleman grabbed Monroe's arm. "You'll have a lawyer tomorrow. But think about what I just said. Do the smart thing."

Twenty-four

"Good morning, Tom."

Tom Weber stopped at Coleman's office door. His sandy brown hair, with a soft wave falling loosely on his forehead, his light brown eyes and tanned face made the six foot lanky public defender look younger than his forty years. His weary eyes betrayed his displeasure at meeting his client again.

"Try to get him to tell the truth," said Coleman. "We know he's our man."

With every step he took towards his cell Tom Weber dreaded his face-to-face meeting with Monroe. He had been his defender last time. It was a case he was not sorry he lost.

This morning, he stopped still and stared at the man he saw sitting in his cell, eyes closed, arms uplifted. The old Dave would have been pacing in his cage, cursing his fate and damning the police. This one looked like a monk. This cannot be genuine, he told himself. Avoiding his obligation any longer was not an option. "Good morning, Dave."

Monroe opened his eyes and extended his arms in welcome. Weber heard the clang of the cell door behind him. *Trapped with a rat,* he grumbled to himself. "O.k., tell me what happened."

As their conversation ensued, Weber tried again and again to focus on the job he was required to do; the convert before him appalled him. He couldn't ever recall seeing a fusion of violence and righteousness repose with such complacence in anyone.

He listened to Dave's declarations of innocence. Using a clenched fist he spelled out each piece of evidence the police had; Dave waved it all away with a snicker.

He went on to profess that it was Father John's murder that motivated him to examine his own life. That was when he started going to church and reading the Bible. One day another ex-con told him about God's Troops and brought him to his first meeting; when he heard the first prayer his life took on new meaning.

"Everything fell into place; everything made sense. All the stuff about God's wrath and punishment for all the evil that is in the world; I know I was a sinner and I deserved to be punished."

He fell on his knees and lifted his face to Weber. "But now I'm in the service of the Ruler of the World."

Weber suppressed the temptation to tell him to knock it off and hurried to complete his interview. He told Monroe he would be back tomorrow for the hearing; maybe he could get him out on bail, but he was not making any promises. As the cell door closed Monroe called out "Tell them I'll take a lie detector test!"

Weber began to walk away but allowed himself to turn around and walked back to the cell. He stared at Monroe looking for something other than the darkness in his eyes. "I'll see you tomorrow; try to relax."

He waved to Coleman and Russell as he left the station. Coleman yelled, "We just got word that Father Andy is able to talk and has recovered his memory of that night; we're going

222

over there now; maybe your client will want to change his plea."

"Keep me informed," said Weber.

As soon as the elevator door opened, Coleman and Russell heard Corita's soft sweet voice singing. They moved faster. With a passing wave to the nurse, they hurried towards Officer Kelly on guard duty; he smiled a very wide smile and opened the door for them.

What a sight greeted them. Corita singing, her face smiling as tears rolled down her blushed cheeks; her mother and father were dancing; Father Andy was laughing.

Mr. and Mrs. Sanchez extended their arms and pulled Coleman and Russell into their circle. A few steps to the right and left, and Coleman raised his hand. "I hate to mention reality. But, we still have work to do."

Instant silence.

"Of course, of course. Come on Anna, Corita. Let's go get something to eat. Detective Coleman and Detective Russell need to do their work. What would you like, Andy?"

With a laugh as hearty as his appetite, he said "Bring me a huge hamburger!"

"Detectives, what can I get you?"

"We're fine; you go ahead."

As they left the room, Anna asked Officer Kelly if he would like a hamburger too.

He replied, "Absolutely!"

She gave him an affectionate hug.

Russell closed the door and Coleman walked to the side of the bed. "Relax, Father; take your time and just tell us what you can remember about that day. Did you know your attacker?"

"I had never met him before; he called me on the phone and said he wanted to discuss some ideas with me about our Cultural Awareness Day. He also said that he was married to a caterer. So I thought he was going to offer some donations towards our fundraiser." He paused to suck in a slow deep breath and reached for his glass of water.

Coleman handed it to him. "Take your time, Father. You're doing great."

"Well, when he came in I noticed he was holding a Bible, so I had an inkling I was dealing with someone who had a problem. As the conversation went on and on, I realized he was somewhat of a zealot, and now I understand, a dangerous one. He opened the Bible and began reading the story of the Last Supper. He kept stopping to give me his interpretation of the verses he had just read. When I stood up he became very agitated and angry. I felt the knife cut into me and I remember trying to push him away. Then I heard the alarm going off. I don't remember much after that."

"The person you're describing fits the man we have in custody."

"How did you find him?"

Just as Coleman opened his mouth, Anna knocked on the door. "Here's your hamburger, my darling, Andy. And a coke." She bowed her head to both detectives, "Sorry to interrupt."

Russell's sleeve was being tugged; he turned to see Mr. Sanchez motioning for him to come into the hall.

"Eat your hamburger. Father; we're fine," said Coleman.

In the hallway, Jorge motioned Russell to walk towards the nurses' station. Officer Kelly gathered some chairs around him, so Corita and her mother, each balancing a hamburger and a can of soda, sat down to enjoy their food.

Jorge took pains to explain to Russell how he would treasure more time with his son, but knew that they had to return to their jobs. He explained that he was worried if their departure would hinder the progress of the investigation. He knew the family would remain for the weekend, but they owed it to their generous employers to take a Sunday evening flight home. Then, he pleaded, "Can you come up with a way to make it easier on my wife to leave her son?"

"We are sure we have the person responsible. He could be released on bail and he may have had an accomplice. So, it will be easier on us if we do not have to worry about your safety; we can concentrate on Father Andy."

"And you'll explain that to my wife?"

Russell patted him on the shoulder. "Let's go back; we still have more to ask Father Andy."

Before rejoining his partner, Russell walked over to Anna. He crouched down in front of her and took her left hand in his. "We are confident that this case will be resolved very soon. I know you will find it sad to leave Father Andy here in the hospital while he fully recovers, but, in fact; you will be doing us a favor. Though we have a suspect he could be released on bail, and it would lessen the demands for security if we have only Father Andy to protect."

Anna's other hand rose to cover her mouth, though not soon enough, to stifle a moan, but Russell told her how the police would surround her son with maximum security. Jorge put his arm around her shoulders as Russell went back into the room. Father Andy was drinking the last of his soda.

Coleman picked up where they had left off. "You asked how we found your attacker. He sent a message to the web site that the teenagers had set up after Father John's murder. He calls himself The Herald, but we were able to trace his e-mail. And we learned more about Dave Monroe when we attended a meeting of God's Troops."

"Oh, I've heard about that group. What a distorted God they see. But who is Dave Monroe?"

"He's the one we have in custody. Everything you said fits, plus you had tried to write a message on a notepad that night; you printed three letters, M-O-N."

"No, No. I remember grabbing that pad; I wrote N-O-W; the man's name is Nowell."

"Pete Nowell!" Panic gripped Coleman and Russell; "Are you sure?"

"No, no, not Pete. I know Pete. He doesn't have a violent thought in his head. This man said he was Pete's brother."

"Pete has a brother, Ed. Are you saying this was Ed?"

"I think that's what he called himself, but I'm positive I'll never forget his face."

"If we send the police artist here, do you think you can give us a picture?'

"Definitely!"

Coleman pulled out his phone. "Father Andy can give us a detailed description; send Tim here to the hospital. Father Andy's room is 406. And release Dave Monroe; he's not our man."

Tim Callero arrived in less that twenty minutes; he set up a laptop on the stand next to Father Andy's bed. "I'm ready when you are."

Fifteen minutes later a familiar face glared back at them. Coleman and Russell were numb; their mouths dropped open.

"Are you absolutely positive?" asked Coleman.

"Absolutely. That is Ed Nowell."

"We'd better move fast," says Russell. "Tim, show that to Officer Kelly."

"Memorize this face," Coleman ordered as Tim turned his screen towards Kelly.

"Is that the man? Is that the one you have in custody?" cried Anna.

"Everything is going to be fine; why don't all of you go back in with Father Andy. Don't worry; everything is under control." He avoided looking in Anna's eyes; he was too afraid he would glimpse his own fear there.

How can time go so fast when you are trying to stop it in its tracks, thought a desperate Coleman. In spite of their speed and the siren, twenty-five minutes passed before they got close to their destination. He cut the siren when they were two blocks away. He swung into the driveway and saw only one car. *O God, please, let it be his.*

In seconds both detectives were beating on the door. "Open up, now!"

"Detective Coleman; Detective Russell; why are you here?"

"Where's your husband, Sarah?"

"Why, what's wrong?"

"We need to know right now where the deacon is." Coleman and Russell realized they were yelling.

"He was called to the hospital. Our neighbor's husband has taken a turn for the worse."

"Let's go!"

"Please, tell me what's wrong. Why do you need to see Ray?" Her words trailed after them.

With the siren blaring, they tore out of Sarah's driveway. She ran after them, then turned and rushed back into the house. She grabbed her keys, jumped into her car and raced after them.

Meanwhile Russell was phoning the hospital; "Room 406, now. This is Detective Russell."

Father Andy picked up. "Hello." Russell asked for Officer Kelly.

"Oh, hello, Susan. How nice to hear from you."

"He must be with you in the room?"

"Yes, I thank you so much for calling. Yes. We are all fine."

"Does he have a gun?"

"Yes, I should be leaving here soon. Hope you can visit before then. Thanks for calling."

"What's going on? Are we too late?" asked Coleman.

"He's there. I think Father Andy was trying to tell us that Deacon Cummings is going to be kidnapping him."

"We better call Beth; she negotiated us out of two hostage situations this year. If anyone can help us now, it'll be Beth."

Within minutes Coleman and Russell pulled into the hospital lot; they checked their watches every few minutes scanning the traffic both ways looking for Beth and her team.

"I see his car, over there," said Russell. Why do you think he came to the hospital? How did he know we had figured it out?"

"Maybe he didn't. The hospital received calls every day about Father Andy's progress. Even though the news of his recovery was not to be given out, I'm sure he knew it would only be a matter of time. When Beth gets here, I think we should go to Father Andy's room as if we were making a visit and assess the situation. By that time Beth's team will be in place and communication will be set up."

They saw Sarah Cummings parking beside them. "We might as well tell her; she might even be able to help us."

Every muscle in Sarah's face froze as Coleman told her about Father Andy's testimony. Her eyes shrieked with the horror of a truth she would rather die than know. All the color faded from her face and she collapsed to the ground.

Russell gently picked up her head and slid his other arm under her; as he lifted her up Coleman opened their car door. With tender care he laid her on the back seat; her hand trembled and she raised it to rub her forehead. Slowly, she opened her eyes and tried to lift her head; then she moaned and fell back. With one arm supporting her back, Russell held her hand and helped her to sit up.

Coleman stood there with a paper cup filled with water. Her hand shook as she put the coolness to her lips.

"Can you talk to us, Sarah?"

She nodded and bit her lip. Most of her walnut colored curls were tangled; one damp curl dangled in the middle of her forehead.

"Can you tell us how he was acting when he left? Did you see a gun?"

Sarah remembered that he was very upset, but she thought it was because of the news about their neighbor. She did not know he owned a gun. The veins in her hands bulged as she gripped the edge of the front seat and pushed herself out of the car. Russell caught her elbow as she stumbled towards her own car.

The van with Beth and the SWAT team stopped in front of them. Russell put his arm around Sarah, and continued walking her towards her car.

As Beth discussed plans with Coleman he gestured towards Russell and Sarah. Visitors walking towards the hospital stared at the police cars, their fingers pointed out the SWAT team to each other.

They hesitated at the front door as they saw Coleman and Russell approach. Both detectives motioned them to keep moving assuring them that everything was fine. Coleman and Russell knew TV cameras would be appearing all too soon.

As they rushed off the elevator, Coleman and Russell stopped in their tracks at the sight of Officer Kelly standing outside Father Andy's room. "Why is he smiling and nodding to the nurse on her way to the nurse's station?" asked a bewildered Coleman.

Officer Kelly turned his head when he heard a hushed "Kelly!" Coleman and Russell motioned for him to walk over to them.

As Coleman explained, his smile faded; his jaw dropped and his face blanched. "But, but—he was dressed as a priest; I didn't even think about that computer drawing. I even opened the door! What are we going to do?"

"We'll figure something out."

They heard the dull thud of a door opening. All three turned to see Father Andy's sister step into the hall. She saw Coleman, Russell and Kelly; her face was petrified in determination; her stiff, determined footsteps propelled her down the hall. She waved them to walk beside her. "I have to bring back a wheelchair; he said I have one minute, or he'll hurt my mother; he looked at his watch as I walked to the door."

Coleman, Russell and Kelly fell into step with her while Coleman asked if everyone was o.k.. She bit her lip as she nodded her head yes. Coleman put his arm around her. "Try to stay calm. We're not going to let anything happen to your brother or your parents, or you." Corita nodded her head; she turned her face toward Coleman and her eyes pleaded for a guarantee.

Corita chewed her lip as the nurse was taking her time getting the wheelchair. "Hurry, please," she blurted out. When the nurse saw Corita's lip quivering and then recognized the detectives beside her, she shoved herself from her computer and grabbed a wheelchair. She opened her mouth and shut it without saying a word; she blessed herself as Corita ran down the hall with the chair.

She bumped and banged the door trying to get the wheelchair inside. Coleman and Russell flattened themselves against the wall. Kelly put himself back in his usual position.

They heard chairs scraped across the floor. They strained to pick up enough words to understand the deacon was instructing the family to remain in the room when he left with Father Andy. Muffled sobs. A plastic cup bounced on the floor.

Realizing that it would take a few minutes to get Father Andy out of his bed and into the wheelchair, Coleman and Russell began walking towards the nurses' station. They turned to face Father Andy's room. Finally, they saw the door opening.

Father Andy's feet came into view. As he turned the wheelchair down the hall Deacon Cummings jerked it to a dead stop. He held up the gun above Father Andy's head. "Don't come near me!"

Coleman and Russell held up their hands until the elevator door closed. Coleman called Beth. "They're on the elevator; Father Andy and Deacon Cummings; they are alone. Get out of sight and let them go. He has a gun. If there are any cameras out there, get them out of sight. Russell and I are going down the back stairs. I don't know why he's taking Father Andy from the hospital, but to get him out of his wheelchair and in to the car will take all his attention; that should give Russell and me a chance to overtake him without endangering Father's life. Make sure he doesn't see any of you!"

Outside a small crowd had gathered; Beth ordered everyone to their cars. She turned to see the Channel 9 van approaching. She ordered them into a side alley behind the SWAT van. Then she ran to Sarah's car and found her crumpled on the floor sobbing. She coaxed her to sit up. "I need you, Sarah. Please, come with me."

Limp and hugging the hollowness in her stomach, Sarah followed Beth to her car. "Sit here in the front; try to breathe. I won't let anything happen to you."

Sarah heard Beth speaking, but nothing made sense to her. *Why would anything happen to her; what about Ray? Who is going to take care of him?* She gulped for air as she choked on her sobs. Beth got in the driver's seat, and reached over to grab Sarah's hand.

The deacon's car was in Beth's direct line of sight but faced the opposite direction. She saw Coleman and Russell, hunched and running to theirs, parked only three spaces away from his. All of a sudden she saw him. He kept looking around and waving the gun. He swung open the front passenger side door; with his left hand, he helped Father Andy out of the chair and allowed him to use his shoulder for balance. He pushed with the gun until Father Andy got his arm inside and then slammed the door shut; he kicked the wheelchair out of his way.

Coleman shouted. "Drop the gun!"

A screech of wheels brought the Channel 7 van to a stop directly in front of Coleman and Russell; "What the hell is going on!" yelled Coleman. "How did they get past Beth and her team?

The deacon smiled. The door of the Channel 7 van opened and a reporter jumped out yelling to the deacon, "Tell us your story!"

"Follow me!" He screamed and slid into the driver's seat. As he roared out of the lot, Coleman and Russell raced back to their car. With their siren blaring they saw the Channel 7 van ahead of them. As they passed it, they caught sight of the deacon running the red light; traffic halted as Coleman and Russell raced after him.

The waning siren caused Sarah to stop crying, but only for a few seconds. Beth touched her arm. "I'll be back. Stay here."

Sarah put her hand over her mouth; she nodded while tears streamed down her cheeks.

Beth headed for Father Andy's room where she found Officer Kelly doing his best to comfort and reassure father, mother and sister.

"We're going to get him back, I promise. Did the deacon give you any hint where they're headed?"

All three shook their heads no. She grabbed her phone on the first ring.

"Looks as if they are headed for the bishop's residence."

"I'll meet you there." Beth turned on the TV as she made her promise again and headed out the door.

Beth gave a swift rap on the Channel 9 van door and a half-minute update. She didn't mention Channel 7. "We'd better get going, now. I'll follow you."

Twenty-five

When Beth returned to her car, she took a moment to study Sarah. She was staring straight ahead, her eyes red; no more tears, her hands clutched together resting on her stomach. "I'm here, Sarah, Please talk to me. You could be a big help to us and to your husband. Trust me; no one has to get hurt here."

Sarah turned her head slowly; confusion clouded her eyes. She sighed and pulled the seatbelt around herself. "I don't know what I can do; I do want to help you."

"Do you have any idea what drove him to this? What does he want?"

"I have no idea. I thought I knew my husband." She choked as she heard her own words and tears seeped out of the corners of her eyes.

"Well, he's headed for the bishop's home. Did he have problems with Bishop Steele?"

"I don't think so. He just wanted the church to be holy, to listen to God."

"And what did he think God wanted the church to do?"

"I'm not sure; I knew we disagreed about changes in the church, but…" The tears flowed down her flushed cheeks. Beth reached over and squeezed her hand.

"Here we are. You stay in the car for now. I may need you to talk to him later."

Beth rushed over to Coleman and Russell who were standing beside their car. By the time they arrived, they told her, the deacon had pulled Father Andy out of his car. "He was gasping for breath and trying to hold on to Cumming's arm for balance, but he couldn't keep up. We could do nothing but watch as the deacon dragged him up the sidewalk and the three steps to the chancery office."

"Sarah has no clue why her husband did this, or why he came here. What happened when they got to the door?"

"The secretary opened the door, she screamed for the bishop. Bishop Steele and the secretary put their arms around Father Andy and helped him inside. The deacon kept waving his gun and looking back at us. We've seen absolutely nothing since they closed that door."

"We'll have phone capabilities in a few minutes." Beth looked across the street; a city park enclosed a lake; a block beyond she saw a school and further down the road were single family homes. She noticed several men pointing at the police and TV crews.

Beth called the bishops' number. She let it ring ten times, but no one picked up. "I guess the deacon is running this show," she said. "The SWAT team is in place, but they can't find a window without the blinds or curtains closed. We can only assume they are all in the bishop's office." She looked at Coleman; "I usually use this megaphone, but the deacon knows you better; do you think he might respond to you?"

"I don't know; besides, you're the expert."

"I'll help you. I think it's the best chance we have to establish contact."

"O.k. Give it to me." Coleman took a deep breath and called out "Deacon Cummings! Listen to me. Let's talk; this does not have to end badly. When the phone rings, please pick it up." He nodded to Beth. The phone rang again and again. He looked at Beth. "Do you think Sarah would be up to doing this?"

"Seems unlikely, but I think she is stronger than she realizes at this point. Give me a few minutes with her."

Coleman breathed a quiet sigh when Beth came back with Sarah. He looked into her moist eyes and saw hope and strength and love. "Thank you, Sarah," he whispered.

Sarah called out to her husband again and again; the awful silence continued.

"We'll keep trying," said Coleman. "You and I; he'll answer one of us." He looked at Beth who nodded and put her arm around Sarah.

Minutes dragged into another hour. Two more TV vans arrived. A crowd of men, women and children gathered across the street; the police roped off the area to keep them from coming any closer. Every few minutes someone shouted questions to the police; the afternoon sun and the humidity pressed on everyone's nerves.

A face in the crowd caught Coleman's attention. "Do you see who's here?" he said to Russell.

"Do you see who else is coming?" Dave Monroe walked over to Dan Salvage and shook his hand.

"I told you he was the one who brought Monroe to *God's Troops*. What if they are in on this?" He called a SWAT team member over and pointed out Salvage and Monroe. "Bring them here," he said.

Coleman and Russell checked for weapons; Coleman stepped back and studied Salvage first, then Monroe. He did not know what to make of the sadness in their eyes. "What do you know about this?"

Salvage spoke up first. "Only that the TV stations said that Father Andy had been kidnapped by Deacon Cummings and had come here."

Monroe shook his head in agreement. "We don't understand; do you think Deacon Cummings had a revelation?"

Coleman's tone was incredulous. "Are you saying you still believe in him?"

Monroe's eyes were steadfast. "He made it all so clear; if we are on God's side, we can make things right. Maybe he is just trying to make the bishop see the truth."

"And what is that?"

"That God has spoken; if people continue to sin, they will be punished; more evils will come to pass."

"Sounds too simple, don't you think?"

"But God is Almighty; he has the power."

"Well, you might learn that God is more complicated than that." Coleman could hardly believe his own ears. *Did I say that,* he asked himself. *What made me say that?* "All right, you can go back with that group across the street."

Nothing yet from the bishop's residence. Coleman heard Sarah and Beth making another attempt while he had been talking to Monroe.

Some members of the SWAT team stood; others crouched in position waiting and ready. Coleman scrutinized the strained faces, rifles on hold and cigarette butts ground by fuming feet. *How much longer can they wait? What does he want? When is he going to make his move?* They all saw him at the window once, about an hour ago, when Sarah had called out to him; he had he pulled aside the drape, just far enough for them to see his face.

A reporter from each TV van came running towards Coleman and Russell. Their shouts became one voice. Bishop

Steele had called the stations; he was going to issue a crucial directive. First Father Andy Sanchez was going to be released.

Earlier, inside the bishops' office, the deacon marched back and forth in front of the bishop's desk waved his gun and called himself the Prophet of the Most High God. Father Andy sat in a chair near the window. Each time the bishop attempted to stand up, he pointed the gun towards Father Andy and shouted at the bishop to sit down and prepare himself for the prophecy.

He went on to explain how it was time for everyone to know the truth. God used him as the instrument of chastisement in regard to Father John and Father Bill. "They had fallen from their exalted role as shepherds and teachers! They ignored the Pope, the head of the church. They altered the teachings of Christ to fit this modern evil and selfish world."

"How did they do that?"

"They allowed themselves to be swayed by the women's movement; they refused to preach the truth that God made man superior to woman. They were so willing to give up their power. I tried to show them that Christ ordained only men; he shared the Last Supper only with his twelve apostles. If it had not been for that woman and her perfume, Judas would have remained faithful."

"What about your wife?" asked Bishop Steele. "Does she not belong to Magdalene's Witnesses?"

The deacon became solemn, his face downcast. "I thought she would see her error; I was sure I would be able to convert her. There is still time; maybe now, she will see the truth."

Bishop Steele recalled Sister Emily's reflection; her words resounded in his heart. How uplifted he was that day. He knew that nothing he would say could reach the deacon now. *O God, help me*, he prayed. *Help me to prevent Deacon Cummings from doing any more violence. Help me to find a way to save*

Father Andy's life. "Deacon Cummings, what can I do to help you?"

"God told me that He saved Father Andy so that a conversion could take place—but it requires your help. His life will be spared when you agree to certain terms, and remember, these are God's terms, not mine."

"What do you want me to do?"

"You will call a news conference to be broadcast on all the local stations. At that time you will say that you have received a Divine directive that will not only deliver this diocese from the punishment it deserves for disobeying the will of the Almighty, but that God has chosen this diocese to be the guiding light for the universal church."

He stopped for a moment as if he were trying to remember something. He stared at the palms of his hands for a long time and then raised his eyes upward and closed them. Bishop Steele slowly began to stand up; the deacon opened his eyes and glared at him. "Sit down!" Then he turned his eyes towards Father Andy and aimed the gun.

"No, No! Please, tell me what you want me to do!"

Returning his attention to the bishop he said, "You will outline the major steps that will bring about this rebirth. First, all Magdalene Witnesses groups will be disbanded at once. Second, Sr. Emily will be removed from her position as parish administrator and will be replaced by a man. Third, God's Troops will be established in each and every parish. A member from this group will monitor all Sunday sermons and any priest who deviates from dogma in any way will be admonished and counseled. Any priest who refuses to conform will be removed from his parish."

The bishop found it hard to breathe; he heard the pounding in his chest; he ignored the sharp pain in his heart. *Oh, God, help me. I must save Father Andy, but how can I do what he is asking of me?*

"What makes you think anyone will believe me?"

"Because you're going to make them believe you! You are the bishop, their leader! Their shepherd! And if you do not then Father Andy will have to be sacrificed."

His agitation is growing, thought Bishop Steele. *I will not be able to stall him much longer.*

"I need some time. If this message is going to sound sincere, it cannot be haphazard. I need time to gather my thoughts."

"Take all the time you need. I'm not going anywhere. Father Andy and I will just sit here and wait." He grinned and pointed the gun at Father Andy's heart. "But don't try any tricks. God will not be pleased!"

"Thank you; I think I can be ready in a half hour. Would you please be careful with that gun."

"Don't you worry about this gun; I know how to handle it. For his sake, I hope you know how to handle your job. Now, get busy."

Bishop Steele sat at his desk, his notepad a blur in front of him. His soul twisted with questions—*if he did as the deacon demanded, would he not shatter the people's trust? How could he speak such words of terror? How could he save Father Andy's life? O God, enlighten me; I am willing to die in his place, if that is what is required of me.*

How he wished he could speak to this man's heart. How could he convince him that God loved him so much? God's love is unconditional, even now, he wanted to tell him.

"Deacon Cummings, may I first ask you a question?"

"Are you trying to waste time? I am getting angry with you."

"Would you take me instead, as your prisoner? Let Father Andy go. You can sacrifice my life and give your own message, right on camera."

"As tempting as that sounds, Bishop, I need you to give the message. I have not lost my mind. How far would I get by killing you on TV? Do not waste my time; and do not insult me. You have fifteen minutes."

"Please, I did not mean to insult you. I will be ready." His heart was pounding so hard he heard it thumping. *O God, I know that you are present here in this room. Help me to do the right thing, the thing that will bring about the most good. I am prepared to give my own life, if that is what must happen.* He picked up his pen. Sentence after sentence poured itself onto his paper.

When he finished, his heart became quiet. His words were firm as he handed his pad to the deacon. "These are my words of introduction; you must understand that if I begin with your demands, the people will know that I am being forced to repeat your words. They will not believe me."

The deacon studied the script. "This is just the kind of drivel they heard from the priests. Where are the three points I gave you? Do not try to trick me."

"I don't need to write those down; how could I forget them? But there is one more thing; no negotiation on this point. You must release Father Andy before I appear in front of the cameras."

"No way! I am in charge, not you! What proof do I have that you will say what I told you must be said?"

"You have my word; I promise I will say all that you told me. By releasing Father Andy, I can convince the police that you will surrender peacefully. I will even help with your defense."

The deacon threw his head back and laughed a chilling laugh. "Defense! I will not need any defense; I am God's instrument; after my work is completed through your speech, God will take me away from this evil world."

The pounding in Bishop Steele's chest began again except the pain was sharper this time. As he prayed he inhaled a deep, slow breath.

"If you want me to address the people of our diocese…" He took another deep breath, "then Father Andy must be released first. If I refuse to speak, what can you do? No one will listen if you appear before the cameras alone. Your message will never be heard!"

The deacon paced back and forth, muttering to himself. At last, he stood still. "O.k., he can go, but I will appear on camera with you. If you have deceived me, you will suffer the punishment of the Almighty."

"Agreed."

Father Andy protested. Bishop Steele pleaded. "Andy, I need you to do this for me. Think about your parents; think about your sister. You should be with them. Please, go. I will ask for your obedience in this act." The grimace on Father Andy's face delighted the deacon.

"Now we can alert the media," said the deacon. "One more thing, tell them I said no police are permitted; I will allow only the TV crews in your office."

After calling the stations Bishop Steele waited for five minutes. He heard for the first time the desolate ticking of the wall clock and found a strange comfort in being reminded that time had not stopped. Then he said, "I am going to walk over to the window now; the reporters should be ready."

Outside, Coleman shouted and pointed to the window. They all saw the drape being drawn back and this time the bishop was standing in the window.

"He's trying to give us a message. Call him, Beth."

The phone rang in Bishop Steele's office. His eyes locked on Deacon Cummings, he walked to his desk. His face reflected the calmness that had overtaken him; his hands were steady. *Thank you, God; I am prepared to do whatever I must to show your love.* He picked up the phone and hit the speaker button.

"This is Bishop Steele. Father Andy will be coming out the front door alone. Ten minutes later, I would like to present a message to the people on live television. Can that be arranged?"

"Yes, of course, Bishop. Are we to come into your office or set up cameras outside your front door?"

"Come into my office; no police, only the TV camera crew."

"I'm sorry. Bishop Steele; I cannot agree to those terms."

"You must. This is what I have promised. I am on the speakerphone, so Deacon Cummings is hearing everything we are saying. You must do as I ask."

"I understand. Can I speak to Deacon Cummings? His wife is here." She put her arm around Sarah who wiped her eyes.

The phone went dead. Beth turned to Sarah. "He hung up. I am so sorry. Please, for now, go sit in my car." Beth motioned to Russell; he put his arm around Sarah.

As they walked away, Sarah turned toward Coleman. Her beseeching eyes latched onto his. *Please, don't hurt him,* they pleaded.

Beth grabbed Coleman and a TV crewman and said, "Get in that van and exchange clothes. I have to have someone in there. She looked around and snatched a baseball cap from another crewman. Here, put this on, too."

Russell yelled, "The door is opening."

All held their breath. They were shocked to see Deacon Cummings and Bishop Steele standing in the doorway with Father Andy between them. One of the SWAT guys lifted his rifle. He had a clear shot; his finger was firm on the trigger. The deacon shoved Father Andy; he fell and the deacon slammed the door.

Russell rushed over to him. Father Andy's face was bleeding and his arm was pinned underneath him. "Let me help you, Father. Here, hold onto my arm."

The crowd held its breath as they stumbled slowly towards the cameras and reporters. Microphones came from every direction at Father Andy; Russell pushed them away. When he shouted, "He needs to sit down," the reporters backed off.

Beth motioned towards the van; "He can rest in there. Get him some water." She was concentrating on her watch, marking the ten minutes before she could send in the reporters and Coleman. At nine minutes, she signaled the crew to start moving towards the bishop's door.

Cameras, microphones, and lights were hauled up the steps. Coleman carried a camera, making sure his eyes did not come into contact with the deacon or the bishop.

Once everything was inside, he watched as the deacon locked the door. His back was stiff; his rigid face was fortified by a harsh satisfied smile. *And to think I was actually beginning to admire him,* thought Coleman, suddenly feeling very cold.

Two men pushed a podium to the right of the bishop's desk. When he heard, "Bishop Steele, we're ready when you are," he walked to the podium carrying his notepad. Coleman noticed the bishop's quick determined steps; *he has a new energy,* thought Coleman. *How can he be so secure; what happened in here? The deacon is close behind; so close.* Coleman instinctively felt for his gun. Sarah's pleading eyes flashed before him.

Across the city, people are glued to their TV screens. On every channel, the anchor person was on alert since Father Andy's release had been broadcast. At 6:10 the screens were filled with the bishop's face. He looked directly into the camera; the deacon stood behind him, smiling. Bishop Steele winced as the deacon rammed the round barrel into his back.

From his spot at the back of the room, Coleman saw an intense glow surrounding the bishop and emanating from within him. *What could that be,* he asked himself as he wondered about the fear that stirred inside. He looked around; *doesn't anyone else see it? Does anyone else realize the danger the bishop is in? Does the bishop realize what danger he is in?* Suddenly, that inner calm that had terrified him, that calm that had lured him to surrender—why was it exploding within him now? *What are you? Who are you?*

He heard the voice of the bishop.

"Good evening. As you all know, the Catholic Church in this city lost two priests over the last several months in a very violent manner. We are so very grateful that a third priest was spared a similar death."

His voice faltered. "And so, now I have a message to all who are listening. God is always present with us, in good times and bad. We often wish that God would not allow the bad things to happen. But then God would not be God and we would not be free."

He gulped as he felt the gun barrel shoved deeper into his back. He stopped talking; his breathing became vigorous.

What is happening to me, Coleman asked himself. *I am losing control; I can't close my eyes; the glow is blinding me.* The calm that had terrified him was now radiating out from the center of his body, slowly consuming him. *Oh, God, help me.*

He heard the bishop talking again.

"Remember what I just said—God is always present to us even when we do not understand." He paused. He lowered his eyes. "Now I have been commanded to give you a directive that will bring rebirth and renewal to our church in this diocese. Please wait until I finish all three points; do not be afraid.

Listen to everything first." He trembled as the deacon jabbed the gun again.

In rapid succession he communicated the deacon's three points; audible gasps filled the office. In living rooms across the city, dazed people wailed.

Coleman couldn't move his arms or legs. *What is he doing,* he cried out in his tortured silence. *How could he agree to do this? I thought he was stronger than this. I believed he was a real man of faith. So, he knows now that God cannot protect him. I was right, all along. I almost believed; I almost believed.*

No one saw the anguished tears in Coleman's eyes. No one heard the howl in his grief-stricken soul.

Finishing the third point, Bishop Steele's unblinking eyes peered into the camera. "I will do all in my power to prevent all this from happening!" Coleman was jerked into the present. *What did he say? Did he really say...?*

Just as his last sentence registered in everyone's consciousness, the deafening blast of a gun stunned everyone in the room. Bishop Steele slumped forward knocking the microphone to the floor. His ashen face creased the pages of his notepad. His beaming eyes stared into the camera.

The deacon whirled himself in front of the bishop and still holding the gun, shrieked, "You have caused me to fail!"

He raised the gun to his own head. Bishop Steele lifted up his arm pleading, "Don't, Ray!" With an agonized moan he smacked the gun out of his hand and fell to the floor.

Coleman found himself launched into the air. He looked down on the deacon stooping to retrieve his gun. *O God, help me. I believe. I believe.* He landed on top of Deacon Cummings, pulled out his handcuffs as he pushed him hard against the floor. Time stopped; the glow folded around him, warm, powerful, peaceful. Embraced! Embraced! *Oh God, my God!*

He had doubted it; he had fought it; now he was its grateful captive.

He looked up; he saw no one in the intense light, but the passionate calm would not let him go. *Don't leave me, please,* he begged, but only he heard his cry. He heard no sound but the answer, *Do not fear, I am always with you,* pulsated within him.

His face was wet and warm; his hands were sweating. He listened to the restful throbbing of his heart. A hushed voice broke out of the light.

"Welcome home, Christopher!"

"Dad? Is that you? Dad? You're here, too?"

Twenty-six

Three hours passed. Russell looked at his partner, collapsed into a soft chair. The waiting room was crowded. Coleman saw faces and heard voices adrift in the fog that encircled him. He remembered the light; he remembered the embrace; and he remembered the voice.

All too soon it was over; he was dragged to his feet. Fuzzy microphones and flashes were all around him; the deacon lay on the floor weeping. A cameraman was kneeling beside the bishop yelling, "He's alive!" An emergency team smashed through the door and ran in with a gurney. Russell pushed through the crowd coming for him.

Russell sat beside his partner, watched him and waited. Waited for him to speak. *What happened to him in the bishop's office? He hasn't said a word since I walked him out of there. I told Deb he was fine, but is he?*

Another hour passed. At 11:30 the doctor walked into the waiting room and looked around at news reporters, police, Bishop Frank McCoy, Sister Emily, Beth and Sarah Cummings, and many other women and men. All searched his face for a hint of good news. His fatigued smile prepared them. "Bishop Steele is in recovery now; the surgery went very well. He will be in ICU for several days, but he's going to make it."

Applause, tears and prayers became a thunderous noise. Russell looked at Coleman; he was standing now, tears rolling down his face, clapping his hands. *He must be o.k. now, thank God,* breathed Russell. *Will he ever tell me what happened?*

The doctor continued to smile and signaled for some quiet. "No visitors until tomorrow afternoon and then only at 1:00 and 5:00 for fifteen minutes; only two people at a time are permitted inside the room." Applause erupted again.

Bishop McCoy turned to the group and waved for their attention. "May I have your permission to be the first visitor? I promise I will take all your good wishes and prayers and I'll give you a full report."

Nods and more applause. The grateful peace within each person was broken by memories of a sobbing Deacon Cummings in handcuffs led away by the police.

At the police station, the officers who had pulled Coleman off Deacon Cummings led the deacon inside; he offered no resistance, his head lowered to his chest. When he was booked on two counts of murder and two counts of attempted murder, he cried out, "I failed, I failed. O God, forgive me for not completing my mission." Taken to his cell, he refused the offer to contact a lawyer. Chief Flannery assigned a guard to suicide watch.

As people began leaving the waiting room, Coleman searched the faces until he found Sarah. She turned away from him and hid her face in her hands. He folded his arms around her, and held her quivering body. "Do you want to see him? I'll take you."

She looked into his eyes, so strong yet so different than she remembered. She shook her head yes, dabbing her red eyes with a crumpled Kleenex.

Russell walked a little faster to get ahead of them. By the time they reached the car he had the back door opened for her.

He gently helped her into the seat and clamped the seat belt around her. She sobbed quietly the whole way to the station.

Both detectives walked with her to the deacon's cell. Sarah dug her fingernails into Coleman's arm as her halting steps brought her closer to husband. They found him with his back facing them and nothing they said convinced him to turn around or speak.

Sarah hung onto the bars; Coleman tried to unfold her fingers. "Ray, I love you. We will get through this together." He did not move nor did he speak. Coleman put his arms around her shoulders and pulled her away.

She turned to Coleman and Russell. They each took an arm and walked with her, her chest rose and fell with each heaving breath. She turned for one last look.

Coleman asked where he could take her for the night. She said she just wanted to go home and she wanted to be alone.

At 1:00 am Coleman was grateful to open his own front door; he noticed the light was on in the living room. Each step towards Deb said *thank you for being here.* He kissed her forehead and she jumped to her feet; he held her quivering body as her tears soaked his shirt. He caressed her hair and pressed his face into its softness. "Let's go to bed," he whispered.

At 1:00 that afternoon Bishop Frank McCoy was outside the ICU checking his watch. When the nurse waved him inside, he tiptoed over to the bed. He looked at his friend, asleep and took his hand.

Bishop Steele opened his eyes and smiled. "Frank," he whispered, as he gripped his hand.

Bishop Frank placed his other hand over Bishops Steele's and wept, "Thank God, Thank God!" He blessed and anointed him and stood there wordless for the fifteen minutes he was allotted.

When he was ushered out he saw a blur of faces gathered near the nurse's station. He hurried to assure them that all was well, when he spotted Sarah standing in the back trying to be invisible. He informed the group that the doctor said Bishop Steele would be moved to the third floor in three days.

As the group walked away, he caught up with Sarah. Her red and hollow eyes let go of more stinging tears, the tears she was unable to block since last night. He put his arm around her waist. "Let take a walk outside."

The day that Bishop Steele was moved out of intensive care, Coleman and Russell came to pay him a visit. Dan Salvage was coming out of the room. He stopped and held out his hand to Coleman; when Coleman took it, Dan gave it a firm shake. "Thank you for showing me the truth; I was so lonely. The deacon welcomed me into his group; I thought I had found a place to belong."

"I understand. How are you doing?"

"I'm going to make it. I was worried about Dave Monroe; I was the one who brought him to the first meeting. But this really has him shaken; he told me that he's checking himself into anger management therapy. I think that's a step in the right direction."

"I'm glad to hear that. What about you?"

"Susan Mahoney and Carol Anderson called me; their husbands are joining the Magdalene Witnesses and they wanted to know if I was interested; I told them yes. Sarah needs us, too."

Coleman and Russell looked at each other, grinned, and said, "We'll see you there."

Russell studied his partner; *I hope that this will be the day that he can let it out; that he can tell me, can tell somebody what happened in the bishop's office.*

They tapped twice on the open door and walked in; Bishop Steele was seated facing the window, an IV performing its silent duty; his body was at rest but his soul was active and lost in contemplation. Coleman was drawn into the serenity embracing the bishop. Now he knew it was true. *Will anyone believe me? Will anyone be able to explain it to me?*

Coleman coughed and cleared his throat; Bishop Steele turned around and his smile was an invitation to irresistible peace. "I'm so glad you came. I owe you a debt of thanks, both of you and especially to you, Detective Coleman."

"I'm glad I was there, Bishop. We came to tell you that Deacon Cummings will be arraigned tomorrow."

"Thank you, Detective." A shadow of disquiet crossed his face as he turned again to the window.

Coleman cleared his throat again. "Forgive me, Bishop, but may I ask what's troubling you?"

Bishop Steele turned to look at him; *there was always something in his eyes that told me that someday we would share the same truth,* he told himself. "I'm not sure I should say this. But... well... maybe it will help me if I tell you. You see, Detective, I know what my faith in Jesus tells me to do in this circumstance, but I am so tortured; we lost so much... so many lives changed forever. Changed because someone had such a narrow vision of God; someone who designed himself a false God; how could anyone believe that the one who created us male and female would favor one over the other?"

"But you think you have to forgive Deacon Cummings."

"I *know* I have to. But when I bring him before my eyes, I feel such revulsion. I watch myself beating him to the floor and screaming, 'Why, why, why?' And then Father John and Father Bill appear, bend down and lift him up. And I know, though I do not want to admit it, I know that each one is a son of God.

"And that's when the terrible power of choice overwhelms me. I can choose to set aside the reality that one of my brothers killed two other brothers and let violence strangle my soul. Or I can collapse into the spirit of God that enfolds me and learn forgiveness from the One who said, 'Forgive them, for they do not know what they are doing."

"Are you saying that God will not punish him?"

"Oh, he will suffer punishment, but not from God. He is already suffering. The consequences of our actions punish us, teach us and change us, even destroy us. God dreams great dreams that will fulfill us beyond our hopes. God is recklessly in love with us."

"You mean that God doesn't care that I stopped going to church, that I questioned how evil can happen if God is good, that I…"

"God cares about all that, but not for the reasons you think. God cares when we make decisions that put our selfish interests first. God cares when we ignore the hungers of people around us and not only physical hunger, but also the hunger for love, understanding, acceptance. God cares if we decide that evil denies the existence of God rather than regarding evil as the proof that freedom is our greatest challenge as well as our greatest gift."

"Bishop," Coleman looked at Russell and back to the bishop and swallowed hard. "Something happened to me that day in your office. I wasn't sure it was real until I walked in here today. When I landed on top of Deacon Cummings; first of all, I don't even know how I got there, but when I did…" He went on to explain the light and the embrace. "It felt so real."

"It was real."

"But there's one more thing; I was so happy; I can't ever remember being so happy. I didn't think it could get any better. Then I heard another voice; one that I recognized."

The bishop's eyes glistened. "Was it your dad's?"

"How? How did you know that?"

"Sometimes we are given a rare gift; we learn how thin is the veil that separates us from the spirit world."

Coleman dropped to his knees. Russell blessed himself and rushed to wipe the tears from his cheeks.

"Now, would you help me get back into bed?"

Just as Coleman was adjusting the bed, Bishop Frank McCoy walked in.

Both detectives spoke at once. "We should go now, but we'll visit you again."

"Please stay. I want you to hear this, too. Frank, come sit over here; I have something to tell you. Detectives, please sit down."

He looked around at the faces of the three men. "I'm not sure how to begin, so I'm just going to say it. I had a vision when I was in the ambulance. It was so vivid, I can remember every detail."

Bishop McCoy, Coleman and Russell glanced at each other and moved to the edge of their chairs.

"I am sitting at the Last Supper beside Jesus. His profile is so familiar to me; then he turns to face me and smiles. I realize I am gazing into the eyes of Pete Nowell! Seated around the table are Sister Emily, Father Larry Strong, his wife, and their children, Sarah Cummings, Marge Peterson, Father John and Father Bill. When Jesus breaks the bread, so does Emily, and Larry, and Sarah, and Marge as well as John and Bill; then they all raise a cup as Jesus says, "Do this in remembrance of me.""

A stillness entered the room. Bishop McCoy, Coleman and Russell were silent, each one entranced by the radiance surrounding Bishop Steele. A piercing light glowed in his eyes.

Bishop McCoy's faint-hearted voice broke the silence. He must ask the question, afraid that he already knew the answer.

"Are you... are you saying that you think this means what I think you're saying?"

"Not think, Frank." Bishop Steele looked at Coleman and Russell, too. Luminous sparks of light danced in his eyes. "I believe it; I believe it with every beat of my heart."

Bishop McCoy laid his hand on his chest; he tried in vain to quiet the intense rapid palpitations he felt there. "I accept what you're saying, Joe, I really do... I do." He caught his breath.

Coleman and Russell were speechless. But Coleman understood; he knew the bond between knowing the truth and being set free.

"I realize what I'm saying and I know what I must do. I've seen the truth; I cannot support the lie anymore."

"But you know what this will mean, what will happen to you."

"I know. But my faith and my freedom is in God not in laws. Frank, you have known me for many years. I have always followed the rules; I have never been courageous, you know that. I will need a friend."

He smiled at Coleman and Russell. "More than one."

Bishop Frank McCoy did not know that he was being the prophet. "I will always be your friend, Joe. And you may learn you have more friends than you imagine."

Meet Sr. Christine Kresho

Sister of St. Joseph for 47 years; currently a Pastoral Associate at Our Lady of Grace Church, Silver Spring, MD; holds an M. Ed from Indiana University of Pennsylvania and B.S. in Education from Carlow College; was a classroom teacher, a principal, a computer teacher, area manager for a computer education company, and Educational Consultant for William H. Sadlier, Inc.; has given numerous presentations at parish, regional, diocesan, and national conferences. Has written student texts and manuals for computer instruction. *At the Last Supper* is her first novel.